THE LAST STARFIGHTER

'Listen, Centauri, I'm not any of those guys. I'm just a kid who lives in a trailer park and wants to go away to college. I'm not special.'

'You *are* special, my boy. You were tested, tested rigorously, and you passed.'

They needed his help! The vast, technologically advanced League needed the help of lowly Alex Rogan, videogame whiz and all-round screw-up. It didn't make any sense!

Alan Dean Foster has been associated with many successful projects, including *Alien: Clash of the Titans, Dark Star, Icerigger, Outland, Splinter of the Mind's Eye* and *The Thing.*

THE LAST STARFIGHTER

A novel by
Alan Dean Foster

Based on a screenplay by Jonathan Betuel

A TARGET BOOK
published by
the Paperback Division of
W. H. ALLEN & Co. PLC

A Target Book
Published in 1984
by the Paperback Division of
W.H. Allen & Co. PLC
44 Hill Street, London W1X 8LB

Printed and bound in Great Britain by
Anchor Brendon Ltd, Tiptree, Essex

ISBN 0 0426 19799 2

For my nephew Daniel,
A fun one . . .

I

The Xurian ship exploded in a blaze of flame which was beginning to dissipate even as Alex drove his gunstar through the expanding globe of hot gas and vaporized metal. They were homing in on him now and he was forced to work twice as hard to dodge their attacks.

If the battle pattern held to form there ought to be a cluster of Ko-Dan fighters gathering for a flanking attack off in the fourth quadrant. He pressed on with his own assault, relentless in his pursuit of the Ko-Dan command ship, clearing one wave after another of the attacking enemy from the battle screen.

There they came! A host of them diving in on him from the side. But he was ready for them. The Ko-Dan were valiant fighters, and they came at you in unending waves, but if your reflexes were sharp enough you could out-manoeuvre them. Alex did so now, twisting a path through the assault as the attacking craft struggled frantically to regroup in his wake.

Too late for them now, he thought grimly. His fingers were tense on the gunstar's controls and he kept his eyes riveted to the battle screen, not allowing his gaze to drift right or left. The screen was all he needed; plenty of power left, and all his weapons still functioned. But the Ko-Dan were crafty. Just when you thought you'd slipped them, another wave of fighters would appear and begin their attack.

But he was through them now, through them all, and his main target lay directly ahead.

'Approaching Ko-Dan Command Craft,' his computer announced evenly. 'Prepare for final confrontation.'

Suddenly a host of lights proliferated on his screen. 'Enemy squadrons in sectors three, six, and seven and closing fast!'

Trying to catch him between them, Alex thought grimly. Well, he knew how to handle that manoeuvre. He thumbed the Evade controls and the gunstar rocked wildly. The images on the battle screen shifted as he swerved to avoid the new attack while still holding a course towards the Command Ship.

Then there was red light washing over the screen and his fingers trembled on the controls. Warning lights began to appear on the battle screen. He knew what they meant: loss of life support imminent, loss of fire control imminent, loss of ... loss of ...

The screen shook from the impact as the gunstar took a direct hit aft. 'Loss of drive,' the computer told him sadly, almost apologetically. He let his fingers slide from the controls. Too late now. Too late to try a different attack plan, too late to avoid the coup de grâce. It was a matter of seconds. The Ko-Dan did not know the meaning of mercy.

The screen shook again and his field of view was obliterated completely. It was over. His ship was destroyed.

He was dead.

Alex Rogan sighed as his battle screen came to life a last time.

YOUR GUNSTAR HAS BEEN DESTROYED. YOUR SCORE ON THIS MACHINE RANKS YOU NUMBER ONE. PLEASE DEPOSIT ANOTHER QUARTER FOR ADDITIONAL PLAYING TIME.

Another quarter. Twenty-five cents a resurrection. Cheap enough at the price. He slipped the coin into the machine. A strong, insistent synthesized voice cut through the stagnant morning air, demanding and full of cosmic import.

'GREETINGS, STARFIGHTER! YOU HAVE BEEN RECRUITED BY THE LEAGUE TO DEFEND THE FRONTIER AGAINST XUR AND THE KO-DAN

ARMADA!'

'Yeah, I know, I know,' he said impatiently. 'Bring on the target lights already!' He leaned both hands against the console and waited for the game to commence.

Off to his left the sign on the trailer park general store popped and sputtered, fizzled and flashed. Sometimes it spelled out ARLIG ARBRI, and sometimes TARGHT IGHT, and sometimes it made sense. Like today.

STARLIGHT STARBRIGHT

The rest of the trailer park sprawled out across the dry ground behind the general store. It was Alex's home, was the trailer park. His mother managed it. His father... he concentrated on the revived game. His father had been gone a long time. A picture or two on the end table in his mom's bedroom. A photographic image. Not a real person. He went after the Ko-Dan fighters savagely.

The trailer park was a self-contained little community located on the outskirts of Nowhereville, California. A small village fashioned out of corrugated steel and fibreglass and plastic. Few transients stopped by to make use of the park's facilities. The Starlight, Starbright was not one of Southern California's vacation meccas, and its inhabitants liked it that way. It was peaceful, and quiet, and safe.

It was driving Alex crazy.

As he pushed and shoved at the controls of the game, the park was waking up around him. Funny, the sounds a community makes as it comes to life. Toasters popping, percolators dripping, juice-makers whirring wetly, younger kids complaining ('Ma, you know I *hate* orange juice with pulp in it... it gets stuck in my brace!'), electric razors shearing male fleece, multiple throats gargling, and middle-aged adults wheezing weakly as they attempt their morning exercises.

Radios began to come alive behind the general store. Country-Western mostly, but some guerrilla rock sneaking in here and there. Pork belly prices cohabited on the air with the news from the Middle East, while unseen hucksters hawked everything from underwear to pickup trucks. Striving to be

9

heard above this din were the defiant peeps of finches and sparrows and the occasional stutter of a hidden roadrunner.

'Strange lights, they wuz, away in the sky,' one voice was declaiming insistently over the local talk show.

'Sure they were, Mrs Granwaters.' You could hear the false sympathy in the DJ's voice, could imagine him winking broadly at his invisible audience as he replied to his guest's declaration. 'Now, how many colours did you say it was?'

An elderly gent clad in T-shirt, faded coveralls and a battered VFW cap opened the door of the trailer nearest the general store on the right side, holding a large filled dog dish. He set it in front of a waiting hound of uncertain pedigree and patted the long-eared head as the animal ate.

When he rose it was to eye the thermometer that was nailed to the outside of the trailer. He used to be able to read the height of the mercury inside the glass tube from across the road. Now he had to squint.

'Already up near ninety.' He eyed the dog again. 'Gonna be a sparklin' day, Mr President. Sparklin'.'

A shout drew Alex's attention to another trailer, though he didn't look up from the game. That would be Elvira Hartford, from the sound of it. He fought to ignore the banal conversation as he blasted whole squadrons of Ko-Dan fighters from interstellar space.

Sure enough, the woman in question stuck her head out of a trailer window. It was full of curlers, giving her the appearance of someone enduring an assault of giant pink caterpillars.

Across the walk that separated the trailers her next-door neighbour Clara Parks was just settling into her sun lounge and lighting up her ancient corn-cob pipe in preparation for the first smoke of the day. Clara had smoked all her life and had put her feelings about the habit in no uncertain terms. She coughed a lot, Clara did, but no one dared to bring up the thought of quitting. Clara kept a .38 special in her bedroom dresser.

Now she peered across at her neighbour, having a fair idea of what was coming. Clara Parks was eighty-four.

'Clara, my 'lectric's out again! Pay attention, Clara, I know you're listening to me! This is *important*. I'm gonna miss my soaps!'

'Settle your britches, woman.' Parks chewed on the stem of her pipe. 'I'll pass it on.' She turned in the lounge chair and cupped both hands to her mouth, dangling the pipe from two fingers.

'Oh, Bill? Bill! Elvira's blacked out again. Pass the word on before the crisis hits.'

The next trailer in line belonged to William Potter, aircraft mechanic, retired. Potter shaved his face the way he'd bombed North Vietnam: sporadically and ineffectively. Since no one tried to get near enough to kiss him, it didn't trouble his lifestyle.

'Pass the word along to whom?'

'Don't get funny with me, Bill Potter,' said Clara warningly. 'Just pass it on.'

'Damn women and their damn soaps,' Potter muttered. He didn't say anything out loud, however, lest it be discovered some day that he was a closet Days of Our Lives freak.

He walked along his porch till he could see all the way up to the Boone mobile and shouted towards it. 'Elvira's got no juice, and if she can't see her soaps, she'll hyperventilate!'

That was usually enough to provoke a response from the Rogan trailer. Jane Rogan was manager, bill collector, mail distributor, sector general, field marshal and repository of all complaints as well as dispenser of favours for the tightly knit community.

She was Alex's mother. She was the Boss.

The girl who emerged from the Boone trailer nearby was much younger than the manager of the Starlight, Starbright trailer park. She was carrying a small ice chest. Her name was Maggie and it was a source of some ribbing from her friends. It was a name you had to grow into. Hard to visualize a teenager named Maggie. Still harder to imagine two proud parents standing over a hospital crib and naming the wrinkled little child in the white hospital room Maggie.

But certain names endure in families as a means of

11

perpetuating the memory of relatives long since departed, so Maggie Gordon was heir to the name of a favourite aunt on her father's side. It didn't bother her anymore. Very little bothered the beautiful, dark-haired Maggie Gordon.

'Thanks, Mrs Boone,' she called back towards the trailer. 'You have a nice day.'

'You too, honey.' Mrs Boone emerged to study the sky. 'Gonna be a hot one.'

Maggie nodded and made her way down the steep steps by peering carefully around the bulk of the ice chest. Mr Boone was just leaving the yard, having prepared for a hard day's fishing. He hefted his battered old rod proudly, like a soldier preparing for parade.

'Got yourself a great day for a picnic, Maggie.'

'I can't wait. If it doesn't get too hot. Catch a big one, Mr Boone.'

He grinned back at her, secure in his age, his pension, and his hobby. 'I'm gonna try.'

There weren't many fish to be had in the small desert lake nearby. That didn't worry Mr Boone. As any true fisherman knows, catching fish has nothing to do with fishing. The catching is an adjunct, a corollary to the actual art of fishing, which consists of killing time on a small boat as simply as possible, utilizing only the minimal amount of energy necessary to maintain life while simultaneously consuming as much cold beer and snacks as the body will tolerate.

Whether you caught any fish or not was, of course, incidental.

When Maggie re-emerged from her own trailer she was wearing a bikini beneath a baggie sweatshirt. A thick towel clung to her neck. The old woman who followed her out of the trailer was an elderly reflection of the young girl. Granny Gordon refused to let life get ahead of her. Unlike many of her contemporaries, she wasted no time running on the spot. The Sony Walkman dangling from her neck was proof of that.

She gave her granddaughter a kiss and a friendly warning.

'You have fun, child, but be careful. No swimming under logs and no diving off the rocks. And you take good care of

12

Mrs Boone's ice chest.'

'I will, Granny. Are you sure you'll be okay?'

'Be news if I wasn't. Say, who's looking after whom here? Maybe you should stay and watch TV and I'll go on the picnic.'

'All right, Granny.' Maggie smiled affectionately. 'I give up.'

'I'll be just fine, dear.' Granny ran a hand through her still thick hair. Not all white. Not yet. 'You just run along and have a good time and don't worry about me. I'll do all the worryin' for both of us.'

'Fair enough. I fixed your lunch and put it in the fridge.'

Granny nodded and did a little dip to barely heard music. Still a little life in the old stems yet, she mused. Wonderful inventions, these new portables. She watched as her granddaughter crossed the courtyard, heading towards the main gate. Lot of life in that girl. Looking after her wasn't work. It was a joy.

With that happy thought in mind she turned and re-entered her trailer, getting out of the sun while getting *down*.

The woman hanging out laundry on the trailer across the way was in her forties, strong of body and personality. Mention women's lib to Jane Rogan and she'd laugh at you, having worked for a living since her teens. For all that life was nonstop, hard work, she was as cheerful as a San Francisco socialite, and a damnsight healthier.

'Morning, Mrs Rogan.'

The park Manager peeked around her laundry.

'Morning, Maggie. You're looking spry.'

'Feeling good, Mrs Rogan. Did you find that picnic basket?'

'Uh-hum.' She fumbled behind her, hunting briefly through mounds of white. 'Here it is.' She handed it over.

'Thanks, Mrs Rogan.' Maggie's eyes searched the parking area beyond the gate. 'Where's Alex?'

Jane Rogan shook her head, sharing a secret smile with Maggie. 'He's up there. Where else?'

Maggie nodded knowingly. 'Right. Hi, Louis.' She moved

away from the open trailer door.

An instant later a rubber dart clung to the metal nearby. It was retrieved by a tousle-haired ten-year-old wearing a disappointed frown. His aim was till off. Either that or the dumb spacegun needed a new spring.

'Morning, spaceson Louis,' said Mrs Rogan. She raised the visor of his space helmet and planted a kiss on his forehead. He wriggled away, but slowly. He was concentrating on his work, which he carried out with all the solemnity of a surgeon attempting the world's first brain transplant. This consisted of carrying the small black and white TV while playing out an extension cord behind it.

Jane Rogan watched with one eye until her younger son had vanished into the garishly painted plywood teepee that squatted near the back of the small yard. As soon as the sounds of morning cartoons began to drift from it, she turned her attention away, satisfied that Louis was not going to electrocute himself. This morning.

Another voice made her turn from the washing.

'Yoo-hoo, Jane?'

Granny Gordon was leaning on the back fence. Everybody called Mrs Gordon Granny, not out of deference to her age or status but because her real first name was Grendil and the old woman would sock anyone who used it.

'Hi, Granny. How's the back this morning?'

Granny put a hand to her spine and smiled faintly. 'Still workin'. Sort of.'

'You ought to go see that chiropractor Dan Robbins keeps recommending.'

The older woman shook her head. 'No thanks. I like these old bones right where they are.'

'What's doin'?'

'Well, Elvira's electric is out again and she's gonna get hyper if she can't see her soaps. She'll make everybody's day impossible.'

'Don't I know it,' agreed Jane readily. 'Pass the word back that Alex'll be over to patch her line in time for her soaps. That'll hold her for awhile.'

'Just for awhile, though. I swear, if they said on those shows that you could walk on water, we'd be fishin' Elvira out of the river before sundown. I'll tell her Alex is comin', Jane.'

'Thanks.' Jane Rogan saw movement off to her right. Louis was taking deadly aim with his spacepistol on a sleeping feline. 'Louis, leave that cat alone and go tell Alex I need to see him.'

'Aw, mom, I wasn't gonna do nothin'.'

'Wasn't going to do "anything", Louis. Now go and get your brother.'

'A dumb messenger, that's all I am.' He climbed to his feet and stared longingly at the unsuspecting cat. Then he sighed and left the yard, heading for the store and taking time off to fire a few desultory darts in the direction of old Otis's chickens. They squawked and fled for cover, making him feel better. When you're real small it's important to know something's afraid of you, even if it's only a bunch of dumb chickens.

As he walked he looked for Mr President, Otis's old hound. Mr President, however, knew Louis from long experience. Since it was forbidden to chew the boy's arm off, the dog had learned to avoid his approach. He watched Louis pass from beneath the cool safety of the trailer's bulk.

Having taken as much time as possible to go from the trailer to the store, Louis finally mounted the steps onto the wooden porch. Store and porch had been there long before the trailer park, but the old wood was solid as iron.

Louis crossed the porch, keeping an eye out for scorpions. His big brother was eighteen. To Louis that put him right up there with their mother, though not with Granny Gordon or Otis. Alex seemed impossibly tall to Louis, who knew for a certainty that he would never, *ever* reach such impressive heights himself. He'd also heard that Alex was good-looking, which just goes to show how much grown-ups know. Because Louis knew it for a fact that his brother was just a malformed klutz whose sole task in life was to make things unbearable for the only important human being on the planet, Louis Rogan.

At times he could be neat to have around, though, like

15

when they went swimming together. Louis conceded that as big brothers went, Alex wasn't all that bad. But today he was going swimming with his own friends, and to compound the bad judgement, he was going swimming with *girls*. That lapse of taste Louis could never forgive.

Now he strained to see past his brother's ribs, looking at the videoscreen that was alive with flashing, rapidly changing lights. The images fascinated Louis. They were so alive, so full of movement and trickery. Alex ignored his younger shadow, letting his fingers dance easily over the multiple controls. Louis watched and tried to learn, knowing that Alex was a master at video games. Once he'd watched during a trip to the big arcade in town while other kids oohed and aahed as Alex ran up several million points on Stargate, a game too complex for his ten-year-old mind to think of trying.

But this new game, this Starfighter, was even more complex, with half again as many controls to manipulate. Yet Alex seemed better at it than anything else. Something one of the other kids had called 'rising to the challenge'. Some kids wouldn't even try Starfighter because it ate their quarters too fast. On a good day, Alex could play the game for hours on just one.

When he wasn't being interrupted, Louis reminded himself. So readily did he lose himself in the game that he'd almost forgotten what had sent him to the store.

'Mom's lookin' for you, Alex.'

'Yeah, sure.' His brother replied without taking his gaze from the videoscreen. His arms hung parallel to the ground, still, relaxed. Only his fingers moved, depressing fire controls, adjusting thrust, guiding the tiny microprocessed gunstar through the maze of enemy fighters. It was very much a virtuoso display. Alex played the game as smoothly as Horowitz did his Steinway.

'Come on, Alex. Mom'll be mad at me.'

'What for?' Bright blue light momentarily filled the screen, fading to reveal a new series of targets attacking faster than ever, relentless and uncaring. 'She told you to come tell me she wants to see me. Okay, you've told me. You're in the

16

clear.'

'Yeah, right.' Louis brightened and tore his gaze away from the motion-filled screen just long enough to locate one of the chairs that sat on the porch. Dragging it over, he climbed up onto the rickety platform. For a breathless moment he was an adult, as big as Alex.

'Look out!' Somehow his brother avoided the wave attack from the left quadrant. Louis couldn't imagine how Alex had seen the attack coming in time to evade. He swayed on the chair, mesmerized by the lights and sounds, waving and bobbing wildly.

After all, it wasn't his quarter at stake.

'Get 'em, Alex, get 'em!'

Get 'em Alex did: efficiently, professionally, avoiding every attack on his own vessel while methodically eliminating everything the game could throw at him, quietly revelling in the simulated destruction and fully confident of his skills.

Louis edged closer and closer to the machine, drawn by the lights on the screen. His small face was aglow with delight. Alex was so good it was more fun to watch him than to play himself. Well, almost. So much pleasure, and all for a quarter. Being good helped, though. Somehow the game wasn't as much fun to play when it only lasted a minute or so.

'Blam, blam, blam!'

'Cool the sound effects, Louis. I can't hear the machine. And move your head, will you?'

Once more the screen showed him the Command Ship. It loomed huge on the battle screen. He tried a different evasion pattern this time, hoping to avoid the squadrons of enveloping fighters which had shot him down the last time. It didn't work. He was dead again.

Dying a lot this morning, he thought.

'Nuts!' He gave the console a whack before jamming both hands into his trouser pockets. 'Not fast enough. I should've had it that time.' A new voice chimed in. Both boys turned to see Otis staring at the screen.

'Heard you almost hit eight hundred thousand, Alex.'

'That was yesterday. Would've too, if Louis hadn't

bumped my hand.'

'Did not! Wow!' Louis pointed towards the screen. 'Seven hundred and ... and ...' His face wrinkled up in confusion. The number was beyond him.

Alex eyed the screen with careful indifference. 'Seven hundred and eighty-two thousand. Almost as good as last night.'

'Yeah, and I didn't hit your hand this time, neither,' Louis shot back.

'No, but you stuck your fat head in my way.'

'Did not!'

'I heard you were in the millions last week on Stargate in town,' Otis said.

Alex shrugged, concealing the pride he took in his accomplishment. 'Yeah, but lots of guys do that around the country. Stargate's easy compared to Starfighter.' He added casually, 'Though I haven't heard of anybody else breaking half a million besides me.'

'Maybe you'd win a national contest if they held one.'

'I guess I might have a chance. But only the big game companies run contests like that. Atari, Sega, Nintendo, Williams. I never heard of the compoany that makes this Starfighter game. Must be some new outfit.'

'Maybe so. Maybe they will have a contest if they get big enough.'

'Yeah. You going to pay my way to it, Otis?'

The older man chuckled. 'Not on my social security I'm not, Alex. Tell you what, though. You keep practising and if a Starfighter contest ever comes up, we'll see about gettin' you to it.'

Alex grinned. 'It's a deal.'

Otis nodded to his right. 'Looks like somebody lookin' for you, Alex.'

He turned, saw Maggie walking out of the side gate carrying a picnic basket, towels and a small ice chest. The chest was sweating, suggesting inviting contents. At the same time a new pickup pulled in off the highway, rolled into the parking lot in front of the store. It was filled with kids Alex's own age, all laughing and joking while fighting not to spill over the tailgate.

'Come on, Alex, they're here!' Maggie broke into a trot, managing her awkward burden easily as she headed for the truck.

For an instant Alex wondered what the hell she was talking about. Then memories from real life came flooding in.

'Silver Lake! The picnic. I forgot.' He started to run after Maggie.

'Hey, Alex.' Louis pointed at the game. 'You won a free credit.'

'What about it?'

'You just gonna *waste* it?'

Alex concealed a smile. The greed was as bright on his little brother's face as a thousand-watt halogen lamp. He deepened his voice, trying to imitate the game.

'Starfighter Alex Rogan requesting permission to turn over gunstar controls to my little brother Louis, sirs.' A brief pause, then he added, 'Telepathic communication confirms OK. She's all yours, Louis.'

Unable to believe his luck, the ten-year-old hastily wrestled the chair he'd been standing on around until it faced the console.

'Oh boy!' He hit the start button, his small fingers waiting tensely above the fire controls. Alien warships appeared on the glass, firing out at him. Grinning, Alex turned to follow Maggie while Otis just shook his head and started back towards his trailer. Louis's excited voice followed both of them.

'Okay, alien dorks, you're dead, 'cause it's me, Louis Rogan flyin' the gunstar now!' A bright red flare filled the screen and Louis's expression immediately became one of inexpressible disgust. 'Oh, *crapola*! Gimme a chance, willya?'

Everyone in the pickup was already wearing swimming gear. Well, he could borrow some, Alex knew, in case Maggie had forgotten his. Or he'd shock them all by swimming in the buff. *Sure* he would.

It was Jack Blake's pickup. Not that he'd expected anything else, just as there wasn't anything he could do about it. Besides owning the pickup, Blake had money for gas. Money for gas, money for beer, for movies, for concert tickets. Which was another way of saying that his parents had money.

What was it they'd learned from the Constitution? 'All men are created equal.'

Bullshit. When did he get equality with Jack Blake? Somehow the writers of the Constitution had left that one out. He'd asked his mother about it.

'There are no guarantees in life, Alex, and it isn't always fair.' That's what she'd told him. Jane Rogan vs. Thomas Jefferson, et al. From what he'd observed of life so far he'd long since decided he'd be better off listening to his mom than any of the founding fathers. Most of them had been rich, too.

The pickup was a big, fat, bright red Dodge Ramcharger, with a chrome towbar on the front and four big bright clear spotters mounted atop the cab. Even the damn rollbar was chromed. Conspicuous consumption.

Blake sat lazily behind the wheel, cowboy hat slightly askew, looking like something out of a sarcastic Waylon Jennings song, the kind Jennings used to sing back before he and Nelson got big, in west Texas towns like Breckenridge. In the back a couple of kids sipped cokes (the beer would emerge from hiding later, at the lake), leaning back in lawn chairs and soaking up the rays.

Just plain unfair, Alex mumbled to himself.

As he passed the row of rusty mailboxes mounted near the store he paused to peer inside the one labelled ROGAN in reflective plastic letters. A daddy longlegs scurried for cover as Alex's fingers probed.

Jack Blake waited behind the wheel of the idling truck, racing the oversized engine. He was fully conscious of his status in the local adolescent hierarchy and gloried shamelessly in it, not yet old enough to realize that it would all vanish the moment he entered the adult world beyond, where they didn't give a damn about ostrich-skin boots or red pickups. For now, though, he was a king, and there was nothing altruistic or benevolent about his despotism.

His eyes traced the outlines of Maggie's body as neatly as Mrs Hawkins's opaque projector traced scientific drawings for projection on the screen in their darkened science class. Foxy chick, Maggie Gordon, even if she did hang around too much with that nerd Alex Rogan. Rogan was harmless, though. Beneath Blake's notice.

Mindy Hammond sat next to him, staring impatiently out the window, anxious to get to the lake. He looked forward to finding out if she'd fall out of her bathing suit. Such thoughts didn't keep him from coveting Maggie Gordon. More important than having either one of them was having what was denied to him. It was the taking that was important, the acquiring, though Blake formed the idea in much cruder language.

'C'mon, Alex!' one of the boys in the back yelled.

'Pile in . . . jump in, Maggie!'

She handed up the basket, ice chest, towels, then climbed agilely over the tailgate, making sure to leave room for Alex to follow. She saw him inspecting the mailbox.

'Did it come yet?'

'Not yet.' Reluctantly, as though it might still appear, Alex shut the front of the box. It didn't close all the way. Mailboxes never did. All manufacturers designed them so they wouldn't close completely, on explicit orders from the post office.

Seeing this, two of the guys in the truck bed began razzing the slow-moving Alex.

'What is it this time, Rogan?'

'Yeah, you joining the foreign legion or signing up for Space Shuttle school?'

'They don't take vidiots for Space Shuttle pilots, Rogan!'

Not one to be left out of the chorus, Blake leaned out the driver's window. 'Yessir, folks, step right up and meet the boy adventurer Alex Rogan, on the last leg of his world-wide trip to nowhere.'

Alex continued towards the pickup, a sour smile creasing his face. '*Very* funny, Blake. If you guys think I'm gonna stick around here, watch you shine your pickups, get drunk and vomit every Saturday night and wind up at City College like everybody else, forget it. I'm gonna do something with my life!'

'You sure are, turkey,' said Blake readily. 'You're gonna go to work for old man Fargi fixin' TV sets. I'll remember what you just said when you come over to fix my big screen Sony.'

'You haven't got a big screen Sony, Blake.'

The driver of the pickup smiled smugly. 'No, but I'm going to, which is more than you can say for you, dumbutt.'

Alex had a brilliant riposte prepared, but the duel was interrupted by a voice not as easily dismissed.

'Alex?'

Wincing, he turned to look back towards his tin house. It was his mom, sure enough, leaning out one window to call to him.

'Alex, Elvira's electric is out again.' Innocent enough on the surface, commanding underneath.

The occupants of the truck were unable to stifle their laughter. His face burned. At least Maggie wasn't laughing, though at this point that was small comfort. He tried to make his reply sound manly and forceful, to no avail. No matter how hard he tried it still came out sounding like a whine.

'Ah, mom. That'll take all day. I was going to Silver Lake.'

She nodded, looked sympathetic as she gazed past him towards the truck full of his friends. Unfortunately, someone had to fix the electric, and Alex was trailer park repairman number one.

'I'm working lunch and dinner at the cafe, Alex. I'll be gone all day.'

That was a low blow, he thought angrily. Why did mothers always have to fight like that? Must be a talent passed down from mother to daughter, one of the many unfathomable maternal secrets boys could never share. She wouldn't think of *ordering* him to do it, oh no.

He sighed, knowing that he'd already lost the battle, just as he knew she wouldn't have asked him to do the work if she could have managed it herself.

'Okay, mom, I'll do it.'

She smiled back at him and he felt better. But only for a moment.

Turning back to the truck he sought Maggie's eyes. Maggie, who somehow managed to look twice as pretty as any other girl in town despite the lack of makeup and the baggy old sweatshirt she wore on top. He forced his reply. It made him sound noble, which was not how he felt.

'You better go ahead.'

'No, I'll wait for you.' Romeo and Juliet, Tristan and Isolde, all the great tales of heroic love he'd studied in school thrilled him no more than those few words from Maggie.

'No, this could take awhile.' More than a while, but he needed to use the lie now, to spare both of them later embarrassment. 'I'll catch up with you later.'

She understood. He could tell by the look on her face. It was a small consolation.

'OK. See you later.'

'Sure,' he muttered. 'Later.'

'Yeah, we'll be lookin' for you to fly over,' said Blake, leading the others in laughter as he peeled the pickup out of the lot and towards the highway.

Alex could still hear the laughter in his ears long after the big engine had faded into the distance.

II

People who spend their lives in big cities see blue sky only on
television. Oh, on rare clear days they may think they're
seeing sky blue, but it's not real, only a fake faded blue like the
kind used in dyed turquoise. To see the real sky you have to
leave the city, get far away from the megalopoli. Out in the
country the universe crowds a little nearer the Earth and the
hues of the spectrum have meaning.

The one other place where colours are always rendered
purely is in any advertisement for faraway regions. This
extended to the starfield map which covered part of one wall
of Alex and Louis's room. It was surrounded by equally
garish, less enlightened posters reflective of the more
mundane aspects of reality. The walls of the boys' room were
more colourful than their clothing.

Especially that particular evening, when Alex finally
shuffled into the room. He was exhausted and filthy. Beneath
his nails were the kind of sand and grit you can't wash out, the
kind you learn to live with for days until repeated baths have
soaked it away. The kind of grime that has the look and
consistency of black concrete. Alex's spirits were lower than
the surrounding desert's water table.

The small desk was filled with notes and scribblings for
school. He slumped down in the used office chair, swivelled
to face the centre of the room as he wrestled with his muddy
boots, carefully removing them and setting them aside so as to
dirty the floor as little as possible.

Then he leaned back, letting his eyes focus on the mobile dangling from the ceiling. It pivoted in the light of sundown, aimlessly reflective, its indecision about how to turn a mirror of his own feelings.

From beyond the thin wall and window came the conversation of neighbours. Alex recognized each one, began to silently mimic the rarely changing words.

'Pleasant day today, eh?'

'Yep. Goin' to be a pleasant day tomorrow, too.'

'Goin' to be a pleasant summer, accordin' to the Farmers' Almanac.'

The talk continued, but Alex had stopped imitating the unseen speakers. Instead he found himself sitting straight up in his chair, frightened and aware. Aware of how that conversation had reached him virtually unaltered on hundreds of similar evenings. Aware that if he didn't do *something*, and do it soon, he'd be fixing 'lectrics and patching water lines and repairing recalcitrant garbage disposals while listening to the same chatter for the rest of his life.

Such simple, cunning traps existence laid for the unwary! His mother owned the trailer park outright. Easy enough for him to ease into handling the books as well as the repairs, to take over day-to-day operation of the business from her. Was that what mom really wanted for him? Was she carefully and efficiently leading him down that safe, secure, lethally dull path? He'd always doubted it before. Now he wasn't sure.

One thing he was certain of, though. If he fell into that waiting trap and allowed himself to take the easy way out of making a living, he'd never escape. Never do anything in the world. It would be exactly like Jack Blake had said, and the laughter that had trailed back to Alex from behind the pickup would follow him, in the slightly more circumspect fashion of adults, for the rest of his life.

Damned if it would!

He slipped on clean shoes and fled from the friendly, warm room that had suddenly turned cold and alien and threatening, rushed outside into the mild air of evening, and forced himself to slow down.

25

There was nowhere to run to, except onto the road or down into the desert. Not that he was running with thoughts of any particular destination in mind. He ran to prove to himself that he, Alex Rogan, was still in control and that life hadn't sealed him up in its smothering blanket of paycheque and taxes and eight-hour workdays. Not yet it hadn't. He was going to do something.

If only he knew what.

It was dark outside, desert nights as black as the days were bright. In the darkness the neon sign outside the general store sputtered into intermittent life. Out back the big halogen lamp came alive, showing the way for residents and visitors alike.

He needed to do something, anything, to take his mind off his sudden terror. But there wasn't anything. Only the radio and the television and one quarter-eating machine.

He'd run away from passivity and bland acceptance, so radio and TV were out of the question. They represented a return to threatening reality, not an escape. On the other hand the game was interactive, depeandant on his movements, on his decisions. Not like in real life, where such decisions were reserved for adults. At a videogame any kid could be in demand, could make life or death decisions (if only in the abstract) on the glowing field of the screen, no matter if they concerned only eating dots, demented gorillas, or a not-too-bright knight in search of his kidnapped princess.

Or defending the frontier against Xur and the Ko-Dan Armada.

The people who'd installed the game one Friday had told him it was a difficult one. At first it had been hard for him, but now he'd grown bored with all but the hellaciously difficult upper levels. Most kids never reached them and watched in awe as he sauntered rapidly through the lower ranges that defeated their best efforts.

Now he played alone on the porch, and the machine responded with whizzes and explosions and mock commands as he methodically worked his way up into the rarified strata beyond half a million points.

'Yeah, yeah,' he mutterd aloud, impatient as always with the basics. 'Let's speed it up, huh?'

'Prepare for target light practice, Starfighter.' The machine warned him in the same tone as always.

Better now. As the play grew steadily more involved he started to take an active interest in the glowing goings-on. Already he'd run up a high score by concentrating on adding bonuses in the preliminary rounds instead of simply blasting his way through each stage.

'Ready,' he murmured, as if the machine could hear and understand. It could not, but it added to the fun. He was relaxed again, calm and confident. His early fear had been wiped out by the need for him to concentrate on every aspect of the game lest he get blown away from carelessness. He'd mastered the game, true. He could play it in his sleep. But carelessness could trip up the most skilful player. Alex had always prided himself on never losing a videogame because of some stupid, thoughtless mistake. The game had to beat him. He wouldn't beat himself.

Someone else had heard the buzzes and pops and whines and had come out to see the light from the screen reflected on Alex's face. Otis lit his final pipe of the day as he strolled over to watch. He liked the games, too, but played only rarely. His hand-eye coordination wasn't as good as it used to be, and he'd worked too many years to start squandering his quarters now.

It was just as much fun to watch the kids play, especially one as good as Alex. The coordination of today's kids never ceased to amaze him.

In addition to liking the game, he also liked Alex Rogan. That prompted him to ask, 'Where's Magie?'

Alex's eyes never turned from the screen, but he heard.

'Good question. Out having a good time, I guess. At least, I haven't seen her since she went off with everybody else this morning.'

Otis concealed his smile. 'Oh, I see. And you never have a "good time", that it?'

'Sure I do, Otis. I have some great times.' Otis had insisted

27

that Alex call him by his first name ever since Alex could remember. 'Mr Davis' was someone else, the man who picked up pension cheques at a mailbox. Otis, on the other hand, was a friend.

'I *love* fixing the electric system, checking the plumbing, plunging toilets and cleaning up animal stuff.' He made a face. 'Otis, I don't even get a *chance* to have a good time around here.'

The game let loose with a flurry of bright lights and electronic sound effects. Alex had advanced yet another level. Now he caught his breath, flexed his fingers while waiting for the next setup to materialize.

'Things change; always do. I ought to know.' Again the smile around the stem of the worn pipe. 'You'll get your chance, boy. Important thing is, when it comes, you got to be ready for it. You gotta grab it with both hands and hold on tight.'

'Real profound, Otis.'

'I don't pretend to be no philosophy professor, Alex. I didn't make as much as some folks either, but I took care of what I made because I knew what I wanted out of life. A hundred bucks invested right is better in ten years than a thousand bucks squandered now. I ain't rich, but I'm comfortable. I don't have to work anymore and I don't want or worry about anything.'

'Did you miss any opportunities when you were my age, Otis?'

'Sure I did. We all do. But nobody ever warned me about missing 'em like I'm warning you now. I figure maybe I'm doing you a favour. Experience isn't worth a thing if you can't pass it along to someone else. There's lots of things in life you can go back and replace, Alex, but not missed opportunities. You remember that.'

He broke off as a big boxy shape emerged from the darkness and slid into the parking lot. Maggie climbed over the tailgate, balancing a moment on the oversized, custom rear steel bumper before jumping lightly to the ground. The picnic basket, empty now, was tossed down to her, followed by the towel and the borrowed ice chest. Goodbyes were made, accompanied by laughter and quips, all part of the aftermath of a good day's mindless fun in the sun. Alex struggled futilely to shut it out, concentrating on the screen.

Otis saw the youngster's expression tighten and knew it had nothing to do with the difficulties of the game. His smile turned sad and he moved away, aiming for the rocking chair at the far end of the porch.

Someone else noticed Alex's discomfiture, however, and had no compunctions about rubbing new salt into fresh wounds.

''Night Maggs.' Blake made sure he said it loud enough for Alex to hear him above the microprocessed mutter of the videogame. 'See you 'round!'

It was small comfort to Alex that Maggie didn't reply. His fingernails dug at the impervious plastic around the control buttons.

His offroad tyres spitting sand, Blake roared out of the lot, not caring if he woke any early sleepers. The noise hid the laughter. Or maybe there wasn't any laughter. Maybe it was only in Alex's mind.

Maggie climbed the steps onto the porch, watching Alex closely as she came up behind him. She took a minute to study the videoscreen, but the nuances of the game were lost to her. Girls didn't go in much for the wargames, no matter what the women's libbers might claim. Girls preferred crushing the nasties in Millipede or the complicated maze games like Pac-Man and its variants.

Maggie didn't much care for any of them. She only took an interest because Alex was interested, though she could still admire his skill.

'Packs low... life support plus two and functioning... photonics low...' The machine delivered its announcements in clipped, precise artificial tones, indifferent to everything else.

Maggie rose on tiptoes to give Alex a peck on the cheek. He smiled briefly, kept his gaze locked on the screen. He was glad of the game. It gave him an excuse for not meeting her eyes.

29

'I thought you were going to meet me at the lake,' she said. 'What happened?' An open question, devoid of accusation. Maggie wasn't bitter, only genuinely curious.

'The same thing that always happens.' He wanted to sound mad but was only tired. Life was grinding him down. At eighteen. 'I couldn't get away. Fix this, repair that... you should see some of the junk that passes for wiring in some of these old mobiles.' He looked beyond her into the darkness to make sure she'd got out of the pickup by herself.

'Where's everyone else?'

'They went to a movie.'

'And Jack Blake just happened to be going your away?'

'What did you expect me to do? Walk back?'

He didn't get the chance to reply because an alien warship unexpectedly sent a salvo of missiles in his direction and he had to evade and counterattack simultaneously.

Maggie noted his concentration, though she had only the slightest idea of the difficulty involved. Then she saw the score and abruptly found herself staring intently at the screen full of little coloured lights and matrix images. She also managed to move closer to Alex.

'Energy weaponry on reserve... life support critical... photonics at peak...' the machine declaimed emotionlessly.

'Look out on the right!' Maggie yelled and pointed, excitedly now in spite of herself. She'd seen Alex play the game many times before but never had the screen been so crowded and full of action. She added absently, 'He said it was on his way home.'

'What was?'

'The trailer park, silly.'

'Issat so? Blake happens to live on the other side of town. He's dumb, but not that dumb. Maybe not half as dumb as I'd like to think.'   Exasperation filled Maggie's reply. 'Alex, I wanted to get back to you, okay? Hey, you're really going great.'

'Am I?'

'Haven't you checked your score?'

'No time. Too busy.' And too busy to watch her arrive in

30

Jack Blake's ramcharger, a small voice scolded him. His gaze flicked upwards and he was surprised in spite of himself. 'Hey, nine hundred thousand plus. Not bad.'

Otis overheard. Despite his initial determination to leave the young folks to their privacy he couldn't keep himself from abandoning his rocker and walking over to have a look. He stared at the screen.

'Nine hundred and twenty thousand. I thought you told me this machine can't score over a million.'

'I don't see how it can,' Alex replied, concentrating on his work. 'It isn't calibrated past nine ninety nine. Maybe we're going to find out what it does.'

'You're going to bust it, Alex.' Otis moved to the edge of the porch, facing the park, cupped his hands to his mouth and shouted.

'Listen up, everybody! Alex is going for the record. He's goin' to bust the machine!'

'You can't bust these machines, Otis.'

'Then what happens if you hit a million?'

'I don't know ... but it won't bust. Will it?'

Otis leaned close to the machine, his pipe smoking like a small steam engine. 'Don't ask me, son. You're the electric wizard around here.'

A couple of the regulars who'd been sitting outside soaking up the evening cool heard Otis's exclamation and, attracted by the thought of one of their own doing something a little out of the ordinary, strolled over to see what was going on. They were nearly knocked over as a gaggle of excited kids dashed past them, all but attacking the porch, pushing and shoving for the best advantage points. Alex's younger brother was in the lead and edged his way up close as strange new sights began appearing on the screen. As quickly as they materialized, Alex methodically demolished them.

'Wow, you never got his far before, Alex!' Louis was so excited he kept bouncing up and down in front of the screen. Alex had to nudge him aside with an elbow. 'The Command Ship! Beat the green shit outta it, Alex!'

'I'm trying to, if you'll keep your nose out of my line of

31

sight.'

'Oh, sorry.' Louis stopped bouncing... for about ten seconds.

There was a bad moment when Alex was positive he'd blown it. Photonics were streaking for his position and there seemed no way out. In the split second available for making a decision he determined to do the unexpected. Instead of fleeing or trying evasion mode he boosted speed towards his attacker. The photonics, calculated to intercept him only if he fled, exploded harmlessly behind him. Before a second wave could be fired in defence, his fingers were stabbing as smoothly as any typist's on the fire control buttons.

The image of the alien command ship exploded and the bright flare of light shrank pupils all around the screen, making some of the onlookers wince involuntarily. The score limned by the red LED readout above the action rolled over past nine hundred and ninety-nine thousand while the synthesized voice inside the console screamed triumphantly, 'RECORD BREAKER, RECORD BREAKER!'

The lights faded, the screen blanked, to be replaced briefly with the words, 'CONGRATULATIONS, STAR-FIGHTER.'

'Wow.' Louis's voice was reverent. 'You really blew it away, Alex. What happens now?'

Trying to sound nonchalant, Alex gave a little shrug and turned diffidently away from the console. 'Got to find a tougher game, I guess. No point in playing this one anymore.'

More personal accolades were heaped upon the champion in the intermittent light supplied by the buzzing neon sign. Though most of the older inhabitants of the trailer park (Otis being the exception) knew next to nothing about the newfangled electronic games, they could recognize skill in another, and it was self-evident that Alex had just done something very exceptional.

Gradually their talk turned to more familiar topics: weather, taxes, the price of gas, the weather, the quality of this year's cotton crop, how many tourists could be expected during the Season, and, of course, the weather. They slid off into the night, chatting amiably as friends do, the quick jolt of excitement already forgotten. Otis gave Alex a contratulatory pat on the back before heading for his own mobile.

Alex turned to Maggie. 'Whattaya think?'

'Not bad. But is there a future in it?'

He slumped. 'Guess not. But it's fun.' He tried for a lecherous grin. 'Want to come over and see my electronic etchings?'

'You know, Alex, I always wondered what a real etching was?'

'Me too, but it's a nice line. Well, how about coming over to watch the crickets sing?'

'Do they sound like Men at Work?'

'Depends on the crickets.'

She grinned. 'Okay, but you have to promise to walk me home. It's scaaarrry out.' The Gordon trailer was one step removed from the Rogans'.

'It's a deal, if my feet hold out. I've been on them all day.'

She was suddenly sympathetic again. 'I'm really sorry about the picnic, Alex.'

'That's oaky. At least one of us had a good time.'

The crickets were not recordable, nor did they sound much like Men at Work, or even their much earlier namesakes. It didn't matter to Alex and Maggie. They snuggled close on the worn porch swing set up in the small fenced area that was the Rogans' front yard, luxuriating in the cool evening air. Around them the trailer park was winding down for the night. It was the end of still another summer day. Maggie said little, preoccupied, and Alex was wise enough not to press her for her thoughts.

Somewhere Dan Rather's pejorations clashed with the Spinners doing Rubberband Man on Otis's stereo. Otis had asked Alex for his opinion on compact disc players but gave up on the idea when he discovered there was nothing out he wanted to hear. Sony didn't seem interested in Otis's favourite music.

Alex didn't care much for it either, except for one singer Otis played over and over. It was a voice that stood out even above the news of the war in Afghanistan and the rise of the prime rate: Billie Holiday. Alex wished he could have seen her in concert. That made Otis smile, because he knew his young friend would never have been admitted to the joints where Holiday had been forced to make her living. But the boy's interest pleased him.

'Yep,' a voice was saying from the region of the Boone trailer, 'that Alex sure is gonna go places.'

'Sure is,' Elvira concurred.

'I'll say,' agreed Mrs Boone. There was a pause, and then Granny Gordon announced the termination of parental radar by calling out, 'G'night, kids.'

A few moments later the lights in the Gordon trailer went out. Mrs Rogan wasn't home yet. Alex waited a moment longer before slipping his right hand innocently around Maggie's shoulder. Seemingly of their own volition, the fingers clenched gently, drawing her still closer to him.

Her face turned up towards his and their eyes locked. He bent forward, lips straining for hers ... and she dodged neatly, pecking him on the cheek. Then she rose from the swing and headed for her trailer.

'Night, Alex.'

His first thought was that she'd made some kind of unconscious mistake. Her aim was off, that was all. But there was more to it than that.

'"Night, Alex"?' he repeated. 'What the hell's "Night, Alex"?' He wasn't as much mad as he was confused. Usually it was Maggie who initiated the kissing. 'Hey, wait!' he caught up to her as she started up the steps towards her small porch.

The spies were out that night. No CIA recruit listened or watched more intently than Louis Rogan from his position at his bedroom window. He was old enough to have some idea of what was happening, was aware there was physicality involved (though he thought of it in different terms). He was as fascinated by the sight as if he'd been witness to a murder.

Maggie continued up the steps but hesitated at the door.

'C'mon, Maggie, tell me what's wrong. You can always tell me what's wrong.'

She eyed him uncertainly. 'Won't get mad?'

'Promise.' He held up crossed fingers, looked solemn.

'I guess it finally hit me.' She didn't want to look at him, discovered she couldn't look anyplace else. 'You're really going away, aren't you?'

'Is that what's bugging you?'

'Isn't that enough? Don't you think that's important?'

'Sure it's important. Of course I'm going away. We're both going away.'

She frowned. 'Both?'

He mounted the steps, put both hands on her shoulders. She didn't back away. 'Yeah, both of us. Who'd pester me if not you? Who'd pester you if I wasn't around? Don't you remember? We already went through all this. I go to college, find a place, get a job, and come back for you.'

'I . . . I didn't think you were serious about that, Alex, I thought you were just talking through your hat.'

'Naw. Always talk through my lips. See?' He stuck out his chin, pointed to his puckered mouth. 'Watch my lips. I . . . am . . . coming . . . back . . . for . . . you. Got it?'

'But what about Granny? She needs someone to look after her.'

'Granny?' Alex nodded sharply at the trailer. 'Granny needs someone to look after her as much as Ma Barker did. Granny can take care of herself, and anyway, you're not the only one she's got. Who do you think helps her out when you're in school?' He gestured towards the surrounding mobiles. 'This whole park's her family. I should have so many friends looking after me.' She was silent, and he found himself nodding at her.

'That's not it. That's not it at all, is it? It's something else. The truth is that you're scared of leaving this place. Scared of leaving . . .'

Suddenly angry, she snapped back at him. 'I am *not* scared!'

He put up both hands, defensively. 'Hey, take it easy. So maybe I'm wrong. You know how to prove me wrong.' He softened his tone.

'Whatever happens, whether you come with me right away, or later, or down the road some time, it's you and me forever right? Rogan and Gordon versus the world. 'Cause I'm not goin' anywhere far enough to keep me from coming back to you, Maggie.'

What now? Was she laughing at him, or crying? It was always so hard to be sure. He had a clearer idea when she put her arms around him and hugged him tight.

'Oh, I love you so much, Alex.'

'And I love you twice as much back, Maggie. I'll always love you.'

This time their lips didn't miss.

Unable to believe his prepubescent gaze, Louis Rogan made an anguished sound as he flipped up the visor on his space helmet, the better to ensure missing none of the sickening display. Weren't they *ever* going to let go of one another? And how could they *breathe*? Maybe they were holding their breath, yeah, that had to be it. But how could they hold their breath for so *long*?

'Di-a-*ree*-ah!' he murmured, thoroughly disgusted with what he was seeing.

But he didn't turn away.

III

One good thing about working in a small town, Jane Rogan thought tiredly as she drove the old pickup into the parking place alongside her home: everyone knew you too well to risk pinching you. Not that some of the regulars in the cafe didn't keep trying to pick her up. At first it had been flattering. Now it was just boring. She doubted any of the men were serious, though. It was nothing more than a carefully choreographed ballet.

'Hey Jane,' Seth Daniel would call out, 'how about bringing some of that over here?'

'Some of what, Seth?' she would reply, the waitress's professional smile glued on her face.

And Seth would grin at his coffee-drinking buddies and say, 'You know what.'

And she would sigh and reply, 'Not on the menu tonight, Seth. Besides, you know your stomach.'

And they would all guffaw while muttering private male obscenities to one another, and the tips would be good, and that was what mattered.

She checked the front seat to make sure she'd gathered up all the mail and put it on top of one of the two big bags of groceries, next to the loaf of generic brand white bread. Then she balanced a bag in the crook of each arm and started for the trailer. She could have called Alex out to help, but she already felt badly enough about making him miss his picnic that morning. So she managed by herself, even though the bags were getting a little heavier each month, in spite of the fact that she always bought the same quantity of groceries.

Once inside, she set the bags down on the kitchen table, put the spoilables in the refrigerator and the freezer, then went to check on Louis. He was lying in bed, eyes shut tight. She backed out, checked Alex's room, wasn't surprised to discover it empty.

Still, a look at her watch caused her to frown. She knew there was no reason for her to worry. Not about Alex. Except ... ever since he'd made that one trip to the college side of town and had come back at three a.m. reeking of beer she'd felt compelled to keep a closer eye on him. Of course, he'd only done that once, and he was of the age to sow a few wild if thoughtless oats, but having been forced to miss the picnic and the swimming he might just be in a state of mind to try something silly and ...

Her worries vanished as he came striding into the living room, a big smile plastered across his handsome young face. He was whistling the theme from Rocky loud enough to wake half the park.

'Shushh, Alex, you'll wake Granny and the others.'

'Wake Granny? Granny Gordon could sleep through World War Three, humble mom.' He gazed ceilingward and adopted a Shakespearean pose. 'Yea, and someday they shall point to this place, to this very abode of tin and glue, and they shall say, *this* is where it all began.' He slipped back into his normal slouch, grinning widely at her.

'Guess what? I finally broke the record on Starfighter. Not the local record, mind you. I pushed it so far it had to back up and start over again.'

'That's nice, dear.' She sifted the mail, some of which she'd already opened and checked. The bills she left untouched, preferring to put aside their malign revelations until the last possible instant.

'Nice?' He gaped at her. Obviously she had no idea of the significance of his accomplishment. When he'd walked into the room he'd felt like Rocky running up the library steps in Philadelphia. Now his euphoria vanished and he felt like

Rocky in Rocky III, getting the stuffing bashed out of him by Mr T.

Mothers had a way of deflating one's ego faster than a blocked punt run back against you for a touchdown.

'It's stupendous, mom, not "nice". We need to call somebody. The paper, the Guiness Book of Records people, the local TV news...'

'I picked up all the mail,' she replied patiently, nipping intimations of imminent immortality in the bud, 'because Mr Perlam's truck broke down.' She handed over a single ragged-topped envelope. 'This came for you and when I saw the return address I got so excited I had to open it.'

'That's okay, mom.' Still feeling good, he accepted the envelope. 'What is it?'

She didn't look at him. 'It's about your loan.'

'Loan?' Suddenly he didn't want to understand. Didn't want to know because he already knew the nature of the letter's contents from the look on her face. He just held the envelope, staring at her.

'Your student loan.' She sighed again, deeply this time, and tried to smile at him. 'I know how much it meant to you, Alex, but you can still go to City College with your friends.'

Weak and sick, he let the letter slide out of its container and forced himself to read the words. 'Dear Mr Rogan,' it said with unctuous politeness, 'we regret to inform you that your application for a loan to cover tuition and related study costs at the University has regretfully been denied due to lack of sufficient collateral.

'Scholarship loans, we must remind you, are dependent on achieving an SAT test score of approximately...'

He crumpled the paper slowly in one hand. Of course his SAT scores weren't what they should have been, could have been. How could they be, when you spent half the nights the month of the testing fixing crappy plumbing and installing fibreglass insulation and exterminating ants? How did they expect him to study, to keep up with the rich kids like Jack Blake with his free time and his personal computer and his tutor and ... and ...

'And I'll always love *you*, Maggie,' murmured Louis wetly from his listening post in the hallway. 'Kissy, kissy, kissy!'

'Louis!' Mrs Rogan shouted.

Ten-year-old or no, Louis saw something then in Alex's sudden glance that made him retreat back into the warm darkness of the hall. It wasn't a threatening look. That he was prepared for and could have coped with. What he wasn't ready to handle was the look of pain on the face of his invulnerable, indomitable big brother. In his preadolescent fashion he was aware that he was responsible for some of that pain, so different from the usual childish torments he and Alex exchanged. It was a numbing realization and he didn't know how to react. He felt queasy, as if he'd just eaten something he knew he shouldn't have.

Alex didn't say anything to him, which was good. The expression on his face was hurtful enough. Twice embarrassed, he turned and fled from the trailer.

'Alex!' Jane Rogan moved after him, halted at the doorway. Sometimes peace and privacy could be more consoling than maternal concern. She was a good enough parent to let him go.

When you're running real hard, fast as you can, and your mind is elsewhere, sometimes you forget to breathe. Eventually the body gets through to the brain and both combine to bring you up short. Alex slowed, wheezing and gasping, found himself halfway to the highway. Behind him coloured lights flashed at the night, Starlight, Starbright, Overnighters Welcome, in intermittent neon swirls.

He uncrumpled the letter, still clenched in his right fist, and read through it a second time. There was nothing personal in it. It was a standard printed rejection form. Even the signature had the look of a stamp. Nothing personal. He let it drop to the road.

Nothing personal, he thought, as an evening breeze carried his hopes for the future towards the ditch that bordered the parking area.

It didn't matter. Just like mom said, he could still go to City College with his friends. But he didn't *want* to go to City

College with his friends. He wanted to go to the University. He wanted *out*; out of the county, out of the state, out of Starlight, Starbright and all it stood for.

He could go to City College and collect his AB, then move on. Two years of juco and then the University would have to accept him, would have to. But that also meant two more years of rusty pipes and blackened electrical outlets. Two more years of 'gonna be a hot one today', every day for the whole summer. Two more years of nothing to do in nowhere. He couldn't take it.

Behind him, something went *spizzit*. Frowning, he turned back towards the general store. At first he was sure it was the big neon sign, finally determined to give up the neon ghost. The buzzing noises came again, but the sign never flickered or dimmed. The sound and the flashing light came from beyond. He headed for the porch.

It was the videogame, come alive with colour and light, practically vibrating with energy. But no one was playing it and there was no one in sight. His first thought was that someone had tried to break into the machine's coin box, but a close look showed no signs of attempted break-in, no denting of the hard steel that protected the collection containers.

Funny too those lights and that buzzing noise. Not like the game responses at all. Abstract yet organized. He decided a power surge was the cause. Sure, that would explain it. Somewhere up the line between the park and the generators at Hoover a big surge had shot through the grid and had thrown the game's delicate microprocessor out of whack.

All he could do was unplug it until the company that serviced it could be notified. If he left it alone it might burn itself out, and he didn't want to chance his mom being held liable for damages due to negligence. They couldn't raise a fuss if he just pulled the plug.

He reached for the back of the console . . . and it stopped. Just went dead, almost as if it were afraid of being turned off and had decided to be good.

Or maybe he'd debated too long and it already had burnt itself out, he thought.

A dark shape suddenly loomed on the road in front of the store, just inside the glow from the store's lights. It caught Alex's attention immediately, large and boxy and unusually long. A rich man's toy, some kind of customized cut-down van. Funny-sounding engine, too.

'Hello,' said a voice. 'Excuse me, son?' A gullwing door whirred open, piquing Alex's curiosity further. He was torn between his duty to check out the suddenly silent game and his desire to see inside that peculiar vehicle. It was an uneven battle.

He walked towards the car, trying to get a good look at the interior without seeming to stare. 'That's a neat car, mister.'

'Thanks. I try to keep it in shape.'

'Foreign job?'

'It is an import, yes.' The man smiled at nothing in particular.

Alex gave it a last, envious once-over before announcing officially, 'Store's closed now.' He pointed towards the highway. 'It's not far into town. There's a 7-Eleven on Main that's open twenty-fours hours. You can probably get what you need there.'

'I doubt it, son.'

Alex tried to see down the road. 'You don't have a trailer broke down somewhere, do you?'

Something inside the car moved and he saw a dimly illuminated face. It was an elderly face, male, lined but without the deep creases of true old age. The owner might have been anywhere from fifty to eighty. His white sideburns were bushy. When he looked up Alex was startled by the clarity of the driver's eyes. They might have been transparent, protective lenses shielding some deeper secret from sight.

The man puffed on a cigarette at the end of a long holder, something Alex had seen only in the movies. As if sensing the boy's interest the driver removed the holder and inspected the cigarette affectionately.

'Quaint affectation. Generates nothing in the way of nourishment, chemical stimuli or beneficial endocrine

42

products, yet it's catchy, catchy.'

'I beg your pardon?'

'Nothing, my boy. In reply to your question, no, I do not have a trailer broke down somewhere. Nor am I here to peruse your establishment for cigarettes or chewing gum. Actually I am here looking for someone.'

Alex remembered some of the tales Otis had told him about his younger days. He'd always laughed at the stories, afterwards, knowing they were nothing more than tall tales spun to wile away the hot summer evenings. Now he wasn't so sure.

'You with the IRS?'

Now it was the old man's turn to look confused. 'The IRS? A perennial; rhizomatous or bulbous herbaceous plant of the family Iridaceae, is it not?'

Alex took a step backward. 'Mister, I think maybe you've had too much to drink tonight.'

'Nonsense! I've imbibed no more liquid than is necessary for proper bodily functioning. As to this individual I seek,' and he gestured towards the porch, 'can you by chance tell me the name of the person who broke the record on that game over there, and where I might find 'em?'

Pride overwhelmed Alex's caution. This old guy was weird, but surely he was harmless. And the fancy rig he was driving... maybe he worked for the company that made the Starfighter game. Maybe there was some kind of electronic relay or something built into the console that sent back the results to some local headquarters. Maybe this old man wanted to give him a prize or something.

'His name's Alex Rogan, mister, and you're looking at him. Who're you? Did I win something for my score? Is that why you're here?'

The man choked on his cigarette. 'Hard to get the knack of this. What, win something? Well, you might say that. Yes, one could say that your achievement has entitled you to receive a singular honour.'

Visions of enough money to pay his way through the University suddenly flooded Alex's mind. Maybe there'd even be some left over. He could buy Louis the stuffed tauntaun he'd always wanted. He could buy mom a new TV, maybe even a new truck!

He forced himself to dampen his excitement. Perhaps the prize didn't consist of cash. It might be some kind of product, or nothing more than a bunch of free plays on the game.

But if it wasn't something big, something important, then why would the company send someone out to meet the top player in person?

'As for myself,' and the oldster smiled broadly, 'Centauri's the name. I invented Starfighter, which is why I'm here to talk to you.'

'Really? You actually invented the game?'

The old man looked pleased. 'Sure did. What do you think of it?'

Alex struggled to sound sophisticated. 'Not bad. It took me awhile to get the hang of it. It's not as complicated as some games but there are a lot of controls to work at the same time and the upper skill levels make you work pretty fast.'

'That's what Starfighters are supposed to do,' Centauri informed him, 'and you've proven you can do it as well or better than anyone else. Better than anyone else around here, certainly.'

'No bullshit?' His ego rose another notch.

'No bullshit, Alex.'

'What about my prize?'

'Ah, yes. Your prize. We must talk about that. It is a matter of the utmost importance.' He gestured towards the rear seat. 'Step into my office.'

Alex started around the hood, hesitated on reaching the other side of the vehicle. The old man *looked* straight, and he seemed honest. How could some creep know about his achievements on the game? And this wasn't Los Angeles or New York.

Still, there was the fancy car, and the fact that it was dark and quiet out. Alex read the papers, followed the nightly news on channel three. He didn't want to end up a surprised corpse in some irrigation ditch.

'Maybe I'd better get my mom out here. If I've won something she'll need to know about it, and if there are forms to sign, I'm not twenty-one yet. I'll need a co-signer and . . .'

'Do you think I am some threadbare charlatan?' Centauri was suddenly angry. 'I am *Centauri*, and you may . . . you must . . . trust me implicitly! There are no forms to sign, and you may inform your maternal parent of the honour you have been selected to receive in good time.

'For now though, time and secrecy are of the essence. Do I look like some metropolitan pervert scrounging the back alleys and streets in search of the innocent to debase? Is that what you are thinking of me, my boy?'

'Well, uh . . . no,' Alex replied, trying to hide the fact that the thought had occurred to him. Then he had an idea which made him feel much better.

'You say you invented Starfighter?'

The old man nodded. 'That's right. Devised the look and format all by myself.'

Then you tell me what appears on the screen on the eighth attack level?'

Centauri didn't hesitate. 'Ko-Dan Pack Fighters in squads of six guarding six landing ships equipped for taking control of civilian targets.'

Alex relaxed. No passing weirdo would know that, even if he'd played the game on occasion. Eighth level was rarifield territory. Some of his initial excitement returned as he climbed into the car.

The interior was more spacious than he'd expected. There was lots of leg room and a complex array of digital instrumentation visible all around, none of which he recognized. Not that he was any expert on what pinafarina might have put on the road that year. The back of the car was solid. There was no rear window.

Something moved away from him and he sensed another presence close by, though he couldn't see a face.

'Oh yes,' said Centauri. 'Say hello to my assistant, Beta.'

'Betty?'

'No, Beta.'

45

'Is he Geek?'

'Hardly.' The old man grinned.

Alex strained but couldn't make out any features in the dark. The car's bulk blocked out most of the light from the trailer park and the instrument panels up front were lit by subdued illumination.

He reached out to shake hands. 'Hello.'

There was a tiny spark that made him jerk his hand back and look quickly at his fingers.

'Static electricity,' said Centauri smoothly. 'You know the problems you can have with these foreign models.'

'Yeah, sure.' While he was engaged in inspecting his still tingling hand, the other passenger had disembarked, still without giving Alex a clear look at his face. He appeared to be a young man, about Alex's size. More than that Alex hadn't been able to tell.

He turned back to the driver. 'Centauri's the name of the star nearest Earth, isn't it?'

'Sure is. Alpha Centauri. And Beta Centauri. I assure you I am not related to my assistant, except through common interests.' He nodded outside. 'He has business of his own to attend to and will not be rejoining us.'

'Funny name,' Alex murmured.

'Now what makes you say that?' Centauri sounded hurt. 'Plenty of people are named after stars. There's Carina, and Andromeda, and Lyra, and...'

'Okay, okay. I take it back. So it's not a funny name. I just never met anyone named Centauri before, that's all.'

'It's more distinctive than Joe, isn't it? Better a distinctive name for a distinctive personality.'

'What about my prize? Or honour, or whatever you want to call it?'

'Ah, yes. I really must congratulate you on your virtuoso handling of the game, my boy. Centauri's impressed, and that ought to impress you.'

'Impress me with a prize,' said Alex, tired of being put off. But the old man seemed determined to ramble on.

'I seen 'em come and go, but you're the best, m'boy, the

46

very best. Dazzling execution, phenomenal hand to eye coordination, a positive instinct for making the right decision at the critical moment. Light years ahead of the competition.'

'Thanks.' Alex was trying hard not to fall under the spell of this wave of tribute.

'Which is why Centauri's here. He's got a little proposition for you. Interested?'

'What kind of proposition?' Alex was suddenly wary.

'It involves the game. Being a Starfighter player. Interested yet? The rewards are great.'

'Sounds good, I guess.' Maybe the company wanted him to give demonstrations or something. Surely they had to pay him for that.

'Bravo! I knew you'd say that.' He turned to his controls. 'Now you must meet your fellows.'

'What? What fellows?' Were there other prize winners besides himself?

There was a *whoosh* as the gullwing doors came slamming down. They locked tight without the metallic snap Alex expected. Everything inside the car operated silently and with great precision.

The engine seemed to whine instead of rumble as Centauri peeled out of the parking lot like it was the final lap at Indy. Nor did he slow down upon entering the highway, ignoring the stopsign at the intersection. Instead, he accelerated, indifferent to the first curves as they began to climb into the hills.

Unexpected acceleration shoved the wide-eyed Alex back into his seat. Inside the car all was silent. He'd never imagined such efficient insulation. At the speed they were travelling there should be a roaring all around them, but wind and noise were completely shut out of the car. As for the seat comforting him, it nudged gently from behind, supporting him with an oddly personal touch. Soon he found that despite their increasing speed he was able to move his arms and legs with ease.

'Hey, what the hell . . .?' He covered his face instinctively as the car leaned into a sharp curve. Somehow it managed the bend without spinning off the road.

'Handles well, doesn't she?' Centauri was as calm and composed as if they were negotiating rural traffic in broad daylight at ten miles an hour. 'Special compensators. All I have to do is drive. Not all these hybrids are built with an eye for that kind of detail.' He grinned. 'This is fun!'

When Alex's larynx finally unfroze he was barely able to gasp, 'What are you doing? You're going to get us killed!'

'Fiddlesticks! Why would I want to do that? Not only is death inefficient, it's counterproductive. You don't have a death wish, do you? I understand it's quite common among you folks.'

'No, I don't.' Alex whispered.

'Well then?'

'Don't,' Alex gulped, unable to take his fear-filled gaze off the road ahead, 'you think we may be going just a teensy bit too fast?'

'Too fast?' Centauri frowned for a moment. 'Nonsense. How can we be going too fast? We're hardly moving.'

Alex watched little white posts flick past his window, one right after another. They were highway markers. He knew they were travelling too fast now for him to think of doing anything, but if this madman ever slowed down... he reached over to check the door handle.

There was no door handle.

'What are you doing?' he repeated desperately. Dimly he recalled something of their earlier conversation. Everything had seemed so normal. When they'd been standing still. Before his heart threatened to leave his body by way of his throat. 'What about my prize?'

'Ah, your surprise, your great honour. Listen, Centauri wants to keep it a surprise a little longer. Allow me that little pleasure. Trust me. You're gonna love it. *Love* it! And who wouldn't? It's the greatest honour ever devolved on mankind and it's yours, all yours. Isn't that something?'

'Will I live to enjoy it?' he whispered, aware he was digging into the seat with all ten fingers.

'Wouldn't be much of an honour if you didn't, would it?

Honestly, I find this preoccupation with death on your part most unhealthy in a Starfighter, my boy. I fail to comprehend your attitude. You're much too young to be thinking about dying.'

'I agree,' said Alex readily, 'so why don't you slow down a little, OK? Please!'

Centauri shook his head, concentrating on his driving. 'Can't do that. Not now. Wouldn't do.' The car continued to accelerate. Now the mountain landscape outside was little more than a blur, dark shapes blending into one another, individual details incomprehensible with speed, the world outside green and brown streaks on black, as swirled together as the colours in a Georgia O'Keefe painting.

'The amusing part of this is that it's all a mistake.' Centauri spoke casually, with apparent disregard for such possibilities as rocks in the road or washouts. ''Cause that particular Starfighter game was supposed to be delivered to Las Vegas, not a fleaspeck trailer park in the middle of tumbleweeds and tarantulas.

'So it must be destiny, fate – luck even – that brought us together. And as the poets say, the rest is history!'

Alex found time to wonder at the old man's words despite the terror engulfing him. 'That *particular* game? What's special about that particular game?'

'Relays. Grid perception. Depth simulacra. Had to have some primitive, ordinary-type arcade Starfighter games made and spread around or some repair and distribution people might've gotten curious. Not your usual integrated circuitry inside that box, oh no!' He chuckled. 'Almost would've been worth it to see the expression on some repairman's mug if he'd gotten inside *that* game, or one of its relatives. He'd think it was some kind of elaborate gag. No gag, though. Oh no, no gag.' He glanced back at his petrified passenger.

'Integral patterned inertia harness secured?'

'Huh?'

'Seat belt on?'

'Oh.' Alex regarded the peculiarly padded straps that

emerged from either side of the high-backed seat, pulled them across his chest and fought for a moment with the strange fastening system. The harness seemed to caress him, adjusting itself to the contours of his body like a cluster of flat tentacles. Initially a disquieting sensation, but the touch was so light it grew soothing. Besides which he was much too scared to pay close attention to anything the straps might be doing. He could barely bring himself to keep his eyes open.

They passed a tall white tower that blew apart from the force of their passing. Fragments covered the road in their wake. A stopsign, or something advertising a store or gas station further up the road. Now it was splinters. Nor was it the first unfortunate object to feel the effects of the car's passing. Their attack was strewn with uprooted bushes, weeds, small trees, and one badly addled raccoon, left staggering in the darkness.

The highway patrolman ought to have been listening to official calls. Instead, he lay back in his seat, the police band on very low, the portable on the seat nearby very loud and alive with AC/DC belting out 'Dirty Deeds Done Dirt Cheap'. Not a lullaby, but still it was all the officer could do to stay awake, despite the Australians' urgent remonstrations.

He was alone in the squad car, no one to talk to and certainly nothing in the way of traffic on the mountain road to keep him awake. Something went *bleep* and he let his eyes slide idly to the radar gun mounted on the dash.

Then something like a horizontal tornado exploded past in a wash of white metal. The squad car rocked in the afterblast, dumping the radio on the floor and reducing the FM wail to a muffled squeal. The squad car slewed around on its rear tyres, ratcheted to a halt on the gravel lining the shoulder.

As programmed, the radar gun had locked in on the passing traveller at the moment of passage. Now wide awake, the patrolman gaped at the gun, not comprehending.

The digital readout read three hundred miles an hour.

He rubbed his eyes. The figure remained. Down on the floor Freddie Mercury was burbling 'Killer Queen' into the carpet. On the police radio the dispatcher was chatting about some minor disturbance in the Gold Rush bar. And the readout wouldn't go away.

The gun was miscalibrated. Had to be. But there was no question in his mind about one thing. Whatever had passed him was not, definitely *not*, travelling within the legal speed limit.

Siren howling, he took off after whatever it was. As he accelerated up the road he retained enough presence of mind not to call his report back into the station.

First he'd see if he could see something.

IV

Alex flinched when they entered the tunnel. It was a long tunnel, one of the longest in the state, and the thunder of the car in the tubular confine shook the supporting concrete until flakes fell from the ceiling.

Centauri was stubbing out his cigarette in something that looked like an ashtray that wasn't. It couldn't be, because when he removed his hand the cigarette had vanished, paper and filter and all, together with all traces of lingering smoke.

'Where are we going? Where are you taking me?' He no longer inquired about the nature of his 'prize', beginning to suspect it was only part of some larger lie.

He was wrong, and yet he was right.

Centauri turned to face him, still smiling, ignoring the narrow tunnel racing past and the road beneath as if they no longer mattered, as though the car could drive itself just as effectively without his help.

'Told you, boy. I want to keep it a surprise.'

'I don't think I can handle any more surprises. I want to know . . .' he broke off, gesticulating wildly at the road.

There was a barrier just beyond the end of the tunnel. He remembered something that had been in the local paper, something about repairs being made to the bad curve on this section of highway. About a detour around the tunnel itself. It explained why they hadn't encountered any traffic.

He couldn't read the words on the rapidly-approaching barrier but he knew what they said.

'Calm down,' Centauri admonished him, his attention still on his passenger instead of the road. 'Are you the kinda kid who reads the last page of a mystery first? Or pesters a magician to tell you his tricks? Or sneaks downstairs to peek at his Christmas presents before everyone else gets up? Of course you ain't! Which is why I'm not going to tell you what your surprise is. Besides which I love surprises. Don't you?'

At the last instant Alex found his voice just in time to croak, 'Look out!'

Centauri turned indifferently, noted the barrier racing up at them. 'Oh, that.'

He touched two buttons on the dash. They lit up when he touched them, which Alex found interesting. He'd never seen controls on a car light up like that. Of course, this was a foreign model and he didn't know much about foreign models but it still seemed strange and . . .

A glass partition snapped down between him and Centauri. The car shuddered. Short, stubby fins emerged from the rear of the vehicle. Other sections of the car were in motion, retracting to reveal peculiar nodules and protuberances or to permit the movement of other external objects.

What would have interested him the most he couldn't see. The rear end of the car adjusted itself to reveal, not an open trunk, but something considerably more sophisticated and solid.

The back of the car glowed with cold energy. As it exited from the tunnel the car left the roadbed, soared over the wooden barrier and torn-up pavement beyond, and vaulted high over the edge of the sheer cliff which dropped away beneath the curve in the road. It did not fall but continued to climb towards the moon.

Suddenly the cool glow at the rear of the car faded. Sputtering noises filled the cockpit. Lights dimmed and winked. They reminded Alex of the neon sign on the front of the trailer park general store.

Glowering at the dash in frustration, Centauri gave it a couple of good whacks with his right hand as the car commenced losing altitude and momentum. Alex made gargling sounds from behind the partition.

A faint rumble rose from astern. All the dash lights sprang to full life and the car began to rise once more. Wheels retracted into the underbelly while metal moved to seal them inside. Antennae appeared on the skin of the vehicle, metal flowers blossoming in the moonlight.

As Centauri leaned contentedly back in his seat the car increased its angle of ascent and split the clouds.

'Damned system locks. Don't make 'em like they used to.' He touched various controls, some of which had just made their first appearance on the dash, and tried to explain to his passenger. 'I tell you, son, you just can't get decent work done these days. A good mechanic's hard to find. Everyone is under a lot of pressure, though. Got to take that into consideration.' He nodded towards the window. 'Nice view out tonight.'

Hesitantly, Alex moved to look outside, acutely conscious of the fact he ought to be dead but wasn't. Far below were the lights of a major city. Beyond lay a broad, dark expanse. The Pacific Ocean. At least, he assumed it was the Pacific.

'Where . . . where's my town?'

'Oh, I'm afraid that's out of view now. Way behind us.'

'It doesn't feel like we're moving very fast.'

'Well at least something's workin' right. Physiologic support systems compensate for our acceleration. You're right, though. We're not moving very fast.'

'Oh.' Alex had reached the point of not bothering to question the impossible, since he was living it.

Something pushed him back in his seat for just a moment. When he could move again he took another look outside, wondering if he'd still be able to see the city. He could not, though he knew it had to be down below them somewhere.

Down below them somewhere, on the Earth.

He was surprised at how small and vulnerable it looked, the Earth. Even as he stared it was shrinking to a point, like a cartoon world vanishing on an animator's drawing board. Again he was jerked back into his seat. The next time he was able to move about and look outside the Earth had disappeared. No sign of the moon, either.

'Sorry about the stop and go acceleration, son,' Centauri apologized. 'Transmission needs work.'

Alex reached a decision, leaned forward and pounded insistently on the partition. 'That's enough,' he said, wondering if he sounded half as hysterical as he felt. 'Take me back, take me home!'

'Now don't be in such an all-fired hurry, son. All in good time. Sit back and enjoy the ride.' Alex noticed his abductor was wiping at his face with a thin rag of metal mesh. When he turned to face Alex again he was still smiling.

Only now his mouth was all wrong. In fact, his whole face was all wrong. Most especially his eyes were all wrong. They were much too big for the face, for any human face. But that was all right because the face they were attached to wasn't in the least bit human. It was grotesque and distorted and resembled some of Louis's wild scribbles, childish parodies of half-remembered nightmares.

The creature that was Centauri continued to smile back at him as it gently polished its eyeballs.

Alex's fist froze halfway to the glass. All of a sudden he wasn't so sure he wanted the glass partition to come down. He settled back in his seat to gape silently at the thing sitting in the pilot's chair.

Minutes passed. The creature used the metal rag on its face again. When it turned a second time, the familiar Centauri was smiling back at Alex.

Some kind of optical illusion, Alex told himself. He had become very calm. Something that looks solid but isn't, quite. The metal mesh activated and deactivated the disguise. Or maybe it was solid, a preset fleshy buildup that could be added to or removed from the alien face simply by applying the rag. Or maybe he was insane, and indulging his fantasies in the coldly logical fashion of the completely crackers. They say the real crazies are the most methodical in their thought processes. He'd read that somewhere.

But he could hear his heart pounding in his chest, feel the

pressure from the car's periodic jumps (he could hardly call it a car anymore) as it shot through the void, taste the dry fear in his mouth. He bit down on his lower lip until it bled and found he could taste that too. The action frightened him. Hurting himself would prove nothing.

Something bright and massive loomed up off to the right. He recognized it immediately. The rings were brighter than he'd imagined them, and far more lovely. Breathtakingly beautiful. As he stared, Saturn receded rapidly behind them.

'Now,' Centauri announced amiably, 'it's time to take some speed.'

'I'm not into drugs,' Alex replied softly.

'Oh, sorry.' Centauri hesitated, thinking, then grinned at his own error. 'Wrong reference. I mean, it's time to *make* some speed. Better?'

'Yeah, better,' Alex told him.

Centauri shook his head, looking very human. 'You people concoct the strangest expressions.' He touched controls. Alex leaned forward. His curiosity was all that remained between sanity and total terror.

'What now?'

'Now we go to supralight drive.'

'Faster than light? That's impossible.' He regretted his words the instant they left his mouth. In the light of his present situation the comment sounded more than silly.

There was no derision in Certauri's reply. 'No it ain't. Why, if it were, nobody'd ever get *anywhere*, would they?'

Alex felt the universe change around him. Stars danced in his eyes and he couldn't be certain if they were in front of or behind the corneas. Maybe both. But the colours were pretty. Space travel as psychedelia. Or psychotic.

'What . . . what happens now?'

'Now?' Centauri was scrunching down in his seat. 'Nothing to do now until we outgabe, son.' He closed his eyes. Alex wondered how that affected the eyes behind the disguise. Perhaps when he stopped staring Centauri would take them out and put them in his pocket for safekeeping. At this point it would have seemed normal.

But Centauri simply crossed his arms over his chest and let out a relieved sigh. 'Enough work for one night. Time for a snooze. Why don't you relax and try and catch some sleep, son? From here on the ride's pretty boring.'

'Sure.' Alex tried to sound composed and in control. Might as well, since there wasn't anything he could do about his situation. Getting out and walking, for example, seemed out of the question. 'Sure, why not?'

But for some reason, he couldn't go to sleep.

He might have dozed off in spite of himself. He couldn't be certain. Consciousness came and went, ebbed and flowed as the lights of a distorted universe flicked past. Stream of cosmosness. His mind was lulled further by the steady tick-tick of the softly lit control panel while the perfect environmental controls of the ship relaxed his body. It was like riding across country with someone else doing all the night driving, the lights of motels and fast-food joints and street signs all melting into a warm yellow visual blur.

The ticking was interrupted by a sharp beep. Outside, the stars resumed their normal appearance. To the right a pale green moon rich with copper ores was sliding past. A sun lay ahead. It was a little whiter than the one that baked the desert around the Starlight, Starbright trailer park.

Centauri awoke, sniffed twice, blew his nose on a handkerchief and settled in to prepare for landing as they dived straight for a cloud-shrouded planet. It was rich with ochre hues and not as blue as Earth.

It wasn't Earth in more ways than one, Alex reminded himself.

Yet the city-lights that hove into view looked no different from this height than those of Los Angeles. There was more than one expansive cluster of lights, though he couldn't estimate population from lights alone. He didn't know anything about population densities, building sizes, or if the local inhabitants simply liked to leave a lot of lights on at night.

They crossed the terminator into dayside, clouds beginning to slip beneath them. Centauri was speaking towards the dash in an alien tongue.

'Hey!' Alex tapped the glass. Centauri looked back long enough to grin and the ship lurched violently, throwing Alex back against his seat. As soon as the shift had been corrected Centauri gave his passenger a disarming shrug. Alex resolved not to distract the oldster again until they were safely down.

He had to content himself with formulating and re-arranging all the questions he'd stored up during their flight, and with watching the alien landscape rush past below. There were brief, tantalizing glimpses of sunlit cities and of other flying craft, all of which shot past too fast for careful inspection.

Signs of civilization came farther apart as they crossed desert, then jungle. Jungle gave way to coniferous forest hugging the slopes of high mountains.

Centauri barked crisply at the pickup in his strange alien voice and they slowed further. Now Alex could examine the vegetation below in detail. He was surprised to see how little it differed from similar dense temperate zone growth on Earth. Only the presence of the occasional oddity like a tall thin tree with a rust-red trunk or a flying creature that resembled a cross between a curious buzzard and a catfish reminded him how far he was from home.

Centauri turned their ship parallel to a grey granite cliff that looked like Yosemite's El Capitan, only much wider. It brooded over rolling, heavily forested hills instead of a narrow glacial valley. They cruised slowly past the unbroken cliff face until a brightly lit rectangular opening showed itself in the solid rock. Centauri nudged a control and the dash responded with a series of high-pitched squeals. A new voice sounded over the dash speaker. Centauri pivoted the ship in midair and drove them into the opening.

Navigation lights illuminated the huge tunnel they'd entered. The ship moved easily down the high, wide corridor. Occasionally another small ship or service vehicle moved past them, heading for the outside. None of the pilots or passengers were human.

'Come on, Centauri.' Alex rapped on the glass again.

'Where are we? What's going on?'

But the old man ... it was simpler to think of him as that ... simply smiled back, amused by his passenger's impatience.

He angled leftward and set the ship down in a hangar cut out of the side of the main tunnel. Alex could see complex machines filling the chamber. Figures moved in and among them, intent on unimaginable tasks.

The dash lights and the steady tick-ticking faded. The door on Centauri's side rose with a soft hum, letting in air full of incense, or something like incense. The atmosphere in the hangar nipped at the senses.

'Centauri?'

Still grinning, the old man stepped clear of the ship and waved back at his imprisoned passenger.

'Hey, Centauri!'

Abandoning his ship and his distraught charge, Centauri walked away, disappearing into the distance like a man with important business to attend to.

'Hey, lemme outta here! *Hey!*' He pounded on the glass partition, then on his door. Maybe that was the accepted method for activating the release. More likely, the mechanism had been released from outside. The door rose, and suddenly Alex wasn't so sure he wanted it opened.

Someone was waiting for him, and it wasn't Centauri.

Two arms, two legs, strange but not bizarre clothing, a human face ... well, humanoid, anyway. The differences were not pronounced, but they were unarguable.

'Hi,' Alex said, smiling wanly. If the features were consistent, then the uniformed being confronting him was female. If they were not, that implied ramifications of shape he preferred not to think about.

She ... it was nice to think of the alien as she ... stared at him and mouthed something incomprehensible. It sounded a little like baby-talk, except he knew it wasn't. Her stance and attitude conveyed her impatience.

He shrugged helplessly and she looked disgusted, provided he was interpreting her expression correctly. For all he could tell for certain his reaction might be sending her into paroxysms of joy. Somehow he doubted it.

Gestures were relatively universal. As she moved her arms, patiently repeating the movements as though for an idiot, he finally got the idea that she wanted him to disembark and follow her.

'OK.' he started climbing out of the ship. 'But shouldn't I wait for...?' He glanced ashead. There was no sign of Centauri. 'I guess not. Lead on, good-lookin'.'

His comment was not understood by his escort, which was probably fortunate, but letting out with a little sass made him feel better. Similar beings immediately swarmed over the ship, tending to outlets and clustering near the stern. One of them muttered something that sounded unpleasant and kicked the lower edge of the main drive. Alex heard something strike the floor with a metallic *clank*.

He straightened as much as he could and tried to exude an aid of complete confidence. 'Perfectly logical explanation for all this.'

They passed rows of metal cylinders stacked two heads high. Something was loading them on a wheel-less platform with the air of a glowing fishing pole. The loader had tentacles for a face and resembled a humanzied relative of H.P. Lovecraft's great god Cthulhu, a character who'd kept Alex awake with the light burning all night on more than one occasion. He moved closer to his more human-looking guide.

They entered a doorway cut extra wide, though whether for appearance-sake or to permit the movement of wide-bodied visitors Alex couldn't have said. His escort turned him over to another female of the same species. This new nursemaid was slightly taller and more massive than the first. She made beckoning gestures and Alex followed meekly.

'Got to do something ... got to make something happen. Can't just follow them around 'til I drop. Talk to them. Try communicating somehow. Maybe this one is more responsive.'

As he struggled to think of how best to proceed they stepped out onto a moving section of floor. It carried them before a short creature wearing a dun-coloured uniform who pointed something boxy and metallic at Alex. A wide beam of light shot from the box, enveloped him from head to foot.

'Don't kill me! I haven't done anything! I . . .'

The light winked off. Abashed, he avoided his escort's gaze. The box wielder disappeared through a small door behind a counter, to reappear a short while later carrying a double armful of clothing which he handed to Alex.

'Mine?' he mumbled.

'Georg-nat,' agreed the alien dispenser, returning to his previous business.

Before Alex could think of another question the floor moved him on. Looking back, he saw the short alien noshing on something like a deli sandwich, except that the contents were moving. He swallowed, determined not to pry too deeply into the dietary habits of those around him.

He remembered his intention to try and provoke some kind of intelligible response from his guide. He cleared his throat and tapped her on the shoulder.

'Pardon me, but does anyone around here speak Earth?'

She made an unintelligible gesture with both hands but did not reply verbally. The section of floor finally slowed and Alex was orderd off. He expected her to join him, but she did not. The mobile floor slab carried her away.

There were plenty of other aliens around, however, all busy at various tasks. Alex spotted a familiar figure in the midst of them.

'Hey, Centauri!'

He started through the crowd, avoiding contact with the non-humanoid aliens filling the room.

Centauri was arguing with the male counterpart of the two females who'd brought him this far. Although Alex couldn't understand a word of it, there was no doubt that the two were locked in some kind of dispute. Occasionally the new alien would gesture forcefully in Alex's direction. Unable to participate, he stood dumbly nearby, holding his bulky load of clothing.

'What's going on? Centauri, what's all the shouting about?' He hefted his load. 'What am I supposed to do with these?'

Centauri didn't reply. That was a pity, because Alex would have found the conversation most enlightening. As he suspected, it concerned him.

What the tall alien was saying at that moment was something that could be translated as, 'Explain this, you chiseller.'

'Chiseller?' Centauri fought to convey his outrage through the confines of his human mask. 'My expenses on this trip were astronomical.'

'Your expenses are always astronomical when you leave this system.'

'No, no, I'm speaking idiomatically.'

'You mean idiotically. Who do you think you are fooling, Centauri?'

'I'm not trying to fool anybody, sightless one. I'll have you know that you're lookin' at A-number-one merchandise here. He's unique, this one is. Centauri guarantees it.'

'Hey, uh, Centauri?' The two aliens continued to ignore the subject of their argument.

'Really?' The tall alien gave Alex a quick once-over. Unaware of the reason behind this sudden stare, Alex smiled witlessly. 'I think this is the ugliest, dumbest, silliest, loudest biped I've ever been unfortunate enough to set eyes upon. The only thing its presence guarantees is the waste of time and effort you've expended in digging it up from the galactic depths!'

Unable to stand his frustration any longer, Alex stepped between them. 'Centauri, dammit, talk to me! What's going on here?'

The old man turned to him, beaming with delight. 'He's saying how pleased he is that you're here, and that if there's anything he can do to make your stay more enjoyable just to give him a ring.'

'Swell, but where *are* we?'

'Oh, you should see your face, my boy! You love it, don't you? I can tell by your ecstatic expression.'

'That's stark fear, Centauri, not ecstasy.'

The oldster was momentarily nonplussed. 'It is? Dear me, and I thought I had all your peculiar simian facial characteristics down pat. Ah well, surface contortions can't mask the true feelings underneath. I knew you would find this invigorating.' He swept one arm grandly around them. 'Welcome to Rylos, my boy!'

'Ry . . .?' Alex started at his erstwhile mentor, slowly letting the import of what had just been said penetrate his brain. 'Rylos.' Recognition flooded his expression. 'Hey, wait. Rylos from the *game*?' He pointed at the tall creature standing nearby. 'He's a Rylan?'

'See?' Centauri turned quickly on the alien officer. 'What did I tell you? He's quick, very quick.'

'What did he say?' the officer asked.

'He immediately identified you as a Rylan.'

'As soon as you identified this world as Rylos. Oh yes, truly a brilliant specimen of the humanoid line. No doubt he'd instantly identify you as an idiot if I informed him that you made your home in an asylum.'

'You're bein' unnecessarily snide.' Centauri looked hurt. 'No matter what you think of him now, you can't deny his enthusiasm. See? He's virtually speechless.'

'Is that an emotional reaction or a reflection of his semantic limits?'

'Entirely emotional.' Centauri utilized a Rylan half-wink. The officer considered the gesture appropriate, coming as it did from a half-wit. 'He can't wait to get started. You have to know how to interpret these alien expressions.'

'I'm sure. He doesn't look very enthusiastic to me. He looks rather frightened.'

'Not at all, not at all,' Centauri insisted. 'He's rarin' t'go. Surely you've heard of the combative nature of these Earth folk?'

'Rumours to that effect circulate in occasional command transcripts, yes,' the officer admitted. 'But somehow this particular one doesn't look the part of the battle-ready berserker.'

'What's he saying?' Alex finally asked.

'He's explaining how delighted he is that you've come, and how anxious they are to show you around.'

'I see.' Alex subsided again, letting his attention drift to the numerous and extraordinary life-forms circulating through the chamber.

'What did he say?' the officer demanded to know.

'He's getting bored with all this inactivity and wonders how soon he can leap into battle.'

'Hmmm.' The Rylan made it sound like a stoned honeybee. 'You personally guarantee this one's abilities?'

'I told you, he was chosen by my own special testing system. His reflexes are inherited, not learned, and he's just primitive enough to know how to apply those abilities instinctively. He'll do the League proud.'

The officer hesitated a last moment, then sighed breathily. 'All right. I suppose I've no choice but to give him a chance. We need all the help we can muster, and if he's checked out on gunstar fire control...'

'Brilliantly, brilliantly.'

'... Then I guess we have to give him a chance to show what he can do. *Auwar* knows it's time to try the unexpected. I've been surprised by the abilities of primitives before. Perhaps this is to be another time. I'll give the necessary orders.'

'Excellent! I'll inform him. I know how pleased he'll be. He can't wait for his first firefight, to bring forth blood and destruction.' He turned back to Alex, switched easily from Rylan to English.

'Good luck to you, my boy. May the luck of the seven psions of Gulu be with you at all times.'

'What're they?'

'Never mind that now. Just hope that they're with you.'

'Why? Where are you going?'

'First, to the john. After that, elsewhere. Don't worry, you're in good tentacles ... hands.' He glanced up at the thoughtful officer.

'Someday you cheapskates will thank Centauri. Trust me on this one.'

64

'As I've said, we've little choice.' He watched Centauri stride towards the far doorway. 'And when I'm demoted in rank for listening to you, rest assured I'll find you.'

'Hey, come back!' A hand came down on Alex's shoulder. It was gentle but insistent. He looked up to see the Rylan face staring sternly down at him.

'OK, so what now?' he asked the alien.

Evidently the decision had been made to move him along. The first female Rylan he'd encountered at Centauri's ship appeared and conveyed him to an elevator. Once inside Alex stumbled and had to catch his balance as unexpected acceleration sent him towards a wall. The Rylan barely glanced in his direction but he resolved not to stumble a second time.

It was a hard resolution to keep, since the elevator behaved more like a runaway motocross bike than a normal lift, bucking and twisting as it travelled through a series of interconnections that ran sideways and backward as well as up and down.

They finally stopped and the doors slid apart. The Rylan nudged him out into another hangar. This one was much bigger than the place where Centauri had parked his ship, and a hive of activity.

Creatures of varying shape and size worked on ships that were strange because they were so recognizable. Sealed behind a transparent wall at the far end of the cavernous room was a waiting area filled with seats of exotic design, created to accomodate exotic backsides. Beyond the seats lay a semicircular chamber alive with lights and glowing screens. Some of the images appeared to hang in the empty air.

As they moved nearer he was able to make sense of some of the images. There was a detailed schematic of a solar system with more than nine planets, a large floating globe which he guessed (correctly) to be Rylos, images of other systems, and a drifting starmap of a portion of one galactic arm. Scattered among these larger projections were graphs and symbols and charts, underscored with scratchings that he imagined to be letters in Rylan or some other alien language. Rylans predominated in the chamber, as they did in the hangar he was walking through. That might be because they were the dominant life-form in this section of space, or simply because this was their home world. Alex still had precious little hard information on which to base his suppositions.

A musical tone sounded repeatedly. His guide gently pulled him aside while a massive ship was shunted past. One thing he did know for certain was the identity of this and the other ships in the hangar. They were identical to those he'd manipulated so casually in computer-generated space on the screen of the videogame back home. They were the same down to the identifying logo on their flanks. It matched the symbol painted on the side of the game console.

'Gunstars. I gotta be dreaming. I gotta be.'

As his mother would so often assure him, wishful thinking would get him nowhere. Wishful thinking, and a nickel. Well, here were the visions of his wishes made whole. They were lined up in even ranks within the hangar, facing a gap which looked out over forest and mountains. Shining like a big fat peridot in the sky outside was the green moon he and Centauri had shot past on their precipitous descent to the surface of this world. That moon was real. As real as Rylos, as Centauri, as the fighting ships standing in silent array before him.

As real as the gulf that lay between this place and home.

Another Rylan beckoned them over, chatted with Alex's escort. Alex had the feeling he'd been weighed and found wanting. He had no way of knowing that they were even talking about him, of course. It was just a feeling he received. His confidence was not raised.

Then the new Rylan spoke to him.

Alex shrugged. 'Sorry. I never was much good at languages. Como se llama? Sprechen sie Deutsch?'

The Rylan muttered to himself and burrowed through a circular drawer that popped neatly out of the wall on verbal command. Extracting something small and brightly coloured, he moved towards Alex with one hand outstretched.

Alex took a wary step backwards, but his guide was there to

restrain him. She spoke anxiously while the other Rylan waited patiently. Waiting for this terrified primitive to get control of himself, no doubt, Alex thought. Angry at himself he stood and waited for whatever was coming.

The Rylan pinned something on Alex's shirt, then reached towards his head. Alex steeled himself and watched. If these people wanted to do something to him there wasn't anything he could do to prevent it.

Carefully the Rylan inserted a small button of soft plastic in Alex's right ear and then stepped away.

'Now what?' Alex gingerly felt the object inserted in his ear. It was so small he could hardly feel it but it didn't seem inclined to fall out. 'Look, this has been a mistake. I don't belong here.'

'Your modesty becomes you,' said the officer who'd performed the insertion. 'Welcome to Starfighter Command.'

Alex blinked, still feeling his ear while trying to balance the awkward bundle of clothing with his other hand. The alien's words had come through to him clearly, in unaccented English.

'You speak English? That doesn't make any sense.'

'I agree, but I am not speaking your language,' the Rylan informed him. 'Your mind interprets my words via the translator button.'

The tiny disc clung securely to the inside of his ear. He let his hand fall. 'That doesn't make any sense either. What would you be doing with a translation of my language? Do you have others of my kind here?'

'No,' said the Rylan. 'The button does not actually translate word for word. It adapts to your own thoughts, transcribing the sense of what I say rather than executing a literal transcription. We have discovered that within a certain range, the internal physical makeup of most intelligent species is sufficiently similar to make such devices practical. Structures may differ, but the transmission of ideas still involves the movement of electrical impulses within brains of varying size. The translator reads the current in your brain and works directly from it, as opposed to intercepting the verbalizations which are the translations of those same impulses into sound by your vocal mechanism.'

'Goes right to the source,' Alex murmured.

'In essence. That is a simplified explanation. Cerebral engineering is not my field. My concerns are with destruction, not interpretation. As are yours.'

'They are? I mean, are they?'

'All will be explained.' The Rylan spared a quick glance for some instrument he wore inside his shirt pocket. 'But not by me. You have to hurry. We don't have much time. There have been reports pouring in most disturbing in nature and frequency. Decisions of great import are about to be made. 'Besides, the briefing begins shortly.'

'Briefing? What briefing?'

'The briefing wherein many of your questions will be answered.' *Schemal*, the Rylan thought, what had Centauri brought us this time? Don't these creatures ever stop asking questions? Such unrestrained curiosity was sometimes an indication of great flexibility. The Rylan hoped fervently this was so. This late adolescent specimen was going to need all the flexibility it could muster in the coming action.

'Now come along and join the other recruits.' He started across the smooth floor towards the large glass-enclosed room at the far end. Alex trotted along in his wake, not knowing what else to do, hugging his burden of clothing tightly to his chest.

'Recruits? What was that about "other" recruits?' He tapped his ear lightly. 'You sure this thing is working right? I could've sworn you said "other recruits". Or is this gadget reading my pulses wrong. Hey, I've got it! You folks are AC and I'm DC, right? I'm mixing up your meaning, right?'

The Rylan stopped, indicated a doorway leaning inward.

'In there?' Alex asked. The Rylan made a gesture Alex couldn't make head or tail of. The button didn't translate gestures. The movement was repeated.

'Of course in there. Where else did you expect to end up?' Then the Rylan turned and strode off down a hallway.

'Hey, wait a minute.' Alex hesitated, then shrugged. Machinery thrummed around him. 'What the hell.' He headed for the door, which opened noiselessly for him.

V

A dozen nightmares turned in the briefing room to give him a quick glance. Their inspection was cursory and they soon turned back to their interrupted chatter, for which he was grateful.

Many of them wore uniforms identical in colour and design, if not in shape, to his own. Others were clad in different attire. Two different ranks, he thought, or different classes. Most of the talkers were humanoid, though a couple were alien to the point of unrecognizability. One wore a complex mask across the lower half of his/her/its face. This was connected by a flexible tube to a square tank strapped across a broad back. Another creature didn't appear to be breathing at all.

The chairs were not lined up neatly and everyone sat according to individual whim. Two of the talkers disdained the use of the furniture altogether and squatted side by side on the floor. No one objected to this choice of unconventional seating, which was after all a matter of personal comfort and not discourtesy. There were more Rylans present than any other species.

A voice blared over a hidden speaker. 'Attention, attention! Ambassador Enduran of the League is here! He will deliver the final address. Please to devote your full attention to the words of the honoured ambassador.'

Muttering in a dozen languages filled the room. Overwhelmed, the button in Alex's ear could only produce a kind of verbal static. He started forward, letting the door close itself behind him.

The being who entered from the far side of the room and walked slowly toward the small rostrum conveyed a feeling of great age despite his erect bearing and fluid stride. He was humanoid, quite human in fact, as much if not more so than the Rylans. From the instant silence that greeted his appearance Alex presumed him to be the just announced visiting ambassador.

He paused in front of the eclectic collection of creatures, all united in common cause, and scanned them slowly. He overlooked Alex, perhaps by choice, perhaps because Alex was standing apart, or possibly because Alex still carried his uniform instead of wearing it. The Ambassador was a powerful presence and Alex found himself waiting anxiously for whatever he might have to say. There was also about Enduran a strong feeling of resigned sadness.

But he stood tall, the single backbone that he shared with most of the chamber's inhabitants unbent by age. He stood surveying them and listening to something only he could hear. Alex wondered if he wore something more advanced than a simple translator button, perhaps some ultra-miniaturized device that enabled him to stay in constant communication with his own superiors.

The Ambassador's hesitation gave Alex a chance to move without attracting undue attention. Trying to keep an eye on Enduran and his path at the same time, Alex started working his way through the scattered seats.

'Excuse me ... sorry ... pardon me ...' He could only hope his apologies were being properly conveyed through the many translators in use in the room. To his dismay he seemed to be drawing more attention than he'd hoped to. This was due as much to his nervousness as to his inability to negotiate the sprawling limbs of various nonhuman listeners.

His usual agility deserted him utterly when he stumbled over a chair support, only to step back on something the size and shape of a garden hose. The hose whipped back like a retreating anaconda, throwing him off balance and toppling

71

him into the lap of something with a face like a tormented canteloupe.

Strong hands caught him and kept him from hurting himself. Alex got a good close look at them as they eased him back to a standing position. They were almost normal hands, if you ignored the peagreen colour and the translucent webbing that joined the fingers. Dull red veins marbled the webbing.

The bulk that heaved behind him did not belong to those friendly hands, however, but to the owner of the bruised hose. Several identical hoses twisted and curled in anger, coddling the one Alex had stepped on. They looked capable of ripping pilings away from piers.

Neither a translator nor an intimate knowledge of alien expression was required to see that he'd stepped on the wrong toe . . . uh, tentacle. Skin rippled on the alien's face and the fury in its eyes was clear enough to anyone who cared to look. Alex didn't care to, but his retreat was cut off and he didn't want to risk offending anything else in the room.

As conveyed by the translator button, there was nothing ambivalent about the alien's tone, either.

'Biped of a thousand heavy pods! I should grind you to g'run dust!' A sweeping tentacle barely missed Alex's face.

He didn't know what g'run dust was but was positive his present condition was preferable. Swallowing, he fought to compose a suitable reply.

'I'm real sorry, uh, sir.' He let out a mental sigh of relief when the creature didn't react. At least he'd got the sex right. 'It was an accident. I didn't mean it. I'm a stranger here. Just got in.' He raised the armful of clothing. 'See? I haven't even had time to change over yet, and I didn't want to miss the briefing.

'Anyway, we're all here because we're on the same side, aren't we? No point in fighting among ourselves, is there?'

The big alien glared at him a moment longer. Then it brought forth a prodigious grunt and sloshed back into its chair, muttering one last phrase about 'clumsy bipeds' and their propensity to trip over everything in sight. But the initial anger had dissipated.

Carefully Alex resumed his course towards the empty chair he'd spotted from across the room. It happened to lie next to the friendly, web-handed alien who'd caught him when he'd first tripped.

'It *was* an accident,' he mumbled.

'I've no doubt of that,' his new-found acquaintance whispered back at him. 'Only a true fool would do such a thing deliberately. You just don't trifle with a Bodati. They just love to fight. That's why so many of them have volunteered to participate in this war, although I understand that the majority of them have to be kept in the rear echelons, employed in support and logistics. They're much too impulsive and reckless to be trusted with a gunstar. They have a racial tendency, so to speak, to shoot themselves in the foot. But it's nice to know they're around in case it becomes necessary to go to a suicide defence.'

Alex digested this information and quickly locked in on the operative word.

'Excuse me, but did you say "this *war*"?'

The alien eyed him uncertainly, its gaze travelling from Alex's face down to the uniform he still carried.

'But of course. Why else do you think you're here?'

'I don't know. I was told,' he said slowly, 'that I was to receive some sort of honour.'

'Ah.' The webbed alien looked satisfied. 'A small problem in semantics. Not that your appointment is anything but an honour, though much depends on your racial mentality. You really don't know what's going on, do you?'

'Not really.'

The alien took a gargling breath. 'You've been recruited by the League to...'

That was more than enough to trigger Alex's memory. The rest he knew by heart. He knew it by heart because he'd listened to a monotone mechanical voice recite the same words over and over with the same inflection each time, speaking from just beneath the surface of a wooden box. A box that sat innocently on the porch in front of the Starlight,

73

Starbright Trailer Park.

That familiar videogame voice was very far away now, as was the trailer park and everything else he could call familiar. It was unnerving to hear those same words spoken by the slick-skinned alien seated next to him, though he should have expected it.

His first thought was for Centauri. For the first time in his young life he considered wringing an adult's neck. If that was a sign of maturity, then he was maturing at an astonishing rate. But Centauri was nowhere to be seen. Alex wondered if he'd ever see the old man again.

Face it. He was stuck.

'. . . defend the Frontier against Xur and the Ko-Dan Armada,' he muttered, finishing the sentence for his alien friend. All was becoming clear now. Much too clear.

This wasn't a game. This was real. Evidently the videogame he'd mastered after dozens of hours and quarters was far more than a toy whipped up in Silicon Valley by energetic hacks to separate teenagers from their allowances. The game looked like other videogames, played like other videogames, but its fire control systems and stratagems were drawn not from some programmer's imagination but from real interstellar altercations. From reality.

He'd been recruited because of his success at the game. He could be sure of that much now. There was an intimate connection between the game and this far-away conflict. For some reason outsiders had been chosen to participate in the coming war, and good ole game-whiz Alex was included among them. What an honour. What luck. What a great prize. The booby prize.

By passing some carefully constructed test disguised as a videogame he'd won the right to be carted halfway across the galaxy for strangers to shoot at. No way, José!

He looked anxiously towards the exit, but all the doors had been sealed. There was an undercurrent of anticipation running through the assembled sapients that he could feel, and he had to admit to a certain curiosity as to what this imposing Ambassador Enduran had to say. In any case, the

74

only halfway clear aisle leading outward from his chair led past the slumping Bodati, and that was a path he had no intention of crossing again.

Besides, this wasn't the game. The game never said anything about a prebattle conference or a visit from some League official. He *was* curious, despite his anxiety. The League was a reality, not just a string of synthesized words.

There was much more to this than repetitive space battles. There were reasons behind the actions he'd mastered on the machine, real beings with matters of importance at stake. A lot more than a lousy couple of quarters, that was for sure. Though he hadn't the slightest intention of getting involved, he couldn't shut out his interest in the momentous events unfolding around him.

Anyway, he was stuck in the briefing room, at least until the Bodati moved. He might as well settle back and pay attention to the speaker. Nothing was wasted. He might get a good essay for English out of it.

His own concerns were soon lost as he became caught up in the Ambassador's speech. This was no game to Enduran or any of the other aliens seated in the room. Worlds were at stake here.

There was sadness in the Ambassador's voice, but also dertermination. Here, Alex knew, was an intelligent creature who abhorred war as the ultimate degradation of civilized species, who nonetheless had been forced to countenance and organize armed resistance. Alex could sense the strain this decision had put on him and found himself sympathizing. The speech Enduran was making wasn't easy for him. He talked of the forthcoming conflict with obvious reluctance, as though the very mention of terms like 'war' and 'battle' caused him physical pain.

'Eons ago, our ancestors, your ancestors, joined together to form the League, an association of civilized, peaceful peoples and worlds. We abjured any further expansion, believing that further growth could only result in an organization too large to be governed efficiently.

'Others outside the League have always been jealous of our

stability and achievements. To protect ourselves from their barbaric incursions the Frontier was established, a region unclaimed by the League which we allowed no others to claim. As you know, it is impossible to define an actual boundary in interstellar space because of the immense distances involved, so the real Frontier was in the mind.' He turned to gesture briefly at the illuminated screen hovering behind him. Lines of light moved about on the screen in concert with his words, illustrating the points he made.

'Each member world of the League was equipped with a shield projector, able to forestall the approach of any ship or cluster of ships determined to be hostile. As many of you are aware, such projections render the drives of all modern vessels inoperative and are capable of incapacitating an entire approaching fleet one ship at a time or all at once, as the requirements dictate. The closer a hostile vessel approaches the more devastating the effects of the shield projector. A formidable and yet civilized weapon.

'Safe from the chaos and ravages of war, we of Rylos and the other worlds of the League enjoyed all the prosperity and comfort that comes to those who choose peace over war. Insulated from these primitive conflicts we have done well. Each of your peoples has done well.

'It would seem to any reasoning creature that peace is preferable to war. Yet there still exist those who believe it is possible to acquire what they cannot themselves create by taking it from others through the application of force. They can build great engines of war but cannot see the folly of their own intentions. Still, even a small mind can bring down a great peace. This is the danger we now find ourselves confronting.

'I am afraid that the time for reasoned words is past. The Frontier remains, impenetrable as ever, the shields as effective as when they were first designed and installed. They stand ready to repel any assault from outside.

'The danger comes from within. We have been betrayed. The Frontier may be endangered from within our own ranks. We suspect someone with access to the most sensitive military information has delivered the design of the shield projectors to the Ko-Dan.'

This disclosure produced much nervous muttering in many languages as the import of it was discussed. Enduran let them talk for awhile before gesturing for silence.

'Security has been increased tenfold around individual shield stations and backups on all League worlds. Our researchers are working overtime to find a method for modifying the projectors which will render them invulnerable to signal distortion or external interruption. But such work takes time and cannot be hurried. It now seems we may not have that time.

'We here on Rylos are especially vulnerable, since the traitor comes from this world. And he does not work alone. The spectre of absolute power tempts many otherwise decent citizens. This is an old pattern, repeated through much pre-League history. Absolute power is an aphrodisiac only the strongest are able to resist.

'Worse, we have grown mature without becoming wise. Peace and prosperity have also brought with them boredom and monotony. There are those who would swamp such personal discontents beneath a wave of destruction. They don't care if they succeed in their aim of overthrowing the League or not. They are interested only in the excitement and stimulation which war brings.

'These are not the dangerous ones. These are the sick, the ill, the misinformed and misused. Yet when their efforts are coupled with the more prosaic evil of the real traitors, the danger they present is all too grave.

'So it is not even the Ko-Dan we have to fear, but our own kind. It seems we are destined one last time to do battle with ourselves. The historians say such upheavals are inevitable, and that we have managed to prolong our great peace to its limits. If we can overcome this convulsion, that peace will return for a long time to come.

'If not,' he executed the Rylan equivalent of a shrug, 'there is a good chance the League could disintegrate into civil war, with some worlds continuing the resistance and others allying themselves with the traitors. What the latter will not see is that behind all such eruptions wait the Ko-Dan, patient and ready to take over every world. This cannot, must not be allowed to happen.'

He pointed over their heads, towards the line of sleek, powerful ships arrayed on the big hangar outside the briefing chamber.

'So we have no choice left but to put aside peaceful methods of settling disagreements and dust off these relics of a more combative age. They have been updated and modernized to the point where they are as efficient and, I am sad to say, deadly as anything that flies. Our ancestors would admire their new capabilities. I cannot.' He sighed deeply.

'Yet it seems they must be employed. We believe they are quite superior to anything the traitors or the Ko-Dan have in their arsenal. Resistance to their attack they will expect... but not resistance of such effectiveness. They know we have relied for hundreds of years on the defensive potential of the Frontier. They should not be expecting us to attack them.'

'How can we be so sure of what the Ko-Dan can bring to bear?' wondered a voice from the rear of the assemblage.

Enduran allowed himself a slight, very human-looking smile. 'Merely because we strive for peace does not mean we do not prepare for war. We have our own servants among the traitors. I am assured that our gunstars, completely rebuilt and updated as they are now, acting under the command of the best Starfighters the League can muster, are more than a match for anything the Ko-Dan have built. *If* we react in time. We are still not entirely sure of how the traitors and the Ko-Dan plan to announce their intentions.' He gazed past them, through the glass wall, to the line of ships waiting in the immense hangar.

'So much intelligence, so much effort and energy, wasted on the restoration of antique war machines. Taken together they have not the elegance or permanence of a single song cycle.' He let his stare drop back down to the waiting pilots and crews.

'What a tragedy. To think that we have come so far,

78

achieved so much, at the expense of our own defence. Because while we still possess these machines and the talent to improve them, the ability to utilize them in battle has been bred out of the majority during the long peace.

'Hence the exhaustive hunts which have brought you together here. Just as these vessels are reminders of our violent adolescence, so are you and the abilities you still retain. You see, you all are also relics. Few are left who can use these ships. Peace breeds contentment, and contentment stifles the fighting reflexes and urges and what we might call the, uh, gift of doing battle.

'Among the billions of citizens of the League, grown contented and easy-going over the centuries, only a few are left who still possess this gift. Only a few. You few.' He let that sink in before adding, 'The future of our civilization, of the League itself, rests on you. You, the most extreme throwbacks, the most primitive and yet skilled among us. It is a talent I have no desire to possess. I pity you for it. I envy you for it. I salute you for it.'

A muffled cheer rose from the assembled fighters. Many of them were outcasts, social misfits on Rylos and the other worlds. Now that which caused them to be shunned was to be their redemption. After this war they would be regarded as saviours; not to be liked, perhaps, but to be respected. All looked forward to the forthcoming conflict.

All, that is, save one, who kept his thoughts to himself and wished desperately he were elsewhere.

Enduran waited patiently for the cheering and the shuddering robust war cries to die down. He'd been told by the psychologists to expect something of the kind, but still, to see such naked expressions of violence among citizens of the well behaved League was a shock.

A fortunate one, though. Without such citizens there would be no chance of turning back the Ko-Dan incursion. He studied the many different visages and expressions and marvelled at the similarities. The urge to combat, to fight, to kill, had been drained from the general population by hundreds of years of peace. Yet a residue of the ancient feelings still remained. He felt terribly sorry for all of them.

'You alone,' he went on, hating what he was doing, hating the carefully calculated manipulation of primitive emotions but at the same time knowing how necessary it was, 'stand between the rest of us and the dark terror of the Ko-Dan. You alone must do what the rest of us can no longer do. You alone must place yourselves between civilization and chaos, between aspiration and anarchy. You alone must resist, must fight, must destroy!' The speech clogged his throat and he could say no more.

He didn't have to. The speech, carefully designed by the amunopsychs, had precisely the effect on the gunstar pilots they'd intended it to. There was a unity of feeling running through the assembly now that transcended such trivialities as racial type and world of origin. These pilots and navigators were defectives, on whom Enduran's words had a powerful effect.

'Victory or death!' shouted one uniformed support officer. The chant was taken up by the others, including the pilots. The force of it shook Enduran. He'd been warned, and the tranquillizers they'd pumped into his system helped him to remain calm, but the feeling of raw violence that now overwhelmed the chamber was terribly unsettling to anyone who regarded himself as a civilized creature.

And he'd been chosen to deliver this presentation because he'd tested out emotionally more resilient than his colleagues. The fury of the fighters' response to the speech would surely have caused poor Masurv of Cann'our, next in line to make the presentation, to faint on the dais.

They were on their feet now, circulating through the briefing room like a living storm, pilots and navs and technicians and engineers, all selected for defects in their emotional makeup. Defects which made them pariahs on their home worlds but heroes of the battle to come. They pounded each other enthusiastically with hands or tentacle tips, slapped backs or carapaces as they strove to bolster each other's spirits. Fighting spirits, Enduran told himself. We have not progressed far enough.

Which was lucky for everyone else.

Alex was on his feet with everyone else, stumbling through the crowd and trying not to get trampled in the excitement. His course wasn't planned and he was trying to reach the far wall without tripping over any chairs or Bodati tentacles. In a few moments he found himself nearly in the clear, on the opposite side of the chamber, where a familiar figure was moving easily through the mob, its attention fixed on a handful of glittering crystalline shapes.

Alex started shoving his way through the remaining crowd, ignoring occasional outcries and not even caring if he offended some belligerent Bodati. The figure he was heading towards was joined by a uniformed alien. Together they headed for an open doorway.

'Centauri, Centauri, wait!'

His recruiter/kidnapper didn't hear him. Or maybe he did and was hurrying out of the room. Alex was clear of the press of alien bodies now. Their cheers and whistles echoed in his ears as he plunged down a short hall and out into the main hangar.

It was filled with noisy equipment being operated by the usual assortment of strange creatures, some of whom were more outré in appearance than the machines they worked with. There was no sign of Centauri, though he thought he saw a half-familiar shape vanishing around a far corner.

He ran, waving and yelling, and not looking where he was going. Fortunately, the alien he ran into was no Bodati.

VI

It was quite humanoid, though completely hairless. The rounded skull and the face with its deep-set yellowish eyes were covered by a thick orange-yellow crust that reminded Alex of desert ponds months after scorching heat had caused them to dry and crack. He was tall (the 'he' another sexual presumption on Alex's part which turned out to be correct) and thankfully devoid of tentacles.

'I'm sorry,' Alex apologized. There was no sign of Centauri now, and no way of knowing which way he'd gone.

'This is a restricted area, off limits to . . .' The alien stopped in mid-sentence, examining Alex more closely as they both knelt to recover Alex's clothes and the small handful of components the tall being had been carrying.

'I don't recognize your species,' he said.

'Human.' Alex stared at a six inch long something that filled his hand. It looked like a cross between an oversized ballpoint pen and an electric toothbrush. He suspected it was neither and handed it over.

'From Earth,' he added.

'Earth what?'

'Just earth. We like to keep things simple.'

I don't believe I'm having this conversation, he told himself. *I don't believe a bit of it.*

'That's a uniform.' The alien gestured with a thick-skinned hand at Alex's bundle of clothing.

'Yeah.' Alex gathered it up. As he rearranged it in his arms the alien caught sight of the insignia on the front. His manner changed abruptly.

'Pardon me, *Starfighter*. I am Navigator/Systems Operator Grig. At your service, sir.'

He performed an awkward salute which Alex found interesting to observe but impossible to duplicate. So he took the thick hand and shook it instead. Grig inspected his freed limb thoughtfully.

'Curious custom.'

'We like it.'

'Individualistic yet intimate, this personal physical contact. Never cared much for it myself, but everyone is entitled to their own mode of greeting, aren't they?'

'If you say so, Grig.' Alex nodded toward the line of silent gunstars. 'You fly those?'

'Me, fly? You mean as an attack pilot? Dear me, no. I am a navigator and systems operator. I run the ship during combat, thus freeing the piloting Starfighter to do what they do best: fight.'

'Your job sounds tougher than the other.'

'Not in the least. I have only mechanical problems to deal with, instead of mental ones. You are named?'

'Sorry. I'm Alex Rogan.'

'Two names?'

'That's our custom.'

'Naming does vary from system to system, culture to culture. I find the use of more than one name unnecessarily duplicitous, though there are those species who make use of a dozen names or more.'

'Hate to have to sign my name like that.' Alex studied his new acquaintance. Grig was more than polite; he was downright deferential. He also struck Alex as straightforward, honest, and devoid of guile. Maybe this was his chance to get a straight answer or two to some questions.

'Listen, Grig, maybe you can help me out. See, I was playing this game back home, a videogame, and this guy comes along, only he's no guy. He's an alien, a non-human. I get into his car, only it's no car, it's a spaceship, and there's been a biggggg mistake somewhere along the line.'

Grig stared back at him. 'My friend, you sound very confused.'

'That's the understatement of the century, navigator.'

'You said there'd been a mistake. What kind of mistake?'

'I don't belong here. I thought I'd won some kind of big prize or something for reaching a score of a million on the game. I thought maybe we were going to go to the downtown motel to discuss it. Then I thought maybe I'd have to go in to LA or something to accept it. So I end up going a lot farther, and there's no prize.' He indicated the pile of clothing.

'I can't put these on. You called me a Starfighter. I'm no Starfighter, just a kid.'

'Starfighter ability is not a function of age, Alex Rogan.'

'Just Alex.'

'Alex, then. It is a matter of a special combination of unusual talents: courage, flexibility under stress, the ability to make rapid decisions while under great pressure, reflexology, mental acuity, determination, and more. I am not qualified to enumerate all of them, much less to explain. But you were brought here to be a Starfighter, it would seem, and you have been issued with the uniform.'

Alex shook his head violently. 'Uh-uh. Not a chance. I'm not putting this on. I don't belong here. I told you, it's all been a big mistake.'

Now Grig appeared uncertain. 'Am I to understand that you are actually declining the honour of becoming a Starfighter?'

'You got it.' Alex said it with a relieved sigh, pleased to at last have made his point to *someone*. 'Besides, how can you call it an honour when the Ambassador from the League refers to it as belonging to "primitives"?'

'Because a talent is rare does not make it less valuable, Alex. We have artists who utilize primitive techniques. That does not make their art less valid. There are concertiflows who design musical superstructures based on motifs thousands of years old. Their flows are no less effective for that.'

'Well, mine is,' Alex insisted stubbornly. 'I don't belong

here.'

'Extraordinary. Unheard of. Not for your presence to be a mistake, but for you to decline the honour of becoming a Starfighter. Only a few have qualified. Primitive you may think it, but the honour remains significant. And you are actually turning it down.' He considered thoughtfully.

'Wait a moment. Tell me again where you are from?'

'I said, from Earth, and we're not at war with anyone except each other.'

'Earth, Earth,' Grig mumbled. 'I am trying to recall. Perhaps in the vicinity of Quarlia.' He brightened. 'Yes, I remember now. An insignificant place, well outside the usual trade or exploration routes.'

'We like it,' Alex said defensively.

'Most curious this is. If I am remembering my galographics correctly, Earth is not a formal member of the League.'

'As far as I know, we're not even an informal member. Everybody on my planet thinks all of you are figments of their imaginations.'

'Typical reaction of those primitive races who believe themselves to be the centre of existence. Nothing personal, Alex Rogan. Alex.'

'No offence taken,' Alex replied. 'I agree with you, Grig. We're not a real modest bunch. Now, don't you agree with me that I don't belong here? This isn't my fight.'

'It's all highly irregular. Earth isn't due to be considered for League membership until its inhabitants mature to the next level.' He eyed Alex with sudden intensity. 'Tell me, how were you recruited?'

'Through a game. A machine. Some kind of simulator.'

'No, no. I don't mean how were you tested. Who actually brought you here?'

'A guy who calls himself Centauri. I thought that was funny because that's the name of the star nearest our own sun, and . . .' he broke off, staring past the navigator.

'And there he goes now.' He waved. 'Hey, Centauri!'

'Ah. Centauri.' Grig relaxed. Everything was falling into

85

place.

'You know him?' Alex inquired as they started to where the subject in question was arguing with a Rylan officer.

'He is known to me personally as well as through his extensive reputation.' Grig's tone was carefully neutral. 'You are not the first to suffer from his manipulations. He is very clever and conceals his doubtful activities beneath a mantle of false simplicity. This matter will be resolved quickly, I assure you.'

'Well, good,' said Alex, feeling better than he had in some time.

The old man was still clutching his handful of crystals, or whatever they were, his glance shifting from his treasure to the eyes of the officer yelling at him. Hearing his name called he looked down the corridor to see Alex and Grig approaching.

Alex was more than a little surprised when Centauri waved back and strode boldly to meet them. Maybe the old man thought his best defence was a good offence and was trying to put Alex off his guard.

Or maybe, despite Grig's words indicating the contrary, the oldster was really a little wacky.

He reached out to tousle Alex's hair fondly. Alex pushed the hand aside and stared grim-faced at its owner.

Before he could say anything, however, the Rylan officer caught up with them.

'For the last time,' he told Centauri angrily, 'take off that ridiculous disguise!'

'Ridiculous disguise?' Centauri sounded offended as he caressed his false face. 'I rather like this appearance. It is most flexible and capable of conveying a great many meanings merely by the contraction of certain muscles.'

'You are a member of the government forces, however slim the attachment,' the officer insisted. 'You will appear in your natural state when on duty.'

'Am I on duty, then? That's funny. I thought I'd just been paid off.'

'Paid off?' said Grig. 'You're up to your old Excalibur

tricks again, eh, Centauri?'

The old man squinted at the navigator. 'Do I know you?'

'Navigator/Operator First-Class Grig, recruited from Sesnet Shipping to run a gunstar's guts.'

'Sesnet, Sesnet.' Centauri frowned. 'Don't know as how I've ever travelled on that line.'

'Maybe you haven't, but you once used it to ship some Uramite sculpture from Shro-al to Wouldd on a liner I was assigned to. I remember your name because it was on the shipping manifest and because of all the fuss at the port when we unloaded the shuttle and the buyer nearly tore the place apart looking for somebody to strangle, preferably you. It seems that all his expensive sculpture had melted in transit.'

Centauri studied the floor. 'The sculpture all passed inspection before leaving Shro-al.'

'I'm sure it did. But the temperature differential between Shro-al and Wouldd was just enough to affect the natural resins from which the sculptures were fashioned. So they melted in Wouldd's strong sunlight, just like you melted into the distance.'

'It wasn't my fault,' Centauri protested. 'That buyer ought to have known enough to have had a refrigeration unit waiting for his danged sculptures. Anyways, what's that got to do with anything?'

'Just reminding myself,' Grig replied easily, 'and this officer here, of how you operate. It seems we have a bit of a problem here.'

'We do?' Centauri's look of innocence was wondrous to behold. 'I don't see any problem.' While he spoke he carefully avoided meeting Alex's eyes.

'Did it ever occur to you,' Grig said quietly, 'that it's against the law to recruit from worlds outside the League? Not to mention doing that recruiting on immature worlds whose inhabitants haven't even learned to stop fighting among their own species?'

'But those are just the kind of backward, jerkwater planets where . . .' Alex's expression darkened further and Centauri coughed and tried to cover himself. 'The kind of unspoiled, uncorrupted civilizations where individual abilities required for Starfighter modes are to be found. D'you think I should've gone hunting for potential recruits on a world like Bissandra, where everybody's either a painter or a poet? It's going to take more than clever couplets to rid us of the Ko-Dan menace.'

'That's no excuse. The fact remains that this isn't Earth's fight.'

'It ought to be. They're real close to being offered membership in the League. And isn't Earth in danger too? Or do you think the Ko-Dan will stop with taking control of the League? They're unsatisfied conquerors. Once they've taken control of the League they'll start moving out into the unorganized systems like Quarlia and Sol.'

'I am not qualified to analyze Ko-Dan politics and motives,' Grig responded.

'You bet you're not,' Centauri shot back, going on the offensive. 'And to answer your question, no, I didn't use the Excalibur test this time. Swords have gone out of fashion on Earth. The new testing mode involves entertainment displays called videogames.

'I don't understand all the fuss.' He nodded towards Alex. 'Say what you want about my motives or methods, but there's no denying one thing: they work. Because this one has the gift.'

He put his arm around Alex while the subject of his sudden affection eyed him warily.

'It doesn't matter whether he does or not,' said Grig.

Centauri frowned. 'What's that supposed to mean?'

'This may come as a shock to you, Centauri, but he doesn't choose to be a Starfighter.'

It was a line of thought Centauri clearly was not prepared for. His shock as he removed his arm from Alex's shoulder was clear.

'Doesn't "choose" to be . . . but he has the gift!'

'Maybe he has the gift, but he doesn't have the inclination. It's still a matter of free choice. No one can be forced to serve as a Starfighter,' Grig reminded him.

Centauri sputtered a reply. 'Naturally, of course. But to have the talent and not want to use it . . . it doesn't fit any of the psychological profiles!'

'Remember what you yourself said about these Earth folk.'

'I know, but this is so far outside my experience that I . . .' he turned on Alex. 'What's wrong with you, son? Are you a coward? Are you crazy? Don't you have any idea of the seriousness of the situation we face and of the singular tribute that's being paid to you?'

'You know what you can do with your singular tribute!' Alex discovered that he was shouting. Maybe Centauri was right. Maybe he was crazy. He was also mad. 'You didn't tell me about any of this! You said I was going to receive an "honour". I thought you meant a prize for making a high score on the game. I thought you meant a real prize, like money or something. You never said a thing about my being chosen or selected or singled out or whatever you want to call it to fight in some crazy interstallar war.'

Grig's tone had turned solemn. 'So you didn't even tell him what this was all about before bringing him in here and attaching him officially to League forces. Irregular, highly irregular.'

'I was late!' Centauri looked from navigator to officer, pleading his case. 'There wasn't time. You know how near the Ko-Dan fleet is rumoured to be. Besides, I didn't think it would matter. I thought he'd love it. I thought in that respect he was a normal human being. They *love* to fight! You should read some of their history. Exquisite aberrations!'

'Nonetheless, this one chooses not to serve,' Grig pointed out. 'The final decision, of course, is not mine to make.' He turned to face the Rylan senior officer who'd been standing quietly nearby.

Now the officer stepped forward and stuck out a hand. 'Return the payment, Centauri. Return the payment, I'll see it's sent back to disbursing, and we'll consider not prosecuting.' He glanced over to Alex. 'You have victimized the ignorant representative of an immature alien race.'

'Hey, now wait a minute . . .' Alex began, but he got no

further. Centauri was giving a superb imitation of having a severe stroke, staggering backward and holding the side of his head with one hand while the other waved helplessly in the air.

'*Return the payment*? You must be delirious! I understand, though. It's the pressure of preparing for the forthcoming battle, of having to relearn ancient tactics. Must be a terrible strain.'

'Not as bad a strain as you'll be under if you don't make instant recompense for your misdeed.'

Centauri struggled to recover some of his fast-fading aplomb. 'Do you have any idea how long it took me to invent those testing games, working undercover on a primitive world, hiding licensing arrangements through dummy corporations while trying to conceal advanced technology from curious native engineers? Do you know how hard it was to merchandise the result, get the games properly distributed . . . only a distribution foul-up enabled me to stumble on this remarkably talented if dense young adult here . . . and see to it that the machine's advanced aspects were not tampered with? Not to mention getting them put in the arcades before Christmas.'

'Christmas?'

'A local holiday corresponding roughly to All-Ether Day on Rylos.'

'Yes, it must be terribly upsetting for you,' Grig put in, succumbing slightly to Centauri's tale of struggle in spite of knowing better, 'and I do sympathize. Yet it remains that you lied to this nice young man, and that he chooses not to pursue the path you have so deceptively chosen for him.'

'I told him he was to receive a special honour, and so he has,' Centauri pointed out. 'So I was a little conservative with some of the details, so what? I saw him fight, using the simplified gunstar fire controls on the simulators I designed. All he needs is a good navigator/operator like yourself to take him into combat. He can be the greatest Starfighter ever!'

'Centauri,' Alex protested, 'that was just a game.'

'A game? Maybe you thought it was just a game, but it was

90

a carefully thought-out, heavily researched test. A test which you took along with hundreds of representatives of other young, combative races. And the test worked exactly as it was designed to. It selected you, my boy, and here you are.'

'Right. Here I am, about to get killed.'

The Rylan officer shifted impatiently from one foot to the other, then gestured with his extended hand. 'Return the payment, Centauri. Or do I have to call Security?'

'No need to rush things. Why so insistent? This is a secured installation. Where could I run to?'

'You always manage to find someplace.'

Centauri chose to turn from the officer and ignore that. Instead, he tried to convince the crux of his current difficulties of the rightness of the course his good friend Centauri had chosen for him.

'Now why talk of being killed. You don't seriously think being a Starfighter is dangerous? You're being foolish, my boy. What could be dangerous?'

'Yeah, what,' Alex snapped. 'It's nothing, really. A simple little interstellar war involving a few billion combatants. What could be dangerous?'

'Exactly my point.' Centauri sounded pleased, managing to ignore Alex's sarcasm with marvellous ease. 'All you have to do is ...'

There was a disturbance in the hangar. In minutes everyone was aware of its presence among them. Hands put tools aside while armed troops scurried to battle stations in case the chance presented itself for them to shoot at more than an uncomfortable feeling.

The light began to change, darkening at first near the centre of the largest open area, then brightening as a flat white glow built into a solid globe of illumination. The light intensified, solidifying.

Alex whispered to Grig. 'What is it?'

'Image projection. Somehow the Ko-Dan have learend the location of our command centre.'

Alex thought a moment. 'The traitors Enduran mentioned. It has to be.'

91

'Yes, the traitors.'

'Are there many of them?'

'No, but there are enough to make a difference, and they are led by one whose philosophy, while abhorrent to all civilized peoples, possesses a certain malignant attractiveness. They are not to be underestimated, nor is their leader.'

'Xur.' Alex stared fascinated at the rotating sphere of dense light and remembered details of the videogame.

'Yes, Xur, but that is little more than a name to you. To us it conjures up the image of a real person, of a great evil. Enduran knows this more than any other.'

'Enduran? Why him?'

'Watch, listen, learn.' Alex held his questions and did as he was told.

Within the spinning globe of light a face began to take form. It resembled another recently observed and Alex struggled to place it. Then he had it, and understood what Grig meant. The resemblance was striking, and frightening.

Enduran had appeared on the floor of the hangar, shaking off the protective hands of the aides who tried to hold him back. The Ambassador approached the projection fearlessly. His expression hinted at anger barely held in check.

The projection reacted to this new presence, smiled humourlessly. 'Hello, father.'

'You have no father,' said Enduran. 'I have no son.'

The image did not appear in the least upset. 'And neither of us has any illusions. No, that is not quite right. You still believe in the invulnerability of your foolish, outmoded "Frontier". It is less solid than the image you gaze upon now, and will vanish just as easily should I will it so ... father.'

'Do not call me father!' Enduran fought to check his emotions. Were he to lose his temper and strike out at a pillar of smoke it would draw only laughter from the traitor. Enduran would never give him that kind of satisfaction.

'You are no longer my son. That much is settled. You have made yourself an outcast, not only from your family but from your civilization, from that which nurtured you. You have betrayed on a level unprecedented in history. Knowing this, why have you chosen to return?'

The projection was amused. 'I wouldn't think that after all you've learned my intentions are still open to question. I thought I made them quite clear when I was thrown out of the Council.' Some of Xur's humour gave way to the blind fury barely concealed beneath his veneer of politeness.

'I have returned to fulfil my destiny, father. The destiny you and the other members of the Council denied to me. I have returned to claim my birthright. I have returned for the good of all Rylans, as my supporters well know.'

'Dabblers in evil,' Enduran responded. 'They see in a return to ancient combat only an opportunity for shallow excitements. Past that they see nothing. I do. You have returned for the good of Xur and Xur alone, with an armada of Ko-Dan warships behind you. I knew you to be a megalomaniac, but I did not think you so complete a fool. Or do you really think the Ko-Dan will let you rule as you wish?'

'The Ko-Dan see in me a ruler more sympathetic to their long-term goals than the present members of the Council.'

'Their goal is nothing less than total domination of the League and all its peoples.'

'On the contrary. Your xenophobia has blinded you, father, as it has blinded all on the Council. The Ko-Dan desire only friendship and good relations with the League worlds.' Xur spoke with assurance, convincingly. Alex began to see how he, like so many of history's successful tyrants, could paralyze the truth with honeyed words.

'Who can blame them if the present government is unremittingly hostile to their attempts to forge a peaceful, mutually beneficial alliance?'

'An alliance which the Ko-Dan would dominate utterly. That is not an alliance: it is an invitation to place ourselves in perpetual servitude.'

'Nonetheless, I believe them,' said Xur breezily. 'One seeks right-thinking allies where one must.'

'They will make what use of you they can and then cast you aside.'

'I think not. You see, father, our aims converge. They wish

for a sympathetic ruler governing the worlds of the League, and I wish to rule. What could be more convenient?'

'It is convenient for you and for the Ko-Dan, not for anyone else. Leave the League in peace. Return to your exile and drink no more at the fountain of Ko-Dan flattery.'

Alex leaned close to whisper in Grig's ear. 'Exile? Hey, Grig, what did he do?'

'He tried to seize control of the League and have himself declared dictator, absolute ruler, king, head tax collector ... whatever the operative designation your people favour. He's a scoundrel and half mad. That is what makes him so dangerous. If he were completely mad or sane he would not be such a threat. But he is clever, Xur is. Too clever. I am convinced he should stay in Rylan space, though ... without a ship or suit.'

'The Ko-Dan wish only to be our friends,' Xur was saying confidently. 'Why not give them a chance?'

'The Ko-Dan are the reason our ancestors created the Frontier in the first place.' Enduran's resolve was as unshakable as his logic. 'As for you, Xur, you have no greater ambition than to be a petty tyrant, a Ko-Dan satrap lording it over your own people.'

'There are those Rylans who would welcome me, father.'

'I am aware of the deviants who follow you. Slavish sycophants revelling in the prospective return of ancient anarchy. League justice took care of them and put an end to your cult. Your followers are few and scattered.'

'League justice!' The flimsy mask of civility that Xur had affected until now was finally thrown aside as his true feelings came to the fore. For the first time Alex was exposed to the naked hatred that motivated Enduran's renegade offspring. 'The League is a refuge for weak worlds populated by weak beings who have lost the ability and the will to control their own destinies. I will return to them the legacy of their own past.'

'That past is filled with war, death and destruction. The legacy of the League is peace,' Enduran said softly. 'But no matter what course is chosen, it is for the citizens of Rylos and the other worlds to choose. They will not let a dangerous and unbalanced child like yourself decide their future for them.'

Xur suddenly turned sly, his expression guarded. It was not pleasant to see.

'And yet it was this "child" who caught your master spy. Or did you think, father, that in my "megalomania" I underestimated the abilities of the League? Far less than they underestimate me. Until now I have not revealed what I know, for I knew you would only replace him who I found out with another, whom I would have to dig out all over again.

'Now there is no longer any need to maintain the game. It is time for all deceptions to be exposed and all screens to be cast aside. Look to your own warboard.'

Against his will, Enduran turned. The main screen in the briefing chamber behind him suddenly went blank, then filled with static. A flurry of activity among those monitoring the screen failed to clear away the interference. When a picture finally emerged, it was clear it was no longer under local control.

The image was faint and hazy with distance, but still recognizable. Enduran could not repress a start as he identified the figure filling the screen. It was a Rylan, seated, restrained, and frightened. A deceptively thin helmet-like device cupped his head, holding it immobile.

'A personal friend, perhaps, father?' said Xur's projection. 'Someone you appointed yourself? Or merely another ignorant tool of League "intelligence"? Not that it matters. It is enough to provide an example of how I shall treat all who oppose me.' The projection nodded and said something in a language Alex's translator was not equipped to transcribe: Ko-Dan.

The helmet shrank. A scream sounded from the warboard, accompanied by a distinct cracking sound that was clear enough even over the great distance the projection was covering. Eyes popped clear of their sockets while Rylan blood gushed in several directions to stain flesh, clothing and restraints. The helmet continued to contract long after the unfortunate Rylan's life had fled, contracted until there was nothing left atop the imprisoned neck save a pinched neck that ended in raw white bone.

No one moved in the hangar or the war-room. No one spoke. Rumours of Xur's barbarisms were well known, but it was something else to have actual evidence of them served up on a large screen in garish colour. Of all the onlookers Enduran was the least shocked. He knew better than anyone else what his son was capable of.

Better than anyone else except perhaps one other.

To Alex it was a scene from a bad horror flick. Knowing it was real and not cinematic make-believe made a number of other things a lot more real. Suddenly he saw Grig as an individual, saw Enduran as a father as well as an eloquent alien. Concepts and visions which he'd only read about in school took on solidity. History was full of blood and the deeds of Xur's emotional relations. Puritan aesthetes cut them out of student texts, with the result that the horrors of the past became sanitized.

Alex saw now how wrong that was. Blood made tyrants far more real than dry descriptions of their misdeeds.

What of the history he was living now? Would it also be emasculated for its appearance in some alien text one day? Or wouldn't it matter because the histories would all be adjusted to fit the wishes of Xur and his imperial descendants?

'Hear me, Rylans!' Xur was all dictator now, fully into the role he'd chosen for himself. 'When the green moon of Galan is eclipsed, the Ko-Dan armada under my command will invade. All who rise and join my cause will be spared to prosper. All who resist will wish for a death as quick as that which you have just witnessed. Your shield projector will not save you. Your false ethics will not save you. Not even your mighty resurrected Starfighters in their antique ships will save you.

'*Nothing* will save you!'

Enduran's reply was quiet but firm. 'We shall see, Xur. We shall see.'

'Indeed was shall, *father*, and the seeing will be most pleasant ... for *me*!'

With that the projection dissipated, Xur's laughter fading to oblivion along with his contorted face.

There was no time for pause and reflection. Even before the last light from the projection globe had disappeared, the hangar had filled with activity. Mechanics hastened through final checks. Programmers activated their systems. Activity monitors regained control of their screens.

The hangar was filled with much movement, little talk, and loud orders. The lights dimmed as power was checked but shone a moment later brighter than before.

Amidst this rush of preparation for battle Centauri turned to face Alex, his expression one of disbelief, and said, 'You *still* wanna go, and miss all the excitement?'

The Rylan officer waited silently, curious as to how the peculiar young alien would react to this challenge. Grig waited too, expectant.

Alex noted that everyone's eyes were on him. They were alien eyes, inhuman eyes. He thought about all he'd seen since being shanghaied from home. Home. The word flooded him with warm, comfortable memories; Louis nagging him, his mom coming home from work exhausted every night, the crickets chirping outside his bedroom, Maggie. Most of all, Maggie.

He let the uniform fall to the floor of the hangar.

From that moment on Centauri never stopped his muttering, though Alex could understand only bits of it. The old man reserved his loudest comments for the return of his payment to the waiting officer. A year's recruiting spent slaving on a backward world, all wasted. Alex felt a little sympathy for him, but only a little.

Centauri had been dealing him from the bottom of the deck ever since he'd set eyes on him. Earlier than that, if you counted the Starfighter game as part of the deception.

He clung tenaciously to those thoughts, to his feeling of righteousness, as the car/starship lifted clear of the Rylan atmosphere and accelerated past the moon the locals called Galan.

'The little brat,' Centauri was mumbling in half a dozen

languages as he prepared for the jump past lightspeed. 'Invent the game, disguise its origins, find the kid, drag him back here, and for what? He doesn't want to be a Starfighter. Take me home! Okay! Home to mommy we go. I give up. Hopeless!'

As the ship rose clear of the ecliptic, the only sound in the cockpit came from the steadily complaining Centauri. If he'd been a bit more attentive, a little less self-pitying, he might have paid more attention to his long-range scanners, might have made sure they were programmed to note things besides the known astronomical bodies which orbited Rylos' sun.

Might even have been in a position to help.

VII

At unexpected coordinates floated bodies that were not native to the Rylan system. They were all quite small, except for a single much more massive object around which they drifted.

This single immense artificial construct bristled with antennae and shafts of metal, serving as a nucleus for the lesser lights that accompanied it. Communications by means of low-power tight beams passed between the monster and its numerous attendants. Orders were conveyed, questions asked, replies made. Information of import passed between the assembled ships.

The busy exchanges were in preparation for a moment which the historians on the command ship were taking care to record to the smallest detail, so that every participant would be guaranteed his or her fair due. An exchange of a more personal nature was about to occur within the bowels of the great vessel that moved ponderously among shoals of lesser ships.

The dark corridor brightened unexpectedly before dimming again. The change did not trouble the nervous, stunted creature making its way along the passage. He knew the route by heart, and could have negotiated it as efficiently in complete darkness as in the artificial light.

A shiny globe tipped the long staff he carried. The black metal orb concealed an impressive array of ultraminiaturized electronic components behind its smooth black finish. It belonged not to the pitiful example of underlife now carrying it through the innards of the great warship but to the underling's master. A master, the underling had decided, no worse than any other.

Unpredictable, though. He preferred masters who were predictable even if they were more abusive. Better predictable abuse than the sudden rages this new master was heir to. There seemed no way to anticipate his abrupt shifts in mood. Privately, the underling was convinced that his new master was more than a little insane.

That did not matter, however. All that mattered was that the real masters, the Ko-Dan, treated this new one in their midst as an equal. It was not for the underling to question this. Only for him to obey. That was all any of the Ko-Dan's subject races could do. The underling had served for a long time.

But audiences with his new master still made him queasy. Two guards stood stolidly outside the command centre. Their presence was more a matter of ceremony than security, since it was ludicrous to imagine a threat to command originating from inside the command ship. But the Ko-Dan were fond of their rituals and traditions, and so he was made to wait near the portal while the words were spoken.

'What seek you here, underling?' asked one of the massive sentries.

'My master, the Emperor Xur.' He waved the black metal staff. 'He ordered me to bring to him his sceptre of office.'

Other ears overheard the byplay. The ritual was shortened by the Ko-Dan commander himself as he spoke from his position inside the centre.

'What transpires?' inquired the noble Kril.

'An underling, Commander,' said the other guard. 'He carries a weapon.'

'Sceptre of office,' the underling protested, keeping his voice deferential.

Another figure, tall and imperious of manner, moved to stand next to Kril. The newcomer looked out of place within the Ko-Dan command centre, but he didn't feel out of place. He found his alien surroundings quite congenial.

100

He waved casually towards the doorway. 'Yes, I sent for my sceptre. Let him enter.'

The senior guard of the pair ignored the directive and looked hesitantly towards his Commander. Kril gestured curtly and the guard responded by stepping aside and slipping on the safety lock on his own weapon.

Wishing he were anywhere else but in this den of power, the underling advanced, holding the sceptre out before him. Xur the Rylan, son of Enduran of the League Council, accepted the sceptre with obvious pleasure. He juggled it in both hands, luxuriating in the weight and feel of the gleaming black metal.

When he'd finished toying with it he grandly dismissed the underling who'd fetched it for him. That poor creature bowed repeatedly as he retreated from the command centre as fast as courtesy permitted, greatly relieved at having escaped without a reprimand or a beating.

Balancing the sceptre on one shoulder, Xur turned to face the expressionless Commander standing nearby.

'A shape and insignia that should be familiar to you, Kril. I made certain the pattern followed precisely that of the staff carried by your own Emperor. Is the likeness not remarkable?'

'Excellent Ko-Dan manufacture,' Kril muttered. He did not care for these posturings, which the renegade Rylan tried to turn into audiences instead of discussions.

'Yes, it certainly is. There is much to be said for a work force that obeys the dictates of its superiors unquestioningly. That sort of devotion has heretofor been alien to Rylos and the other worlds of the League, but we'll change that, won't we?'

'Yes, *we* will,' agreed the Commander.

Other eyes watched the byplay. Finally one senior officer could stand it no longer and began muttering dark threats by way of his subordinate. Kril noted the grumbling but chose to ignore it so long as the grumbler remained discreet. He could hardly blame the officer for expressing aloud the feelings of many of his comrades.

To his Rylan counterpart he said only, 'It takes more than a sceptre to rule, Xur, even a backward world like Rylos.'

'Backward, yes. So backward you would not think of approaching it so openly were it not for the aid of my backward self and my backward allies.' Kril tensed but again chose not to respond.

'But you are right, Kril. It does take more than a sceptre to rule. After all, what is a sceptre? Nothing more than a harmless standard of office.'

He touched a concealed switch. A thin shaft of green light emerged from the sceptre's black globe. It was the visual manifestation of a high-powered sonic needle, strong enough to heat the air around it. It could cut through just about anything. Xur waved it around the room with disconcerting casualness, but Kril never flinched.

The voice of the outraged senior officer became audible. 'How long must we be forced to endure this fool . . .!'

Kril whirled to pin the officer with his eyes, making him shrink back inside his psyche. Realizing he'd overstepped his bounds, the officer executed a voiceless apology. However much the Ko-Dan officers disliked taking orders from and suffering the antics of the renegade Rylan, they were compelled to do so unless Xur's granted rank was reduced. For the moment, he drew his strength directly from Imperial Degree. If not the person, that rank had to be given full respect.

Everyone in the command room was conscious of this silent exchange and its import for all of them. The officer accepted his rebuke silently. It was to be only a momentary humiliation, however. The word they had been waiting for since they'd first arrived on the outskirts of the Rylan system was passed from Research.

'We have a break in the energy shield defending Rylos,' a technician announced. Immediately the confrontation between Commander and officer was forgotten amidst general excitement.

'How long will the break last?' Kril inquired.

The technician communicated with his superiors in the

command ship's laboratory section and replied, 'Insufficient data for conclusive evaluation, Commander.'

'Is it weakened sufficiently to permit an attack?'

'Yes sir. Countershield believe they can suppress its effects until we can destroy the projector itself.'

Excitement gave way to methodical preparations. 'Are the assault schedule and squadrons ready?'

'They've been ready for many cycles, Commander,' came the reply from Logistics.

'Then the time has come.' Kril's eyes glistened with anticipation. This would be a moment the recorders would permatize in special script. 'All sections prepare for first assault. Mass drive activation if . . .'

The sound of a fist slamming against a console cut off the rest of the Commander's order. An enraged Xur glared at the aliens surrounding him. Ko-Dan they might be but in this time and place *he* was master, by decree of their own Emperor. He would not see that authority usurped. Especially not at this critical moment. He wanted to savour it, as he had savoured it in his own mind for many long, frustrating, empty years. No alien interlopers were going to deprive him of that long-awaited pleasure.

He was conscious of their eyes on him, knew that if Kril would permit it any one of them would cheerfully rip his flesh from his bones. But they would not dare act without Kril's permission, and Kril knew better than to allow his emotions to gain control of his mind.

So when he spoke to them he was not afraid, and he enjoyed their discomfort.

'My Ko-Dan friends. Lest you forget, allow me to remind you that it was your own Emperor who in his wisdom gave me command of this armada. Only I know the secret of the Frontier and the shields which protect the League worlds, just as only I know the location of the ancient Starfighter base and the shield projector. Only my people on Rylos can execute the critical manoeuvres necessary to ensure our triumph.

'Therefore only *I* will give the order to fire!' He let them stew in their own fury for a long moment before adding, 'Is that understood? By *all* of you?' He looked squarely at Kril as he spoke.

It was not in the nature of the Ko-Dan to tremble, out of either fear or fury, but the effort it took for Kril to reply without losing control was self-evident to every officer in the command centre, and their already high admiration for their Commander rose proportionately.

'Forgive my presumption, Xur.' It was voiced in a tone barely above a whisper, but it satisfied the Rylan. It also pleased him to be magnanimous, knowing that such treatment could only humiliate the Ko-Dan Commander further.

'You are forgiven, Commander Kril. We are all anxious to begin the final battle.' Unable to watch any longer, several of Kril's senior officers turned back to their instruments, fighting to suppress their own anger at this Rylan upstart's actions.

Having prolonged Kril's debasement long enough, Xur turned grandly to the proper station. 'Now is the time to use the mass driver. Fire!'

The fire control officer hesitated just long enough to glance at his Commander. Kril gestured imperceptibly. This infuriated Xur, but there was nothing to be done about it. He could never prove that the officer had requested permission first from his own Commander before engaging the driver.

'Fire!' Xur screamed at him, trying to regain the domination so recently won and off-handedly lost.

Taking care that the Rylan could not see his expression, the Ko-Dan fire control officer passed along the requisite orders.

There seemed no need to build a starship the size of the Ko-Dan command vessel. Traditional weaponry could be mounted on much smaller, more manoeuvrable ships, including world-threatening atomics.

But there were sophisticated methods of rendering atomics harmless, just as there were ways of diverting energy and particle beams or small explosive projectiles. Rylos possessed such defences in abundance.

Yet if an attacking ship could get into position near enough to a target world, there was a weapon so ancient and overpowering it could overwhelm any traditional defence. A weapon which had been in use since the beginning of all civilizations. Advanced technology merely upgraded that weapon in scale.

The weapon was mass.

The chunk of heavy metal ore which was moved from one end of the command ship to the other passed through a line of immense supercooled magnets. They accelerated the hunk of platinum-iron to tremendous speed. As soon as it left the command ship's foreward hatch on its carefully calibrated course, a second mass of similar size and shape was moved into position at the command ship's stern. It was soon following the first towards Rylos.

It had taken some time for the Ko-Dan to locate a local planetoid of sufficient composition and size to fit their need, longer still to section it into chunks small enough to fit into the mass driver which ran through the longitudinal axis of the command ship. The resulting pieces were still very large indeed.

Superfast heavily armed fighters might still have intercepted the incoming masses safely out in empty space and destroyed them, except that the League had relied on its shield system for so long it no longer kept such vessels active. The League had nothing ready to counter the Ko-Dan threat with ... save some half-rumoured rebuilt old ships called gunstars.

Awesome as the power posed by the mass driver was, however, the Ko-Dan did not intend to rely on it alone. A second attack was about to make itself felt on Rylos.

A far more subtle one.

It had been too long since that world had been required to deal with anything more solid than a theoretical assault, so the technician in charge could have been excused for his delay in reporting the objects that suddenly appeared on his screen. Once their reality had been confirmed, though, he displayed no reluctance to file his report.

'I show incoming solid objects, largely metallic, in sector three-one.'

A suboffizer ambled over while other technicians glanced up from their stations.

'Track them,' ordered the suboffizer. Together the two Rylans watched the screen. 'Composition?'

The tech scanned his readouts, waited briefly for a computer analysis. 'Heavy metals, unrefined. Not starship hulls. Too much mass in too small an envelope and shape does not conform to any known Ko-Dan or League type. Furthermore, mass seems to vary slightly among incoming objects.'

'Course deviation?'

'None. Is the shield still functioning?'

The suboffizer looked across the room, receiving positive replies from several stations.

'So it would seem. Then why no course deviation?'

'Could they be coming in on some new kind of drive? Or even without using drives?'

'I don't know, but I don't like it.' Around the room, instruments and consoles began shouting for attention. 'Whatever they are, they're heading straight for Rylos. No question about that. Give me an impact approximation.'

Another long minute of study and subsequent analysis. 'Right for the base, sir. For this portion of the continent, anyway.'

'*Sanprash*!' The suboffizer grew livid. 'They must be aimed at us. There's nothing else of military importance for a thousand *milots* along this coast. It has to be the Ko-Dan, attacking! Somehow they managed to pinpoint this location!'

'Xur's underground at work,' muttered another technician angrily. The suboffizer ignored him.

'Never mind. We can handle it, no matter what they're throwing at us. It'll be a good test for the revamped gunstars and their crews. We ought to thank Xur for the target practice.' He turned to a voice pickup and his words were broadcast throughout the defence complex.

'Alert! We are under attack! I repeat, we are under attack!'

Alarms began to sound as he continued. 'Incoming spheroids of varying metallic composition. Intercept and destroy, intercept and destroy. Navigations prepare for onboard reception of intercept coordinates.' He looked back to the technician.

'Make sure the intercept point is at least two-dozen planetary diameters out. We want them to have plenty of time.'

'Understood. Schematics forthcoming.' Like everyone else in the room the tech was relaxed, confident. They'd been preparing for this attack for over a year now. 'Incoming objects have passed through a destabilized section of the shield. They must be driveless. We may not have enough time for a two dozen diameter intercept.'

'Make it a dozen, then. We'll still have plenty of time to stop the first ones.'

Out in the hangar, Starfighters and Navigator/Operators were donning helmets and running last-minute equipment checks. Gunstars were prepared for final powerup, computers detached from central control.

The subofficer's information was relayed to the command centre nearby. An engineering officer made a last check of a certain console before speaking to the technician working next to him.

'Deflector shield powerup?'

'On-line. Standing by, sir.'

'Activate.'

'What about Plomerr Precinct, sir?'

The officer's expression never wavered. 'We're the target here, not Plomerr. Our first priority is to protect the gunstar base. We'll just have to hope those pilots can get to these incomings first.'

'Yes sir,' said the technician slowly. He had family in Plomerr Precinct.

Around them others worked smoothly at tasks long rehearsed. Everything was functioning according to design. Everyone was at their proper post.

Everyone except the monitor making his way along the

service conduit that ran behind the main warboard. He did not really belong there, nor was the small package he carried so gingerly part of the intricate maze of circuitry and components that combined to provide the Rylan Defence command with necessary intelligence.

Selecting a site, he placed the package in a gap between two fluid-state junctions. Then he retreated as fast as his feet would carry him.

Not far away, on the other side of the board, the general officer in charge of defence was feeling confident. He was in the process of requesting an update on the trajectory of the incoming objects with an eye towards sending a few of the gunstars racing back along that path in search of the Ko-Dan armada.

He was preparing to issue the necessary orders when the console he was studying exploded in his face, shredding it along with that of the technician manning the instrumentation.

Considering the small size of the explosive package, the resultant detonation was substantial. It effectively demolished the warroom along with all local communications.

A second similar package exploded simultaneously in a heavily guarded power station buried deep within the same mountain range. When the station went up, the power to the defensive shield protecting Rylos evaporated.

In the ruined warroom the technician who'd initially detected the incoming attack staggered clear of his demolished console. He was bleeding and dazed, as were most of his colleagues.

There was another console nearby, away from the central command area. It looked relatively intact. The technician stumbled over to it and flailed at the controls. At first it ignored his insistent demands, responding only after emergency power gave it life.

The technician worked with it until he had produced a duplicate of the plot he'd had on his own console. It showed the incoming masses with emotionless clarity. They were as big as first suspected and travelling very fast.

When the first one reached a certain point on the screen, it disintegrated, along with most of the flank of the mountain in which the command base was located. Succeeding masses of heavy ore reduced rubble to powder. Mixed in with the ruined rock were the gunstars, their pilots, and the unlucky technician, together with the hopes of the League.

Other eyes watched avidly as pinpoints of light representing the heavy masses impacted one after the other on the surface of Rylos. There was measured, restrained jubilation on board the Ko-Dan command ship. Then the crew bent to their tasks. There was still much to do.

In addition, by concentrating on their work they were able to shut out the sight of the strutting, bombastic Rylan in their midst. To hear Xur talk one would have thought he'd reduced Rylos's defences all by himself, down to hurling the pieces of moon at the planet's surface with his bare hands. Those forced to listen longed for the day when permission might be granted to expose the interloper to the sight of his own intestines.

They said nothing, keeping their desires concealed. One of their number had already been reprimanded by the Commander. None of the crew intended to tempt Kril's anger a second time. Such were the rules that the Ko-Dan lived by.

Those rules were worth adhering to. They had made the Ko-Dan masters.

By now the invading armada had moved close enough to Rylos to show the planet and its satellites on highpowered visual scanners. They were not yet near enough to see the extent of the damage they'd inflicted on the surface, but further confirmation was unnecessary. Abstract imaging was documentation enough.

'A direct hit, Commander,' reported the fire control officer. 'All strikes successful in succession. No manifestation of a defence, either ground-based or spatial. It appears that we can attack at will.'

'Thank you,' Kril replied. 'Further use of the mass driver should not be necessary. I expect to begin negotiations leading to a formal change of government soon. They are clearly defenceless and have no choice but to submit or face progressive annihilation of population centres. The change-over to Ko-Dan administration should be brief.

'With Rylos subdued, the rest of the League should rapidly follow suit. This is a great moment for the Empire of the Ko-Dan.'

Xur wasn't listening. At the moment he wasn't listening to anything except the hatred in his own mind. He stared at the viewscreen which showed his now helpless home and exulted aloud.

'At last it is done! My return is complete. Soon all talk of a "Frontier" will cease, as will the concept of the Frontier. It is revealed now for what it always was: a screen consisting of nothing stronger than words.

'They will all bow to me, to Xur. They will bow to their new Emperor or I will darken the sky with their ashes! I will raze the cities of Rylos until all will to resist has been crushed. I will ...!'

While Xur raved in the middle of the command centre the Ko-Dan smiled to themselves and quietly worked at their stations. One communications officer was concentrating on a single, tight-beam coded channel that emanated from the surface of Rylos. It was the fleet's only means of communicating with their Xurian allies below.

Now several monitors came alive on his console. He listened intently, waited for the computer to transcribe the code into Ko-Dan. As soon as this had been done he left his seat and hurried to report to the Commander in person.

'What is it?' Kril's tone was relaxed now. The successful destruction of the secret League base enabled him to view Xur's tantrums with contented detachment.

'The report is full of uncertainties, Commander. Our contacts on Rylos are having difficulty making observations while staying in touch with us because of the havoc caused in the sensitive area by our recent attack.'

'I sympathize. The destruction must be extensive. Yet it must be important or they would not take the risk of

110

contacting us now.'

'Again, this observer wishes to make it clear he is not positive, but he thinks that one ship may have escaped from the Rylan base just prior to our assault. A very small ship, of indeterminate specifications. It *could* be piloted by a Starfighter.'

Xur whirled from the screen and the world it revealed.

'*Could* be? A Starfighter escaped?'

Kril sighed but held his temper. 'It is only one small ship. What can one ship do against the armada?'

'You don't know our history. You don't know what these gunstars are capable of if directed by the right combination of instincts.'

Kril didn't try to hide his contempt. 'I was assured all such instincts had been bred out of your citizenry.'

'Out of most Rylans, yes, but not out of the more primitive peoples of the League.'

'Still, one ship ...'

The deadly needle of disturbed air appeared above the knobbed end of Xur's sceptre. 'None must escape. None! None *will* escape. It is not a matter of concern, but our victory must be total, absolute. There must not be a suggestion of resistance left for the people to rally around!'

Krill turned to Detection and Surveillance. 'Suspect escaping craft recently cleared destroyed Rylan base. Examine all potential flight tracks at atmospheric point of departure and initiate a search of the surrounding spatial vicinities.'

'Yes, Commander,' replied the Scanner in charge. 'What are we to do if we locate evidence of passage?'

'Track it,' Xur snapped. 'If it goes to supralight take an energy reading and approximate place of re-emergence into real space. Report to me.' He turned to Kril, smiling. 'I will handle this in my own way. With your concurrence, of course.'

'Of course,' murmured Kril, smoothly maintaining the sham of Xur's dominance. As for dealing with the possible escapee, that did not concern the Ko-Dan Commander. He was content to let Xur amuse himself with its destruction. After all, as he'd already stated, what *could* one ship do against the armada?

VIII

It was dark at the crossroads. They had re-entered the Earth's atmosphere over the Southwestern United States after midnight, local time. They had set down safely on an unused dirt road, rumbled out onto the highway heading towards the trailer park, and promptly broken down. Centauri's hybrid vehicle had carried them halfway across the galaxy, only to break down a mile or so from Alex's home.

Alex stood and watched as Centauri puttered around under the hood, wondering if the alien was fooling with a dummy internal combustion engine designed to fool curious mechanics. Either that or he was actually fixing a device capable of interstellar flight with the aid of a few hand tools. The old man's spindly legs (was that flesh-coloured makeup on those ankles a mate to the mask that covered the alien face?) and gartered sock were the only portions of him that were visible beneath the edge of the car.

Alex listened longingly to the crickets and frogs chirping in the nearby ditch. He stared out into the familiar night, hands jammed deep in his pockets.

'Sure I can't give you a hand?' He turned back to the stalled vehicle. The rear licence plate said RYLOS; Centaurian humour at its most basic.

The old man spoke from beneath the car. 'Ever done any work on a missealed sisendian toroid?'

'Uh, is that anything like a transmission?'

'Not really.'

113

'Then I'm afraid I wouldn't be of much help.'

'I didn't think so.' Centauri's tone was rich with indifference. 'You've done quite enough already, thank you. As for this blasted toroid, even your Einstein couldn't figure it out. On the other hand, I can ...'

Something bright flared beneath the vehicle and the odour of ozone filled the air. A bright spark jumped from the car to the road sign across the intersection, melting it like candle wax.

'Yeah, I see that you've got everything under control. Suit yourself.' Alex turned to gaze down the highway. 'It's only a couple of miles from here. I'll walk it. So long, Centauri. Nice knowing you.'

'Wait a minute, boy, wait!' The old man struggled out from beneath the vehicle, wiped sand from his false face and fumbled in a pocket until he produced what appeared to be a slimline digital watch. The time on the watch, a quarter to two, was correct. Centauri might be a liar and a conman, Alex mused, but he certainly was a finicky one.

'Here.' He held out the watch.

Alex shook his head. 'Gee, I can't take a present from you.'

Centauri shook his head, spoke sadly. 'Humans ... they're *so* perceptive. He reduces me to poverty and thinks I'm giving him a present. What a world this is.'

'Then what is it?' Alex asked, a mite belligerently. 'It looks like a watch. If that isn't a gift I don't know what it is.'

'If you'll shut up a minute, I'll tell you. It functions as a watch, sure, but that's only concealment. It's very subtle, this little toy. The real components aren't in the body, they're in the facing, the cover.'

Intrigued, Alex accepted the 'watch', inspected it closely. 'It's transparent. There's nothing inside the crystal.'

'It's your thoughts that are transparent, boy, which leads me to believe there's nothing inside your head. What makes you think a simple little short-range communicator can't be built out of transparent materials? Anyway, the crystal really isn't transparent. It just bends light waves around it. So it looks transparent.' He moved his fingers over the crystal,

114

careful not to touch it.

'Then what's it for?'

'I told you. It's a short-range narrow-line communicator. One way only, simple signal generation. If you prefer, think of it as your second chance, my boy. Should you change your mind regarding the employment I so dilligently secured for you, just tap the crystal in this brief sequence.' He demonstrated twice, until Alex nodded. 'It will reach me so long as I remain suborbital.'

Alex started to hand it back. 'Then keep it. I won't be needing it.'

'Just think it over, my boy,' Centauri pleaded with him. 'If nothing else, it *is* a perfectly serviceable watch. You don't own a watch, do you?'

'Sure I do. It's back in my room. Only ... the batteries burnt out.'

'This one doesn't need a battery. It runs off the electrical impulses running through the muscles in your wrist. It'll keep running as long as you do.'

'All right, I'll hold onto it, if you insist.' More than anything else Alex was tired of arguing. 'But I'm *not* changing my mind.'

Centauri moved to the gaping gullwing on the driver's side of the car and put one foot inside. 'You're walking away from history. History! Did Chris Columbus say he wanted to stay home? No! And what if the Wright Brothers had thought only birds could fly? And did Geloca say that the Yulus were too ugly to save?'

'Who's Geloca?'

'Never mind. That's not the point. The point is that history is made up of critical decisions executed by extraordinary beings at just the right moment.'

'Listen, Centauri, I'm not any of those guys. I'm not a Hannibal or Akbar. I'm not extraordinary. I'm just a kid who lives in a trailer park and wants to go away to college. I'm not special.'

'You *are* special, my boy. You were tested, tested rigorously, and you passed. With, as you say, flying colours,

115

though I fail to see anything aerodynamic about colour. I do so love your quaint human expressions. My boy, you are extraordinary.'

'Bull. I know how to make a quarter last, that's all. I'm just your average kid.'

'And if that's all you think you are, then that's all you'll ever be!' Centauri snapped angrily, unable to contain his frustration any longer.

He slid behind the controls and revved the false engine. The mock V-8 sputtered and came to life above the noise of the real engine. Centauri quickly dampened the sound. Then he turned the car around and headed back out onto the highway, muttering to himself loudly enough to be heard above the engine's whine.

Alex watched him slip away into the night, unable to push the old man's last words from his mind. Oh, he was clever, Centauri was! Appeal to Alex's vanity and ego when all else fails. His final words had been delivered with as much careful calculation as the first. All that talk about 'honours'. Just a chance to get himself killed in a fight that had nothing to do with him or his world. Hadn't Grig as much as said the same?

He wondered what Grig was doing now. A sombre type, so different from the ebullient Centauri. Alex wondered if all Grig's people were like that, precise and dry and courteous to a fault, or if it was just characteristic of Grig himself.

He'd never know, never have the chance to find out. Not now. A chance to explore the whole galaxy and he'd turned it down.

No, that wasn't fair. Maybe he wouldn't have, if he could have gone exploring without being shot at. Asking him to participate in a war so far removed from his own experience, his own concerns, was downright unfair. And no matter what the game claimed, he wasn't the militaristic type. He'd never even considered joining ROTC at the high school.

Could Earth remain apart from the fighting? So many worlds were involved. From what he'd learned during his brief visit to Rylos most of the civilized galaxy was in danger of being overrun by the Ko-Dan. There'd been talk of

116

admitting Earth to the League some day. After its inhabitants had matured.

Was he acting maturely in refusing Centauri's offer? Or was he behaving in a manner Grig and the Rylans and the rest would regard as adolescent? As no better than 'human'?

In addition to the greater concerns, he felt for Enduran. How would he react to Alex's refusal to help if he could? His own son was the leader of the traitors fighting against the League. In what category did Alex's refusal place him?

Dammit, it wasn't his responsibility! He hadn't asked for Centauri to come and yank him away from his normal, untroubled, everyday life.

His boring, monotonous, uncertain, dull everyday life.

The crystal protecting the digital readout that Centauri had given him caught the moonlight as he walked along the side of the road. Angrily, he jammed his hand in his pocket so he wouldn't have to look at it. The crystal had become a rectangular transparent eye that stared at him accusingly.

They needed his help. The vast, technologically advanced League needed the help of lowly Alex Rogan, videogame whiz and all-around screw-up. It was a bad joke. It didn't make any sense.

Primitive instincts, Enduran had called them. Primitive instincts he and the other potential Starfighters retained, instincts lost to the majority of League citizens. Not lost. Outgrown.

Was Centauri right? Would he prove as effective behind the fire controls of a real gunstar as he had behind those of the videogame? Where did computers have to make way for the more flexible decision-making ability of a living mind? Of a primitive mind that walked a thin line between civilization and barbarism?

His mind?

The neon sign flashed Starlight, Starbright over the front of the general store and office, welcoming him home in weary blue and yellow. The crickets were joined in their night-time song by sounds of toilets flushing, people arguing, televisions blaring out the evening's canned idiocies. Dust billowed

117

around Alex's feet.

Somehow everything looked different. Everything was changed. Yet as he looked and listened he knew everything was exactly as he'd left it. It was he who had changed. His little journey had altered his perspective. Somehow all the daily problems that vexed him no longer seemed so important. Not even going to the University seemed important.

Damn you, Centauri. You can't make me feel guilty.

'Hey, Alex, I thought you were gonna help me with this antenna?'

Otis stood near the rocking chair on the far end of the general store porch.

'Fine, Otis ... sorry. I forgot.'

Otis saw something in Alex's expression. Old Otis was very perceptive. He frowned as he stepped down off the porch and approached the youngster.

'Hey, you look kind of funny, Alex. Where you been?'

'For a walk. Couldn't sleep. Nothing wrong with that, is there?' He increased his pace and hurried into the park, leaving a puzzled Otis standing and staring after him.

'What about my antenna?' Otis called to him, gesturing with the metal grid.

'Later, okay?'

He was heading for his own trailer when another figure cut past in front of him. He swerved to follow.

Maggie! Sure, he could tell Maggie. She might not believe him at first ... hell, she might not believe him at second or third! But he didn't think she'd laugh outright at him. At least she'd listen.

Besides, he didn't care what she said. He was too happy to see her.

'Hey, Maggie!'

He finally caught her on the steps leading into her own trailer. That's when he saw the expression on her face.

'Maggie, is something wrong?'

She hit him hard, right across the right side of his face. He wasn't sure if she'd been crying or not, but she was as mad as he'd ever seen her.

'I told you,' she said tightly, glaring up at him as he felt his cheek burning, 'me and my . . . how did you put it . . . "strange sexual urges", aren't talking to you anymore. Is that clear enough for you, Alex Rogan?'

The trailer door closed behind her with a metallic *bang*. Slowly Alex recovered his senses enough to close his mouth, which had been gaping dumbly. It took longer before he was able to stumble down the steps towards his own trailer, wondering what the hell was going on.

She'd hit him before, but always in play. Never like that. She'd intended to hurt him. He wasn't angry at her for doing it, because he was too confused to be angry, and too stunned to respond.

Later. Sure, later. Fix Otis's antenna and find out why his best girl had tried to knock his teeth down his throat. Two items filed for future consideration.

He opened the door to his trailer quietly. It wasn't locked. Nobody in the Starlight, Starbright trailer park locked their doors. There was no need to. He tiptoed through the living room, past the tiny kitchen and its ticking wall clock. At the far end of the narrow central hallway the door to his mother's room remained shut. As hard as Jane Rogan worked, it would have taken more to awaken her from a sound sleep than the noise of one of her sons prowling about.

With considerable relief he cracked the door to his bedroom and stepped inside.

And got another shock. The room was a disaster area, a complete mess. Jane Rogan insisted on neatness from her boys because it was a good habit to acquire and because she didn't have the time to spare to spend cleaning up after them. Alex made it a point to keep the room as neat and tidy as was possible for any eighteeen-year-old living in cramped quarters with a younger brother, and Louis usually did his best to help out.

But something had gone badly wrong. It looked like the police had made a hasty search of the premises. Clothes were scattered everywhere on the floor, school supplies had spilled off the side of the single desk, bits and pieces of plastic model kits crunched underfoot as he entered and his books were strewn all over the place.

As he picked his way through the mess his gaze rose to the small figure sleeping on the top half of the bunk bed. Louis lay asleep on his side, his mouth open, one arm dangling over the side of the bed. A dozen or so Playboy magazines lay scattered around him, forming a second blanket of slick paper.

Alex checked his anger. Let Louis sleep. There was no point in waking mom. He'd take care of his younger brother in the morning. It was just like Louis. Alex had only been gone for a little while and ...

How long had he been gone? What about Einstein? What about the effects of travelling faster than light? What about relativity?

Nuts, what about it? He was too tired to care, much less to try puzzling out the great unanswered questions of modern physics in his demolished bedroom. He had more important problems to solve, the rationale for Maggie's fury being foremost among them.

He sat quietly on the edge of the lower bunk and started working on his running shoes. It would be good to sleep in his own bed, listening to the night sounds of the trailer park, far far away from Rylans and Xurians and Ko-Dans and other figments of a deranged imagination. Maybe he could even slip in a quick bath without waking his mother. A bath would feel great.

Already the memories were starting to fade, to become less imposing. In his mind Centauri's ranting and raving was changing into dialogue spouted by some refugee from a Saturday morning cartoon. A few days should see him back in the groove of lazy normality. The events of this night would be as one with memories of special Christmas presents and busy nights at the drive-in with Maggie. Nothing more.

Something moved beneath the covers on his bunk. Something large and irregular in shape.

He leaped off the bed, whirled to stare at the shifting sheets and blankets, his eyes wide.

'Who's there?'

The last thing he expected was a nervous reply. There was something about the voice that was familiar, though he couldn't quite place it.

'Hey, keep it down!' the voice told him anxiously. 'You're gonna wake Louis! That could be awkward.'

The sheets were tossed aside and a figure sat up in his bed. Alex didn't know what to expect: an old friend playing an elaborate practical joke on him, a Rylan, Centauri himself.

It wasn't any of them. It was just another guy, dressed like Alex, staring back at him.

In fact, it looked exactly like Alex Rogan.

It was a mirror-image of himself, come to life. There was no doubt about it. It was unarguably himself, Alex Rogan, down to the smallest mole and the slight change in hair colour at the sideburns. It sat on the edge of the bunk exactly as he might have and stared back at him. Alex stared at this duplicate of himself and swallowed hard.

Maybe he was too tired to be frightened. Maybe it was a good thing he was so exhausted. Certainly it was a good thing that in the past hours he'd seen so many marvels and impossibilities that one more couldn't shock him any worse than anything he'd already seen.

He did not run gibbering from the room. His reaction was more matter-of-fact than anything else.

'Hey, you look like me!'

The perfect double made shushing sounds while glancing up and back to make sure their little brother was still locked fast in sleep.

'Of course I look like you. I'd be worthless if I didn't. I'm the Beta Unit.'

'What the hell's a Beta Unit? I know what a Betamax is, but not a Beta Unit.'

'I recognize the reference, but there is only the most tenuous of relations. Centauri didn't tell you?'

'No, Centauri didn't tell me. Centauri doesn't tell people things,' Alex murmured angrily. 'Why did I think that you had something to do with Centauri?'

The double hesitated a moment. 'You're being sarcastic now, aren't you? Sarcasm is difficult to recognize.'

'It shouldn't be. Not when Centauri's involved. You still haven't explained what you are, besides me.'

'I am a BS-RS.'

'I'll buy the first half of that. What about the rest?'

'I don't think you buy any of it, unless you're being sarcastic again. I am a brain-scan regenerated simulacrum. An exact duplicate of you. Only not as *loud*.'

The noise made Louis turn lazily in his bed, the dangling arm rolling to flop against the far wall. Alex fought to keep his voice down. It would not do his younger brother's development any good at all if he awoke in the middle of the night to confront two Alexes sitting on the bunk beneath his, staring anxiously up at him.

'We met before,' the alien said. 'Don't you recall?'

Alex shook his head slowly, thinking. 'Somehow I think I'd remember you.'

'I was in the car, Centauri's vehicle. Remember now? In the back. We touched hands, I took a fast impulse and retina scan, the final impression was complete, and then I got out fast. After which I became you ... unfortunately.'

'Unfortunately for whom?' Alex frowned. 'A brain-scan regranulated ... can't you put that in plain English?'

'All English is plain; a scientifically unsophisticated language.'

'That's okay. I'm a scientifically unsophisticated guy. Lemme give it a try, though. You're a robot?'

His double looked offended. 'I *beg* your pardon! I am a state-of-the-art, top-of-the-line Beta Unit, fully programmable on short notice with slipsoidal epidermis and complete self-adapting internal cultural acclimatization features designed specifically for work on backward planets.'

'Which means?'

'Which means that to you morons I'm a robot.'

Alex pondered this a moment, then brightened. 'I didn't remember promising to help Otis fix his antenna. So you're the one who made that promise.'

'That's what I liked the first time I was told I was going to be working among you humans. You're so quick on the uptake. Of course it was me. Who else?'

'What else have you been doing while I was stuck chasing Centauri through a cave on Rylos?'

'Oh, wonderful things. Eminently suitable to a simulacrum of my class. Patching electric lines and fixtures, plunging toilets, repairing fences, chasing stray dogs; no wonder you wanna get out of here! What a dump, and a backward dump to boot. And I thought this was gonna be a cushy assignment; big metropolitan area, everything nice and clean, the pick of local museums, my choice of exotic native lubricants and electronic stimuli ... you don't even have cable out here! If I hadn't been able to pick up transmissions from a couple of your geosynchronous satellites I would've gone bonkers by now.'

'Sure, you've had it tough. I'll bet you've spent half that time watching cartoons.'

'As a matter of fact,' the Beta Unit replied drily, 'your animated entertainments feature the drollest portrayals of primitive robotic notions I've ever encountered. From an archeological standpoint it's been fascinating. The fascination wanes rather rapidly, however. Hey, what are you doing back here, anyway? I wasn't notified of any impending return.'

'Are you kidding? There's a war going on up there, and if you're on the wrong side they stick your head in an alien vegematic! How's that for the reactions of an advanced civilization?'

'Sadly, among organic sapients technological advances always outpace the social. A truism of advanced societies, I fear. One to which your own racial history can attest.' The Beta Unit's eyes narrowed.

'Hold it just one minute. You mean after all this moaning and groaning about making something of yourself, about getting out of this trailer park, you get your big chance, a chance afforded very few primitives, and you punk out?' He clucked his lips. 'How depressingly typical.'

'It's not my fight! And how did you know I wanted out of here?'

'Centauri's programming was very thorough. In addition to qualifying for Starfighter rating on the test machinery, a potential recruit must also be of the proper frame of mind. That is a more subjective measurement, however, and one Centauri apparently misjudged on your part.'

Alex looked away. 'Whether I want out of here or not has nothing to do with this. This war still has nothing to do with me or my world.'

'Oh, save the whales, not the universe, is that it? And if you think this conflict between the League and the Ko-Dan has nothing to do with you, wait a few hundred years until they reach this part of your galactic arm. Of course your lifespan will have ended long before then, won't it? You won't have to worry about it, will you?'

Alex turned on his double. 'If you're so hot to defend this League or whatever the hell it is, why don't *you* go up there and fight, instead of sitting here running off at your mechanical mouth?'

'First, I do only as I'm programmed to do. I don't enjoy the luxury of free will. Though after seeing how some beings utilize it, I'm not sure I want it anyway. Second, simulacrums can't fight, on any level. We're not allowed. Besides which it's been shown that we can't respond to the needs of combat as well as organics. We're not flexible enough in our thought-patterns.'

'Tell them you're me. Pretend. I won't tell.'

'You think it's that simple? Externally, yes, I am you. Internally I'm a dead giveaway. If I were to try a stunt like you suggest I'd be reduced to scrap inside a week. A machine that doesn't work right is valuable only for parts. Sure, I have a lot of you, Alex. But not the intangibles that make up a Starfighter.

'Anyway, I wouldn't try it. I pride myself on working right.'

A shuffling of covers sounded from above and a small shape

mumbled sleepily.

'Alex, be quiet, willya?' Louis was half conscious, half still in dreamland.

Alex whispered, 'Sorry, Louis.' He whispered it twice, and found himself regarding himself thoughtfully.

The truck ground to a halt outside the general store, the driver muttering to himself as dust rose from beneath the rear wheels.

'Damn brakes. Got to get the bastards some new pads. This okay for you, buddy?'

The hitchhiker he'd picked up down the highway nodded, opened the door on his side and jumped lightly to the ground. The driver eyed him one last time. Scruffy-looking type, the kind you might encounter on any road hoping for a lift. Looked out of place, somehow. Maybe a foreigner trying to see the good ol' US of A.

Because he'd felt sorry for him, the driver had picked him up. It was against company rules to pick up hitchhikers. He did it as often as possible.

It was unusual to run into somebody standing thumb-out this late at night, though. He shrugged. None of his business what the guy was up to. Just somebody else in a hurry to get somewhere. Nobody took their time anymore.

A boxy wooden console on the porch nearby began winking its lights while emitting a series of regular, urgent beeps. The driver squinted at it.

'Video whatzit. Hate them suckers. My oldest kid, he pumps his lunch money into 'em all week long. Thinks we don't know. Crazy.' He gestured at the subject of his ire. 'That one must be on the blink.'

The hitchhiker nodded in agreement as he stared at the flashing, humming game.

'Yeah, well, take it easy, mac,' the driver said. 'I hope you know someone here. It's a long hike to the next place to sleep.'

The hitchhiker turned. For the first time since he'd been given a lift, he smiled at the driver. It made the driver suddenly uncomfortable. He got the feeling that one more comment, one more question, might be one too many.

Naw, that was silly. This guy was quiet, but hardly threatening. 'Don't talk much, do ya?'

The hitchhiker shook his head and the driver shrugged indifferently. 'Suits me. I like a quiet rider now and then. Take it easy, mac.'

He revved the engine, backed the truck up in the broad, dirt-paved parking lot in front of the motel, and headed out towards the highway. The hitchhiker watched and waited until the lights of the truck had been swallowed by distance. Then he turned to study the trailer park. After several minutes of motionless examination, he headed for the first fence.

Behind him, the videogame continued its inexplicable electronic antics.

Moving in a preplanned arc through the trailer park, the hitchhiker passed the first lightless mobile without incident. The second still had lights showing and he bent low to make certain he passed well beneath the line of sight of anyone inside.

As he ducked below the last window a voice inside suddenly blared, 'Drop it or you're dead!'

The hitchhiker froze, momentarily frightened as well as confused by the unexpected challenge. More words followed upon the first, but they were unrelated to the challenge. In fact, they made next to no sense at all. Another loud voice followed clicking noises.

'Herrreee's Johnnnny!'

Now very puzzled indeed, but considerably less frightened, the hitchhiker rose slowly until he could just peer over the window sill into the trailer. At one end of the room an elderly human sat in a chair holding a small plastic rectangle. This he kept aimed at a video device squatting on the far side of the room. Each time a button on the rectangle was depressed, frequency shifts took place within the device and a new image appeared on the primitive glass face.

Relieved, as well as mad at himself for his reaction, the hitchhiker once more crouched below window level as he resumed his prowling through the park.

Alex and his Beta had resumed their conversation, keeping their voices down, each conscious of the impressionable ten-year-old sleeping on the overhead bunk.

'. . . And one other thing,' Alex was saying angrily, 'what'd you do to Maggie?'

'Maggie? Ah, the young woman. Not all primitive instincts are unpleasant.'

'I don't like what you're saying, friend.'

The Beta raised both hands defensively. 'Merely an unemotional analysis of observed habits based on known mammalian standards of beauty. Nothing personal. That would be impossible in any case.'

Alex wasn't sure how far he should trust this character, no matter what he was made out of, much less the facile disclaimer. After all, the Beta was an exact duplicate of himself. It was only natural to wonder just how far that duplication extended.

'What'd you do to her?' he repeated.

'Do to her? You primitives, I never will understand you. Listen, we're sitting outside, looking up at the stars. I'm trying to offer a little basic astronomy lesson . . . I know the names of all those stars, after all . . . and does she pay attention and ask pointed, intelligent questions? No! She sticks her tongue in my ear!'

Alex winced. 'What did you do?'

'I screamed. I was startled. I guessed immediately that was not the proper reaction, but I was unprepared. My programming is not one hundred percent in those areas of knowledge that were deemed peripheral to my central function, the job of imitating you.'

Alex relaxed a little. 'That explains Maggie's reaction when I saw her. I guess she was a little startled herself when you screamed.'

The Beta unit nodded unhappily. 'More than a little, I fear.'

'So what do we do about it?'

'I will apologize to her tomorrow,' the Beta assured him.

Neither of them noticed that Louis had awakened. He sat on the upper bunk and rubbed sleepily at his eyes.

'Like hell you will!' Alex rose from the bed, glaring at his double. 'You won't be apologizing to her or doing anything else, because you won't be here tomorrow. You're going back with Centauri right now, tonight.'

As he moved towards the door he began tapping the crystalline face of his new 'watch' in the sequence Centauri had shown him.

'What's up, Alex?' Louis mumbled dazedly into the darkness. There was something not quite right about his brother's mumbling, though Louis was still too sleepy to identify it.

At the door Alex turned to face the upper bunk. 'Back to sleep, Louis, or I'll tell mom about your Playboys!'

Alex had voiced the ultimate threat. Blackmailed into total submission, Louis fell back on the mattress and stared across the dimly lit room at his angry brother.

'Okay, okay!'

From below the upper bunk his brother added, 'You're blowing it, Alex. You're ruining everything. I knew I was replacing a primitive, but they didn't tell me just how *much* of a primitive!'

Just conscious enough to be confused, Louis swung his head over the edge of the bunk. Seated below, to his great surprise, was his brother. So then who had just shouted at him from near the door?

He knew his older brother could move quickly when he wanted to. Alex had been on the High School wrestling team. But *this* fast?

'I said,' the Beta told the hanging face, 'back to sleep, Louis, or I tell mom about your Playboys!' The Beta Unit had quick reactions of his own.

The ten-year old had had enough. He retreated immediately, taking care this time to stash the pile of thick magazines in the gap in the trailer's inner wall, the one neatly concealed by the big Star Wars poster. Then he threw the covers over his head and began snoring loudly, lest Alex think he wasn't taking the threat seriously.

Still tapping on the crystal facing Alex headed outside, as the Beta Unit debated what to do next. He was directed to remain in Alex's place of habitation. Presently, that meant the bedroom.

But things were not proceeding according to plan, not at all. Alex shouldn't have returned. Didn't his unexpected return cancel the original set of instructions? At such times the Beta was designed to operate independently, reacting as it saw fit to a new set of circumstances. It now elected to do so. Rising from the lower bunk, he followed his original outside. Alex was nowhere in sight. The simulacrum searched. Which direction?

While the Beta was trying to make up its mind, Alex was already alongside Otis's trailer, standing beneath the awning that had been erected to keep off sun more than rain. Monotonously and seemingly to no effect, he continued tapping on the crystal.

He frowned and turned to face the general store. Something was flashing brightly out front, and it wasn't the familiar erratic blinking of the old neon sign. Well, he'd check it out in the morning. He'd worked on the wiring to the big sign often enough to be able to repair it in his sleep by now. He'd begged mom to get it replaced, but she refused, saying that those old neon signs were becoming classics. Alex knew what she was really saying was that they didn't have the money to replace it.

Something cold and irresistible caught him beneath the chin and wrapped itself tight around his neck.

IX

Alex exhaled in surprise as he found himself rising into the air. His legs kicked wildly at emptiness. Fighting for his life he managed to turn in the powerful grasp just far enough to find himself staring into a bulging alien face. The eyes were placed far to either side of the skull, like those of a hammerhead shark, while the teeth visible in the low slung mouth were thin and pointed and very sharp looking.

As he stared bug-eyed at the apparition something went *snap* inside his head. The alien visage was replaced by that of a kindly older man. A second snap brought back the vision of alien gruesomeness. The creature fumbled at something buried inside a shirt, cursing as Alex witnessed a recurring series of visual shifts from alien monstrosity to elderly hitchhiker.

After several seconds of useless manipulation of the concealed device the alien gave up in disgust. It was no longer necessary to maintain the disguise anyway. He raised a pistol towards the target's face.

Alex saw the muzzle of the strange weapon coming up, wrenched and shoved with all his strength and managed to slide free of the single-handed grip. He dropped to the ground, stumbled back against the cold wall of the trailer. Above, the alien let out a violent hiss and realigned his aim.

Alex jumped for the stone wall that ringed Otis's precious vegetable garden. Something smacked against the rocks behind him as he dived. The smell of fused silica filled the air as the quartz in the rocks melted. Rolling fast, Alex ended up on his feet and ran blindly from the trailer, towards the store and the nearby ice house.

From the roof of the trailer the alien fired again, missed again, cursed again and rushed in pursuit of the target, easily clearing the gap between the roof of Otis's trailer and the ice house.

Alex pounded around the side of the old wooden building, frantically searching for better cover while hammering at the crystal facing.

'Please, Centauri, come in! Centauri, help! Something's trying to kill me!' He heard footsteps overhead and moved to his right ... where he tripped, landing hard on his side.

He wasn't injured and was on his feet again in an instant. No thought of running for the bushes now. Everything seemed to be in working order. Nothing sprained, nothing broken ... unless you counted the bits and pieces of strangely coloured crystal that sparkled in the moonlight. He looked at his wrist: the facing had shattered on a rock.

Dust fell on his face as he looked up. Standing on the edge of the ice house roof, aiming straight down at him, was the alien assassin.

So this is how it ends, he thought. I retreated across half the galaxy to avoid getting involved in somebody else's war, and something out of a bad dream shows up right here to kill me anyway. He wondered what the reaction of the trailer park's inhabitants would be in the morning when they found his body here, sandwiched between the general store and the ice house. He only prayed it wouldn't be his mother who found him.

A sharp whistle split the silence. The monster on the roof hesitated and turned curiously.

Standing nearby and thumbing his nose at the killer was the Beta Unit. The confused alien hesitated, but only for a moment. It was not easily put off by distractions. Clearly one of the two targets was a simularum. Well, he'd dealt with them before. Many who feared assassination used simulacrums to try and deceive their killers.

131

On this backward world that would not be a problem. It didn't matter which of the two was the original. All he had to do was destroy both of them.

Again he took aim at the human face staring up at him, aiming for a clean burst through the braincase.

A violent buzz sounded. Something exploded close to the alien. It threw him off-balance just enough to make his shot go wild, passing close enough to Alex's skull for him to feel the heat. Without waiting to see what had happened, Alex broke for the tenuous safety of the store porch. Additional explosions landed all around the alien.

The killer recovered, kneeling on the roof of the ice house and aiming into the night, trying to find a target as brilliant light suddenly swept over him. Another blast sliced off an arm. The alien faltered for a second, calmly switched his weapon to his other hand and continued firing.

As Alex came panting around the front of the store, there was Centauri's car fishtailing in front of the porch. The old man was firing through a port in the gullwing door, his weapon letting off one buzz-blast after another.

A weird, stifled moan floated down from above and behind Alex. Slowly and moving cautiously to his right, he edged out from underneath the porch until he could see the roof of the ice house. The alien's other arm had been shot away. It was staggering as it searched for an avenue of escape. As it trembled another blast from Centauri's gun struck it square in the back, spinning it around. It glared down into the parking area, the alien eyes finally locking on Alex. It was a cold, fishy stare and it went right through him.

Then the thing keeled over on the ice house roof. Smoke or steam poured from the body. It twitched once before tumbling over the side of the building to land with a dull *thunk* on the gravel below.

Centauri stepped out of his car, keeping his gaze on the steaming alien body. A quick search revealed that the fight had passed unnoticed by the sleeping citizens of the park. There were no awkward witnesses.

Alex wasn't as confident and searched the darkness beyond

the store. Surely someone must have heard the noise, Centauri's pistol at least.

Then he imagined what someone like Otis would have made of the peculiar sounds. Mobile homes and trailers were not blessed with thick walls. More than once arguments flared when the sound of one television show overlapped another in the trailer nearby. If anyone *had* heard the late-night fracas, they'd probably ignore it, thinking it was old Mrs Hadley watching the late-late show with the sound turned way up so she could listen without having to use her hearing aid.

What mattered was that no one materialized to stare curiously at the unexplainable corpse, for which Alex was grateful.

Centauri continued to aim his pistol at the smoking remains until he was satisfied that it was incapable of further movement. Then he slipped the small weapon back into the shoulder holster from which it had been pulled, trading it for a monogrammed handkerchief which he held over his nose.

Alex wondered at the reason for the handkerchief until he'd joined his rescuer in staring down at the body. Then his own nostrils wrinkled up and his eyes began to water.

'Yuck!' He hurriedly retreated from the odour.

'Illiterate comment, but evocative,' said Centauri. 'Foul stench, isn't it? Dirty creatures. Primitive predators who had wrapped themselves in the flimsiest trappings of civilization. Their real nature is much more difficult to camouflage.'

'Do they make good Starfighters?'

'Hardly. Their moral sensibilities are far too undeveloped, and their ability to distinguish between what is good for the individual and what is good for the group is atrophied.'

Alex hurried to change the line of questioning. Centauri's description of the morals of the monster lying dead before them sounded too much like the evening news.

'What's it doing here?'

'I thought that would be obvious by now. Get a good look at it, Alex. You can bet your sense of peace and well-being you'll be seeing others like it.'

'Huh? What are you talking about?'

'You asked what it was doing here. I thought you'd have figured it out by now. Apparently I was wrong. I tend to forget that while you are fast on the uptake with mechanical devices, your other mental processes have not developed quite as rapidly.

'This is a Double-Z Designate, judging by his method of operation.'

'Does that tell me anything?'

'It tells you that this is a recruited murderer. Usually a very efficient one. Compliments of Xur.'

'Xur! Why is he trying to kill me? How does he even know about me? If he knew anything about me he'd know I don't want anything to do with him or his war.'

'Nevertheless, this creature was sent to find and kill you. By Xur's order. No doubt the traitor keeps tabs on such useful throwbacks. This one must have been operating conveniently close to your system, hence his ability to locate you so quickly.' Centauri coughed into one hand.

'Evidently our flight from Rylos was picked up and plotted by Xur's Ko-Dan allies. There aren't that many inhabited worlds in this sector. Any supralight ship leaves a tell-tale track. It would appear that this thing detected ours.'

Behind them, smoke still rose from the alien torso. It twitched imperceptibly. One eye half opened. Armless and immobilized from the waist up, the alien searched the ground on which it had fallen. Nearby lay the deadly pistol that had almost slain Alex.

Slowly the alien slipped one of the peculiar terran shoes off a foot, exposing prehensile toes. The foot moved slowly, quietly, towards the weapon. Toes gripped it firmly as the alien fought to raise the muzzle.

Ignorant of the activity behind them, Alex and Centauri continued their conversation.

'But why is Xur after me?'

Centauri emitted a heartfelt sigh. 'Because whether you believe it or not, Xur knows that you're a threat to him.'

'I can't be! I turned in my uniform. I don't want to be a

Starfighter!'

'Ah, but Xur doesn't know that. He only knows and is evidently convinced that at least one *potential* Starfighter exists on this backward world. You. Merely by living you constitute a potential threat to him. Xur is not the kind to leave potential threats undealt with.'

'But I don't want to fight him. I'll sign a treaty with him.'

'Why should Xur bother with a treaty? Treaties take time and effort to put together, and one like Xur can never feel safe with them. Much simpler just to have you killed. I'm afraid you have no choice any more, my boy. Xur will consider you a Starfighter whether you choose to pilot a gunstar or an old Ford.'

A new voice joined in. 'You gotta go back, Alex, if only to protect yourself,' said the Beta Unit. 'If you stay here, you're dog food.'

'Trust Centauri, my boy. I assure you I had nothing to do with this. It's not my style. Just bad luck that the Ko-Dan detected us leaving Rylos.'

'How could they know there was a maybe-Starfighter on board your ship, though?' Alex wanted to know.

Centauri shrugged. 'There are many ways. It is well known that the Rylan defence command has been infiltrated by Xur's people. The command itself was organized in haste. Furthermore, it's clear that we were detected not just leaving Rylos, but leaving from the vicinity of the secret Starfighter base. Xur may be quite mad, but he is also madly clever. He is known to leave nothing to chance.

'If he knew your true feelings, it is true he would realize he has nothing to fear from you. Alas, he doesn't know that. So he assumes the worst. A small caution on his part. What is the liquidation of a single primitive in the context of his plans to make himself Emperor of the worlds of the League? Even if he could now be convinced of your determination to stay out of the coming conflict, it's unlikely he'd go to the trouble of rescinding the order to have you killed. Xur would rather have you eliminated than admit he might have made a mistake.' Centauri sighed.

'No, no, my boy, it's too late for talk. I do feel sorry for you.'

'But what can I *do*?'

'Trust me. You have no choice anymore except to trust me, because within hours this place will be crawling with ZZ-Designates with one thought foremost in their microscopic, predatory little minds: kill Alex Rogan.'

'Kill Alex Rogan,' Alex mumbled. Something moved out of the corner of his eye and he jumped, only relaxed slightly seeing that it was a gopher.

'He's right,' the Beta Unit told his original. 'At least you'll have a fighting chance up there in a gunstar.'

'Exactly.' Visions of full payment danced again in Centauri's head. 'And meanwhile down here they'll all be running around like mad trying to get Beta.'

'Beta?' The double frowned.

'Beta.' Alex eyed his duplicate.

'Of course,' said Centauri, wondering at the confusion. 'What do you think he's here for?'

'Now wait a second, Centauri,' the Beta started to protest.

Centauri stared at the simulacrum. 'You are programmed to follow directives. Personal survival is not programmed into your system. What is this, some kind of electronic mutiny?'

'No mutiny,' the Beta Unit replied. 'I know what my job is. It's just that you could be a little more diplomatic about it. Remember, I have Alex's feelings as well as his body.'

Centauri muttered something about Ormex & Co. not making simulacrums the way they used to, raised his voice and smiled as he spoke to Alex.

'Well, my boy, the choice is yours. Either join the fight against Xur and the Ko-Dan or,' and he gestured absently towards the smoking corpse nearby, 'get used to this smell.'

'You see,' the Beta said insistently, 'you gotta go back, Alex. At least you have a fighting chance up there. I'll cover for you down here.' He tried to smile reassuringly. Alex's skin crawled as he watched his own lips curve upward. 'It's my job, and I'm good at it. Xur's jerks will go nuts trying to catch me.'

136

'Maybe the next ones won't know how to find me,' Alex suggested hopefully.

Centauri shook his head slowly, looked genuinely apologetic if not entirely displeased by the turn events had taken.

'Afraid not, my boy. Now that you have been located it's a virtual certainty that your position and description have been relayed to a central distribution point. This thing's companions will know where to look, all right, as well as who to look for.'

The pistol clutched in flexible toes on the ground nearby finally steadied on its target. As it did so Centauri noticed the movement of the alien leg where there shouldn't have been any movement. He yelled a warning as he jumped at Alex, shoving him aside with one hand while drawing his own weapon with the other to return the fire.

The impact of the blast from the alien's pistol sent him staggering backward as Alex went crashing to the ground. Centauri fired repeatedly. This time he didn't stop after amputating the offending limb. He continued to fire until the alien body had been chopped into small, smoking chunks and didn't stop until the shrunken remains finally burst into sputtering, blue-tinged flame.

Alex was on his feet as the old man stumbled. The Beta Unit caught him from the other side. It took both of them to keep him upright.

'Centauri! Beta, get a doctor!'

Blood seeped through the side of the old man's jacket, but with the help of the two Alexes he managed to make it to his vehicle. They let him slump against it and moved back while he stood by himself, breathing hard and deep.

'No doctors!' Centauri gasped while gingerly feeling his side. 'No native cures or witch doctors. They wouldn't know what to make of my insides anyway.' He put one hand over his lips, coughed twice, then forced a smile.

'Excellent duplicate, actually. I can't tell you apart. I take back what I said about Ormex's designers.' He glanced towards his ribs. 'I'm okay, boys. It's just a scratch. Looks worse than it is.'

Carefully he walked around to stand next to the driver's side, turned to confront Alex.

'Face it, Alex. You're a born Starfighter. Whether you like it or not, you're a part of this war now. You can stay here and battle Xur's minions one at a time or come back with me and fight on behalf of all the civilized worlds. Your special talents are needed. *You* are needed. It's time to grow up, Alex.'

The subject of Centauri's discourse turned his face to the night sky, thinking hard. It was a painful decision to have to make, but wasn't that what growing up was all about? Making painful decisions?

'What if I'm killed out there, Centauri? What about my mom, and Louis?'

'Two people. A trillion lives are on the line out there, Alex.'

'Yeah, but they're not my people. Not my family.'

Suddenly Centauri sounded very wise. For a moment he put aside his snideness and spoke in dead earnest.

'That's where you're wrong, Alex. Intelligence and civility unite all creatures. Those are the ties that bind, that mean something. As for yourself, if you should be killed, well, everything dies eventually. Stars die, whole galaxies perish. Existence is brief, time is relative. Only truth goes on.'

'I like existence as it is, even if it is brief.'

'The Ko-Dan feel differently, Alex. They're not civil. They're not part of your family, as the citizens of the League are whether you think so or not. You're worried about Louis? What happens when he grows up and has to face the Ko-Dan here, on your own world? Because they'll come here, Alex. The Ko-Dan and the mentality they represent are never satisfied. All that stands between backward worlds like your Earth and eternal subjugation are the united peoples of the League. Help them now, Alex, and in doing so, help your own world's future.'

Alex nodded at nothing in particular, then wrenched his gaze from the stars to look across the gleaming hood of the ship. As Centauri said, he no longer had much choice in the matter. Might as well do the right thing for the right reasons.

'All right, Centauri. Let's go.'

138

The oldster nodded, and Alex was pleased to see he wasn't smiling in triumph. Maybe he took pleasure in Alex's change of mind, but he was tactful enough not to show it. Gullwing doors opened on the vehicle and he slipped inside.

Alex started to get in on the other side, found himself stopped by an irresistible hand. The hand fell away, turned sideways. He gripped it with his own.

'Good luck, Alex,' the Beta murmured.

Alex smiled as they shook hands. 'You too ... Alex.'

He turned away and lowered himself into the car.

'Let's do it. I'm ready.'

The old man spoke without taking his eyes off his instrumentation. 'I hope you are, my boy. I hope that you are.'

Once clear of Earth's atmosphere Alex found he was already impatient to reach Rylos. How quickly we become jaded, he mused. Been on one interstellar jaunt, you've been on 'em all.

His complacency vanished when they reached Rylos and descended to the portion of the northern continent where the supposedly secret Starfighter base was located, Centauri coming in from behind the sun to avoid detection by any lurking Ko-Dan ships.

At least, the secret base *had* been located there, Alex corrected himself. The mountain in which it had been buried looked like a volcano that had blown itself apart. Whole forests lay flattened like toothpicks on the surviving slopes, and the topography had been rendered unrecognizable.

Centauri dropped lower, scanning the approaches.

'Looks bad. Xur's hand in this. Somehow the Ko-Dan broke through the energy shield that's supposed to protect Rylos. Bet it was an inside job. The Ko-Dan couldn't have done this without help. It's tough to fight both ends from the middle.'

'I don't follow you.'

'Sabotage, my boy. It's not just the League against the Ko-Dan. It's the League against the Ko-Dan and Xur's followers. Ah, there.'

139

The entrance Centauri located was partially blocked by debris, but still passable. He slipped inside, narrowly missing several immense chunks of granite that had fallen from above. He coughed hard and squinted at the controls.

Alex leaned forward, concerned. 'Are you sure you're all right?'

'I'm fine, just fine, my boy.' He coughed again, quickly wiped the drop of blood from his lip so his passenger wouldn't spot it. 'An unfortunate memento of my younger days. A little matter of money owed and a misplaced knife.'

They were moving slowly down the twisted tunnel, deeper into the mountain. The lights were dimmer than Alex remembered. Whole sections of wall had caved in and in places the ceiling had collapsed, forcing them to rise higher in order to clear the blockage.

'Centauri, the base . . .'

'Yes, it's very bad, my boy. Very bad. You could tell that from what we saw on the way down. Still, destruction doesn't appear to have been total. We Rylans know how to build well. The entire internal structure of the mountain was reinforced and buttressed. Xur's spies may not have known how extensive the reinforcing was. We build well. If anything of the planned defence is left at all, then there is still hope.'

They finally reached the remnants of the main hangar. Centauri tried to turn the ship and set it down gently, but his reflexes had grown lethargic. The little vessel bounced twice, barely avoiding more debris, as startled Rylan workers tried to wave it to a halt.

'Centauri!' Alex leaned over the seat and tried to help. The ship's controls were simple enough and he'd had three chances to watch Centauri operate them. Pull here, push there . . .

They finally stopped less than a yard from a cracked metal wall. Alex let out a deep sigh of relief and slumped back in his own seat.

'That was close. Wouldn't it be funny if we'd come all this way only to finish by running into a dumb wall. Right, Centauri?' There was no reply. He leaned forward again, gently shook the motionless driver. 'Centauri?'

Still the elderly alien did not respond. Alex pulled his hands away. They were covered with blood.

He stared at them, then at Centauri, then jabbed the door release. As soon as they'd opened far enough he stumbled outside.

'Hey, somebody, help! Somebody get a doctor, we need a doctor here!' He felt his ear to make certain the translator button was still in place and was gratified as well as a little astonished to discover that the tiny instrument hadn't come loose during his flight from the alien assassin.

Was there another word for doctor he should use, or was he too excited for his words to translate properly? He ran around to Centauri's side of the ship and was about to start pulling him clear when a familiar figure appeared, running toward him.

'Grig!'

The alien slowed, his near rigid lips straining to convey his surprise. 'Alex. You came back. I'd hoped you might. I did not think you would.'

'I had to.' Alex was too embarrassed to relate the whole story. Besides, there was still a chance to redeem himself in the eyes of those he respected. 'Centauri's hurt pretty bad.'

Grig helped him pull the limp body clear of the car. Then the alien rose and shouted something Alex's translator didn't transcribe. Whatever Grig said must have been effective, because Rylan medics appeared immediately and bent to tend to the injured Centauri.

Alex stood watching, feeling frustrated and angry and helpless. Grig assisted the medics.

'My fault,' Alex muttered disconsolately. 'He took a shot that was meant for me. It's my fault.'

Grig spoke sternly. 'Look around you, Alex. Hundreds lie dead in this base alone. This is war. It is not your fault Centauri was hurt. I am certain he was only doing his job.' He nodded toward the supine figure. 'He was protecting something valuable to the war effort. An important resource.'

'But I'm *not*,' Alex started to protest. Polite as ever, Grig interrupted him.

'He believes that you are important. Believes it strongly enough to sacrifice himself to save you. I hope he will not be proven wrong.'

A faint wheeze issued from the figure on the floor. 'You see, you see? Centauri brought him back ...'

'Yes, we see.' Grig exchanged a glance with one of the medics. 'You did well, Centauri. You always do well. Now rest for a while. Conserve your strength.'

Centauri's false human face broke into a wide, satisfied smile. He looked to Alex. 'Does he have my payment? Does he?'

'I've a fortune held in wait for you, Centauri,' Grig assured the oldster. 'Your initial payment and a big bonus for performing recruiting work beyond reasonable expectations. Now please lie still.'

'He's not fibbing, is he, Alex?' Centauri murmured anxiously. 'I've dealt with his kind before and you're never sure where you stand with 'em. They're so damn courteous you can't tell when they're trying to cheat you.'

'No, your payment's here.' Alex fought back the lump rising in his throat. 'Full payment, and the bonus. Just like he said. All for you.'

The old man relaxed a little. 'Ahhh ... at last. Alex, I want you to know that I brought you back for the good of the League. For civilization's sake. It wasn't just the money.' He coughed and his smile cracked. One of the medics broke something out of a thin plastic tube and jammed it against Centauri's upper arm.

'Of course,' the figure on the floor added in a whisper so weak Alex had to strain to make out the words. He fiddled with the translator control, wondering if there was a hidden volume control somewhere. 'Of course, it doesn't hurt to be rich. Filthy, disgusting, obnoxiously rich. I always wanted to be rich, Alex. So rich that ... that ...'

Grig waited until one of the medics gestured, then rose and stepped aside. The tired old body below was at rest at last, content.

'You are rich, Centauri. Richer than ever you could imagine. 'Til the next existence, you old reprobate. I'm going to miss you.' He turned to face the young human standing nearby. 'I'm sorry, Alex. How he held himself together long enough to get you both back here is a minor miracle.' He put a gentle hand on the boy's shoulder and urged him towards a doorway.

Alex looked back over his shoulder. The medics had moved on to other work. Centauri lay quietly on the floor of the hangar.

'Are they just going to leave him there?'

'For the moment, yes. They have done what they could and there are wounded to save. It won't bother Centauri. Very little bothered Centauri except missing the chance to make a profitable, slightly questionable deal. He was an avaricious soul, but a benign one.'

'He saved my life.'

'Because he thought you could save others. We're going to find out, Alex. No time for mourning. Our remaining orbital defences won't stop the Ko-Dan. You've seen what they can do to a mountain. Imagine what that same weapons system could do to a major city.'

Alex allowed himself to be led through twisted passageways and down corridors with cracked floors and shattered ceilings.

'We weren't away from Rylos very long, Grig. What did happen here? I thought you were ready for the Ko-Dan. When I left, a whole roomful of Starfighters was preparing to go out and intercept the Ko-Dan armada.'

'We were a few minutes too slow, Alex.' Grig struggled to explain the disaster. 'We went from the heights of confidence to the depths of despair in a moment. The Ko-Dan attacked from long range. Simultaneously, our defensive shield was sabotaged by Xur's fanatics. So was Starfighter Control. None of the gunstars had a chance to get out before the mountain was hit. All were destroyed or damaged by the first strike. The main gunstar hangar is solid with shattered rock.

'In one stroke we had been rendered helpless. That Xur

143

knew exactly when and how to attack suggests careful intelligence work by his agents. It's too late to do anything about that now. You've come back none too soon.'

'Fat lot of good I'll be able to do now,' Alex murmured, appalled at the destruction around them. Centauri's death had brought home to him the issues at stake in this conflict far more forcefully than his words ever had. The growing conviction that he had to do whatever he could to help was reinforced by everything he saw around him.

The last thing he wanted to do was insult Centauri's memory by lying to protect himself. 'Yeah, well, there's nothing noble about my coming back, Grig. I didn't have much choice. Xur detected Centauri's ship leaving Rylos just before he attacked, I guess. It's a small ship. Maybe it looked like a gunstar on their radar, or whatever kind of tracking devices the Ko-Dan use. Centauri said it would look suspicious to them, and I guess it did.

'So Xur plotted our course, tracked us somehow, found me and tried to have me killed. If it wasn't for Centauri and a Beta Unit he'd left behind to replace me I wouldn't be talking about it now.'

'But you are here,' Grig pointed out quietly, 'and it seems you've changed your mind about ... certain things.'

'Yeah. Don't get me wrong. I still think Centauri picked the wrong guy. But now I understand why he was so anxious to try and recruit any help he could find.'

'Then you *are* willing to give it a go?'

'Huh?' Alex threw him a sideways look.

'Here we are,' Grig said. He ducked beneath a beam that was leaning at a crazy angle across the corridor, rummaged for a moment behind a shattered barrier, and returned with a handful of clothing.

'Give what a go?' Alex pressed him.

'Fight,' Grig said.

X

Alex stared at the uniform. It was identical to the one he'd been handed eons ago, in a similar room, by a different alien. It was more than familiar.

Grig generated one of his stiff, thin smiles. 'Yes, it's the same one. I made a point of knowing where I could find it. In case you changed your mind.'

Alex took it, blew dust off the shirt. 'Do I have to? I mean, isn't it silly?'

'Not as silly as standing here arguing about it,' Grig told him, making Alex feel very immature indeed. 'Besides, my people are sticklers for the proprieties. If you're going to do battle on behalf of the League, you should feel and look the part. The uniform is a small concession to my sense of rightness. Don it for me.'

Alex shrugged. 'OK. No big deal.'

'Then you're still ready to participate in the fight?'

'Well, yeah, okay, sure.'

'Perfectly splendid that is.'

Alex turned to examine the destruction surrounding them. Two dazed Rylans were struggling to move small mountains of twisted metal.

'But with what? You said yourself that the gunstar hangar was completely destroyed.'

'I promise you this much; we will not have to fight with words. Come.'

He followed Grig out of the devastated storage area and into a still functioning elevator. The alien ran his fingers over the controls. A brief spark flared and he drew his hand back

145

quickly. A hidden motor hummed and sudden speed made Alex lurch to the side. They were moving, and far faster than during his first such journey.

No point in wasting the time, he thought, as he climbed out of his jeans and shirt and into the uniform. Grig watched with some interest, always interested in such minutiae as the peculiarities of a new lifeform.

'You mentioned something about a Beta Unit. Am I to understand that one is taking your place back home?'

Alex mulled that one over a moment before replying. 'Well, he's *trying*. I don't think Centauri got all of his programming straight before assigning him.'

'Any serious difficulties?'

He thought of Maggie. 'Maybe, but we can't worry about that now.'

'It is at least doing an adequate job of substituting for you, though?'

'Yeah. Adequate.'

Grig looked satisfied. 'Then we may safely assume that Xur thinks you're still on Earth. When his hireling does not file a success report, a second will be sent to make certain, then a third, and so on until your death is confirmed.'

'That's what Centauri told me,' Alex mumbled uncomfortably.

'Don't worry. A good Beta Unit will keep them fooled as well as occupied, and keep Xur's attention away from here. That could work to our advantage. Theoretically.'

The elevator finally began to slow and Alex had to brace himself as their speed diminished rapidly. Grig did not have to use his hands on the elevator walls. Practice, Alex mused.

The doors opened onto a well-lit chamber. Instrumentation lined the far walls.

On a second lower level a single ship sat gleaming in its docking bay. The walls enclosing it were cracked in several places and the floor underneath had buckled, but the ceiling was intact. To all outward appearances, so was the beautiful, sleek ship.

'Some damage occurred even at this distance,' Grig

commented, 'but Xur's people thought there was nothing out here except construction equipment and design facilities, so this place wasn't hit as hard as the main base.'

Alex stared at the untouched ship, scanning their surroundings as Grig led him downward. 'Where are we?'

'In the design silo, on the far side of the mountain range from the main base. A lot of experimental work was done out here, mostly with upgrading and refining the improvements made on the old gunstars. No one's working here now because they're desperately trying to make a portion of the command centre functional.' He drew himself up proudly.

'I worked here myself, helping with the practical aspect of new improvements. You need more than good theory to improve ship design.'

They reached the cockpit level. It was open, waiting. Beckoning. Alex turned on his companion.

'It's a fine-looking ship. What now? We wait for instructions?'

'What do you think we ought to do ... Starfighter?'

Alex hesitated. His gaze roved from the curving high-backed seat to the patient alien standing next to him.

'This is *my* gunstar? You expect me to fly this?'

'Only in combat. Why not? Everything is computer controlled. Space flight is too complex to leave entirely to us mere organics. We can only monitor the ship's decisions and make a few important adjustments. The ship does everything else. What do you think of her?'

'Like I said, she's beautiful,' Alex admitted readily. He studied her lines. 'Different from the ones I saw before, though.'

Grig was pleased. 'You are observant, but that is only to be expected. Starfighters excel at noticing details. Yes, this one is different. She's a prototype, actually. Different internally as well as externally from her sister ships. The others were updated gunstars. You could say this one is the first entirely *new* gunstar.

'She's just been certified operational. It was intended that she be held in reserve, except in case of dire emergency.' He

147

didn't have to finish the thought.

'How's she different? Besides on the outside.'

Grig considered a moment before replying. 'She has much greater range, greater manoeuvrability, additional simplification of basic instrumentation, advanced fire control facilities, more power, and a slight weapons modification.'

Alex nodded as he strolled over to the side of the ship. He leaned into the open cockpit. The instruments that stared back at him were more extensive and complex than those he'd mastered while standing at the control board of Centauri's video test game.

'I don't recognize any of this stuff.'

Grig stepped past him and eased himself into the seat facing the curving console. 'That is not surprising, considering that this is the Navigator/Monitor's station. My position. I'll guide us from here, handle life support and drive, all the other little details. All a Starfighter has to do is ... fight.'

'Then where do I sit?'

Grig finally relaxed inside. Alex had said 'do' instead of 'would'. The young human had finally committed himself. Now Grig could shift his thoughts from coercion to instruction. He turned and pointed.

'In the gunnery chair, up there.'

Alex followed directions, picked out a small, tightly curved seat located higher up in the body of the ship. He searched in vain for a ladder or walkway.

'Great. How do I get to it?'

'Like this.' Grig touched a button and the section of walkway under Alex's feet began to rise. He balanced himself and was ready to step in when the lift stopped just outside the hatchway leading to the gunnery position. Grig let the lift retract as Alex snuggled into the chair.

It enveloped him like a warm blanket, moulding itself to his contours as hidden sensors noted his shape and made internal adjustments. For a different species it would have provided a different configuration. It took only a moment. The human form was not a complex one.

Muted whines rose from within the body of the vessel. Glancing down and forward, Alex saw Grig's fingers working busily at a line of controls. Simplified or not, there was plenty to check out, much to prepare. There was no ground crew standing by to help them.

Alex had a sudden nasty thought. 'Are you sure we're supposed to be doing this, Grig?'

'What an odd question. Do you think that someone of my experience would do anything against orders?'

'Anyone ordered you not to take this ship up?'

'We're wasting time,' Grig said firmly, 'and Rylos has precious little remaining to it. Pay attention. I'll swing the display around for you.'

Alex glanced nervously to his left, then his right, and missed the display console's approach as it swung down to face him. His chair also moved.

'Ouch! Whoa.' He leaned back from the display module and rubbed his forehead where he'd been bumped. Lights winked on all around him as the ship's weaponry was activated. He tried to settle deeper into his seat. As he did so the display module vanished.

'Hey, it's gone!'

'Don't worry,' Grig told him. 'It's still there, but it's suspended in a xenon-based mist designed to protect the systems from damage. Most of the ship's vital instrumentation is shielded that way. Localized force fields lock the mist in place and all important internal connections are photic. Just don't wave your hands around a lot. Lean forward and pick up the screen again.'

Alex did so and was rewarded by a succession of soft clicks. 'What was that?'

'Retinal lock-in. Now the screen will follow your eyes whenever the ship's weaponry is activated. Even if you're wounded and fall sideways you'll still be able to fight because the screen will stay that same distance from your eyes, no matter where you go. It'll reflect all combat information back towards you.'

Alex leaned to his left as far as the chair allowed and was

149

fascinated to see the screen move with him. The grid image on the screen stayed in perfect focus the same preset distance from his face. He tried moving just his eyes, looking towards the floor, and it shifted lower to stay in sight. It was a lot simpler than pushing buttons.

'Gotcha. Now what?'

'Put your left arm into the left arm lock and grasp the combat flight controller. It overrides the ship's guidance system as well as my own.'

Alex slipped his left arm into a flexible sleeve and let his fingers feel the indicated instrumentation. Several lights came alive off to his left.

'Looks okay, but I didn't push anything on.'

'The systems responds to your touch,' Grig informed him. 'When it's powered up all you have to do is make physical contact to activate everything and let go of it to relinquish control.'

'Okay.'

'Now slip your right arm into the other arm lock.'

Alex did as he was instructed. More lights sprang to life around him. He was sitting inside an electronic Christmas tree. It was quite pretty, so long as you didn't think about what it represented.

'Got it.'

A small control panel slid into position beneath his right hand.

'At your fingers now are the ship's weapons systems.'

Alex moved slightly to inspect the panel and was startled to see that he recognized it.

'Hey, fan lasers, photon bolts, particle beams . . . just like on the game back home.'

'Nothing so primitive,' Grig assured him. 'Centauri's test game would use terminology familiar to you. The weapons you actually control are far more advanced and much more deadly than anything your people have yet developed or even thought about.'

'Oh,' said Alex, impressed.

'However, you may refer to the weapons system by familiar

names if you wish. It doesn't matter what you call them; only how you employ them. What did you call the first system?'

'Fan lasers.'

Grig managed to sound amused. 'Toys. Kids' stuff.'

Alex swallowed. 'What exactly can this ship do?'

'You'll find out,' Grig assured him.

'Well, at least the controls are familiar.' He moved his thumb towards a large red button protected by a flip-up bar set off to the far side of the panel. 'Except for this ...'

'Careful, careful!' Grig shouted. Alex hastily withdrew the exploring thumb. 'That is for the ...' the alien hesitated. 'How's your knowledge of the theory of high energy physics?'

'Pretty shallow,' Alex confessed.

'Let's just call it the blossom, though there's nothing so delicate about it. A defensive weapon of last resort. Hopefully we won't have to use it.'

'I'll go along with that.' Alex studied the button warily. It looked like a big fat red spider now, hunkered down on its legs, just waiting for a chance to jump out and bite him on the back of his hand.

Yet there was a morbid fascination to it. He tried to imagine what it might do. Grig had referred to it, at least for Alex's benefit, as the 'blossom'. He conjured up an image of a burning flower but discarded it as unsatisfactory. It did give him something to concentrate on, however, as Grig took the ship through final checkout. A steady whine was now coming from the stern, audible even though Grig had closed both hatches and sealed them in tight. Like bugs in a bottle.

That image wasn't very nice either. He turned his thoughts elsewhere. 'How come you know so much about this ship when it wasn't even included with the others?'

'I told you. I helped with some of the final refinements. In fact, I was working here with the design staff when the main hangar went up.'

When the main hangar went up, Alex echoed silently, trying and failing to imagine what that instant of shock and destruction must have been like.

'You mean the whole hangar's gone? I know it looked bad

back there, but I didn't think it was all gone.' He paused. 'What about the other hangars, the other bases?'

'What other bases?' Grig asked him.

Alex's thoughts were moving fast now, one right on the heels of the other. They collided with some rising, uncomfortable suppositions. 'You mean all the gunstars were located in that one hangar?'

'Yes. We were overconfident and underexperienced. Remember, we relied on our long-range defensive shields to protect us from assault for so long.'

'Well then, what about the rest of the Starfighters? The ones I sat with when Enduran spoke?'

'They were all in the hangar. That one hangar.' Grig's tone was flat and unemotional, wholly professional.

'You mean they're *all* dead?'

'Death is a primitive concept. We still have little real knowledge of what lies on the other side of the line of existence that we call life. It is like different states of matter. Nothing is destroyed, only changed. You end up facing the universe in a different guise. Myself, I am something of a romantic. They were good souls all, your fellow fighters. If they hadn't been, they wouldn't have been Starfighters. I rather like to think of them as battling evil in another dimension.'

'"In another dimension".' Alex swallowed before asking the inevitable next question. 'How many are left? Surely some of them got out? How many?'

'Counting yourself?' The ship shook beneath Alex's backside now, trembling with energy held in check, eager to show its strength. He wondered if the engines were prototypes too, and if so, how thoroughly they'd been tested.

If nothing else they were more thoroughly tested than he was, he thought.

'Yeah, counting myself.'

'*One.*' Grig touched a switch. A section of mountain vanished ahead of them. Despite the internal compensation system Alex was slammed back into his seat as the gunstar exploded skyward.

The surface of Rylos receded behind them with astonishing rapidity. Alex was nestled so snugly into his seat he couldn't turn to look out of the transparent dome covering the gunner's position, but it was simple enough to activate the perpetually positioned display screen to provide him with the view astern as well as forward. It was not a flat image. He saw fore and aft hemispheres as the screen neatly cut the globe of the universe in two halves for easy viewing. Fore and aft, of course, were relative terms only, extrapolated from the ship's longitudinal axis.

There was a voice in his ears, reaching him via concealed speakers. The tiny button in his left ear continued to translate for him.

'Who is this?' the voice demanded to know. 'Who is taking up the last gunstar? That ship is still classed experimental and is not qualified for flight. Identify yourself!'

Alex could see Grig turned slightly towards a voice pick-up. 'This is League Navigator/Monitor Grig. Hi.'

'You're taking up the last gunstar without . . .!'

'Thanks ever so much. We appreciate your concern.' The angry voice was banished from the ship when Grig nudged a control.

Alex had heard enough. 'Now wait a minute, Grig. What the hell do you think you're doing? What the hell are *we* doing? There's no fleet, no other Starfighters. I thought I was coming back to help the others and now you tell me we're the others. We don't have a plan or backup or anything. It's just one ship. One lousy little untested ship. You, me, and . . . that's it?'

'Precisely.' Grig was unperturbed by Alex's tone. He adjusted something on his console and the starfield slid eighty degrees before straightening again. The gunstar did not bank and roll like the fighters Alex had seen on TV in World War II movies. There was nothing to bank and roll against.

'Xur thinks you're still on Earth. He knows that the main base and Command Central, together with all the Starfighters and their ships, have been destroyed. His spies will have so informed him. This will be classic military strategy, a surprise attack when least expected. They think they have us beaten, helpless, unable to resist.'

'They're right!'

'So,' Grig continued easily, 'the last thing they'll be expecting is a counterattack. It will throw them badly off balance. They'll start to wonder what else they've missed.'

'Yeah, I'm sure they'll be terrified,' Alex mumbled.

'It will be something of a shock.'

'It'll be a slaughter, that's what it'll be!'

'That's the spirit!' Grig told him. 'I knew you had the makings of a true Starfighter. You have all the base primitive emotions, the blind desire to strike back, the relentless drive to ...'

'All the fear,' Alex said, interrupting him. 'All the terror. You don't understand, Grig. I meant it'll be our slaughter. One ship against the whole armada! It's worse than crazy!'

To Alex's consternation, his declaration only seemed to please Grig that much more. 'Ah yes, just think of it! One gunstar against the armada. I've always wanted to fight a desperate battle against incredible odds. It appeals to my sense of irony.'

Alex groaned.

'Besides, you badly underestimate your own abilities. Centauri knew his business. And you said you found the fire controls familiar.'

'Yeah, sure, but that was just a *game.*'

'You destroyed everything the test unit could throw against you. You must have, or Centauri would never have brought you into this. Forget reality, Alex. Make a game of it if it helps. Concentrate on your fire control and your display screen. Remember the game? It should've had test lights as one phase.'

'Yeah, it did.'

'Then let's try a few. They are actually drone targets. You might want to squeeze off a few bursts while you have the chance, work any bugs out of the weapons systems. This being this vessel's maiden voyage, we don't want any surprises with fire control when we attack the armada, do we?'

'Oh goodness, gracious, no,' Alex replied drily. 'That would be *ever* so disconcerting.'

'Exactly my point,' Grig agreed, blithely oblivious to his companion's sarcasm. The alien nudged several controls. Alex heard something go *thump* near the ship's stern.

His screen immediately lit up to show three shapes moving rapidly from the rear of the gunstar. They swung around and assumed positions forward, scattering and waiting, always staying just ahead of the racing ship.

'They'll dodge,' Grig warned him. 'They're quite fast.'

'I know that, but they look so big,' Alex replied.

'Actually they're very small. You're looking at false images projected by the drones. They're designed to simulate the actual size of enemy vessels. Proceed on the assumption you're firing at a real target.'

'Okay.' Alex leaned slightly forward and tried to imagine the fire controls under the fingers of his right hand were those of the videogame console on the porch back home. They *were* the same controls. They looked the same, felt the same, were located the same distance from each other, and responded to the same amount of pressure. Centauri had designed his game well.

The drones dodged the first burst of fire from the gunstar's weapons with ease. Nerves, Alex told himself. C'mon, this is no game. Get a hold of yourself and concentrate.

He fired again, barely nicked the centremost of the three lights. They were so damned *fast*. Or were they? Were they really any faster than the lights on the console back home? Or was it his reaction time that was way off?

He couldn't help it. No matter how hard he tried to convince himself otherwise, he knew this wasn't the game in front of the general store, knew he was playing for a lot more than a few quarters. The uncertainty stole down from his mind to take control of his fingers.

Grig was there to help calm him, to try and allay his festering self-doubt. 'Steady, Alex. Take your time.

Remember the timing from the test machine. This is no different. Your weapons function in a similar time-frame. Relax and react just like you did back home.'

'Terrific,' Alex muttered in reply. 'I'm about to get killed a million light-years from home and a gung-ho iguana tells me to relax. What next, Grig? You going to tell me to use the Force?'

'I don't know what that refers to,' his mentor replied, 'but it sounds vaguely supernatural. There is nothing supernatural about this ship's weapons systems or the track-and-fire computers that operate them. You were not chosen by Centauri because you manifested any supernatural abilities. Your talents should include preternaturally fast reflexes and decision-making ability coupled with outstanding peripheral vision both optic and mental. Use *those*, as you did when you operated the test game, and stop babbling.'

'I am not babbling!' Alex shouted angrily, taking grim aim at the target lights.

This time they exploded in quick succession; ping, ping, ping, his fingers running over the fire controls as if they were guitar strings. He blinked at the screen. No question, it was clear.

'Hey, that wasn't so hard.'

'Not for you,' Grig agreed. 'Not for a Starfighter born. *I* couldn't have done it. But then, I'm a Navigator/Monitor, not a killer.'

'Uh, yeah. Thanks for the compliment ... I think.' Alex allowed his fingers to stray over the fire controls, barely brushing their smooth surfaces. Memories flooded in on him: blinking lights, computerized images, sound-effects and synthesized voices.

It *wasn't* all that different from the video game. Centauri had duplicated the fire control system of a real gunstar. In some ways this was easier than the game. The screen, for instance, that followed his line of sight no matter where it wandered, provided an image a hundred times sharper than the game screen. Maybe ... just maybe ... he had a chance to live up to Centauri's expectations.

The difficult part was going to be thinking of the coming battle as nothing more than a game.

XI

'Hand me up that wire cutter, will you, Alex?' Otis steadied the antenna with one hand and reached down with the other.

'Coming right up.' The Beta Unit paused a moment to study the odd assortment of primitive metal tools Otis had laid out nearby. Stored information connected the image of the only possible cutting tool with the older human's request. It matched a similar image retrieved from Alex Rogan's hastily scanned memory. He chose the instrument and handed it up.

'Thanks, Alex.' Otis began tightening the bracing wire attached to the antenna mast. Beta held the rest of the antenna ready.

While Otis worked, the Beta inspected the flimsy metal. An extremely simple device designed for recovering short-range electromagnetic transmissions. He shook his head wonderingly. The antenna was about as sophisticated as a mortar and pestle, and plucked transmissions from the air with about the same degree of efficiency.

Something tapped him on the shoulder. He jumped, holding the antenna like a weapon. Bright, curious eyes stared back at him.

'Oh, Maggie . . . it's you.'

'I should hope so. You expecting someone else?'

'No, of course not.' The Beta stared past her, searching the bushes across the way. 'How ya doin'?'

'I'm doing fine. It's you I'm starting to worry about. Are

158

you feeling okay, Alex? You've been acting awfully funny here lately.'

'I'm always funny. You know me. Good ol' fun-loving Alex Rogan.'

'I didn't mean mean funny ha-ha. I meant funny-weird.'

'What's the difference?' he countered lamely, brushing dust from his jeans. Ploy four-six: change the subject. He pointed past her.

'Hey, did you hear something over there?'

Maggie listened hard, eyeing the innocent bushes. A light breeze stirred the dry dirt around her feet. 'Like what, Alex?'

'Like a Double-Z Designate . . . uh, never mind.'

She considered him a moment longer, decided pursuing the matter would get her nowhere and went off on a different tack, exactly as he'd hoped she would.

'Alex, I just came over to say that I'm sorry I slapped you last night.'

'Slapped me? With a right cross like that you ought to be training for the Olympics.' He grinned to show her she shouldn't take him seriously.

She grinned back, a little embarrassed. 'I didn't mean to hit you so hard. Honest.'

He put his hand over his left heart and declaimed in his best melodramatic tone, 'All is forgiven, madame.' They were discussing inconsequentials again and he felt able to let down his guard slightly. 'Hey, forget it, Maggs. I deserved it. I'm the one who should apologize.'

Her grin became a smile and her eyes spoke to him. The Beta found such nonverbal communication fascinating. It was no less effective than standard vocalized communication and much more economical. While rather plain, the human face was extraordinarily expressive.

'That's settled then,' she said confidently. 'We can make it up to each other tonight at Silver Lake.'

'Yeah. Right.' There was something new in her expression that he could not interpret. Alex's memory wasn't very helpful on that score. Oh well, he'd learn all about it tonight, he decided. Meanwhile he chose to respond by duplicating the expression as best he could with his own facial muscles.

This must have satisfied her, because she kissed him before she left.

There now. That wasn't so difficult, he told himself. Alex would be proud of him. His manufacturers would be proud of him. He was coping with a difficult situation extremely well, if he did say so himself.

Idly, he wondered how they were going to 'make it up to each other' tonight. No doubt another interesting learning experience was in store.

He was about to hand the rest of the antenna up to Otis when the noise he'd heard earlier was repeated. Though he had Alex Rogan's body, his senses were considerably more acute. He hadn't just been trying to divert Maggie. He *had* heard something.

But another detailed scan of the bushes and the road still showed no surprises. Feeling uneasy, he started for the door of Otis's trailer. Programming commanded him to take cover the instant he sensed something but could not identify it.

Far back in the trees and scrub, a cousin to the first alien killer Centauri had dispatched lowered the monocular with one hand and the long-snouted pistol gripped in the other. It mumbled something half aloud, perhaps a few choice words of disappointment that its quarry had taken cover, perhaps a phrase or two counselling patience.

A local vehicle was coming down the roadway nearby. The alien crouched low behind a rock, grateful for the surplus of cover this primitive world afforded. Somehow he had to get closer to the target while remaining unsuspected. He studied the vehicle with interest.

It was against all laws and regulations for a visitor from an advanced system to expose himself to unsophisticated primitives, but that was a League tradition, and the League was about to undergo some drastic shifts in policy. The killer knew that his master couldn't care less if he had to expose himself to half the local population. All that mattered was getting the job done.

If any of the natives happened to catch a glimpse of him in

his unmasked form, that was their tough luck. They were going to be seeing quite a bit of the Ko-Dan and their allies before long.

The ZZ-Designate looked forward to the future. This world looked amusing. After concluding his assignment, he decided, he might stay a while. The inhabitants made funny targets. There was sport to be had here.

XII

Alex watched the screen as it filled with images representing the incoming Ko-Dan ships. A superimposed grid located the armada precisely and readouts ticked away the distance remaining between the invaders and Rylos. The script meant nothing to Alex, but seemed ominous just the same.

'The armada will come through like this, according to predictors.' Grig spoke carefully, methodically. 'Unless opposed, they will reach geosynchronous orbit around Rylos in twenty time-parts. Squadrons of small attack ships will precede the command craft, which houses the mass driver.'

The last translation used a term vaguely familiar to Alex. He asked Grig to elaborate.

'That is the weapon that was used to destroy the Starfighter base. Actually a very primitive notion, made useful in modern warfare only because of the intervention of advanced technology. It's difficult to defend yourself when the enemy is throwing irresistible objects at you from an immovable object. Think of it as the ultimate catapult. A very flexible weapon. It can fire anything you can fit inside it.'

'Then how do we cope with it?'

'We don't,' Grig informed him. 'It poses no danger to us. Only to fixed objects like ground-based installations . . . and cities. Our danger will come from ships armed with weapons similar to our own.' He adjusted a control, trying to locate the Ko-Dan command ship.

'You said the command craft will be preceded by

162

squadrons of smaller ships, fighters. How many ships? Or maybe I should ask, how many squadrons?'

'Oh, it's not the number of squadrons that concerns me,' Grig replied easily. The view on Alex's screen jumped, then steadied. Grig finally had the Ko-Dan command ship in focus. It was most impressive. The view leaped forward so realistically Alex almost ducked, then slowed and crawled across the skin of the alien vessel until it stopped on a large opaque blister located near the bow.

'It's this command centre that worries me. From there combat information is relayed simultaneously to every Ko-Dan ship, enabling them to act in concert against any attacker. The centre is comprised of a series of ultra-sophisticated plotting computers operating in tandem. Give them enough time, and they require very little, and they will predict a pattern of movement for any intruding ship, enabling the fighters to concentrate on it as one.'

'How can it do that?' Alex inquired, 'when any attack is bound to be made at random?'

'No machine or organic pilot functions in a purely random fashion. Each utilizes preferred manoeuvres without doing so consciously. The Ko-Dan computers will pinpoint enough of a pattern to predict where an attacking ship is likely to be at any point in time. That takes the initiative away from any attacker, and initiative is vital to the success of any Starfighter assault.'

'So we've got to destroy that command centre before it has enough time to analyze our movements.'

Grig nodded. 'And deal with the fighters while they're trying to regroup for concerted action. That is the Ko-Dan's weakness: they tend to hold back while receiving instructions from higher up. They can't help it; it's part of their mental makeup. Usually it works for them. They overwhelm any enemy with mass attacks. But they've never had to deal with a Starfighter before.

'After we take care of the command centre we'll finish off the smaller ships before they can move in and attack Rylos itself, then return to take care of the command ship before they can move the mass driver within precision range.'

'Seems to me they were precise enough from farther out when they destroyed the base.'

'They need to drop into low orbit to make their threat as believable as possible. It is one thing to be on the receiving end of such a weapon, quite another to be able to look up in the night sky and watch it cross over your head. The Ko-Dan do not really want to destroy Rylos; they want to conquer it. There is no glory in ruling rubble. So psychological weapons are as important as technological ones.'

'I see.' Alex did some mental figuring. 'Wait a second. We knock out the control centre to prevent the fighters from acting in concert, but to get to the command centre we gotta get through the fighters.' He slumped. 'That makes it simple. We're dead.'

'Don't fret. I'll have it all figured out by the time we reach attack position.'

'Sure you will. While you're making notes, keep in mind I'd like any remains sent to...' he broke off as a steady humming noise suddenly penetrated the cockpit. 'What's that?'

'Sensor. We're nearing the outer limits of Rylos's inner defensive shield.'

'I thought the Ko-Dan already broke through that.'

'Temporarily, long enough for them to destroy the base. Now the shield is back in place again, until they break through the next time. They are playing with us, I fear. This time the armada itself will come through, convinced they'll be doing so unopposed.' He emitted an alien chuckle. 'Aren't they going to be surprised!'

'Oh yeah,' Alex agreed flatly. 'They'll be terrified out of their socks.'

Another buzz replaced the steady humming. Grig's main monitor screen came to life. Two images appeared off to port.

'What is it?'

'I'm not sure.' Grig studied the screen. 'Highly irregular to see cargo ships this far above the ecliptic. I can't imagine

164

where they're headed. They may not be aware of the Ko-Dan presence.'

'How's that possible? Surely everyone within communications range knows about it by now.'

'Everyone within range, yes, but these visitors may be on their way in from outsystem and may have just emerged from supralight drive. I'll try hailing them on sealed beam.' His hands worked instruments.

'This is gunstar one of Rylos. Identify yourself, please. You are in a combat area. Ko-Dan armada is close at hand. Repeat, identify yourselves. You should leave this sector immediately and procede in to Rylos.'

'Can't the Ko-Dan pick that up?' Alex asked anxiously, watching his own screen. Indeed, he couldn't take his eyes off it. Literally.

'Not unless Xur's spies have burrowed deeper into League technology than so far suspected.'

Abruptly space lit up outside the ship, bright silent flares erupting off to their left.

'What was that!'

'Contradiction of my aforementioned,' said Grig as he threw the ship onto a different course and boosted their speed. 'Unless they have simply been ordered to attack any vessel not attempting contact on an approved Ko-Dan channel.'

Alex stared at the battle screen. 'Hey, they're coming towards us! Shouldn't we take evasive action before they catch up with us?'

'They are not catching up with us,' Grig replied as he concentrated on the controls. 'We are catching up with them. They are trying to get away.'

'Uh ... maybe we should let them?'

'This is no game, Alex,' Grig admonished him. 'These are not Ko-Dan fighters. They are Xurian ships, traitors, Ko-Dan allies. I've jammed their transmissions so they can't report back to the rest of the armada, but we have to stop them quickly. Stand ready, Alex. There are your first live targets.'

'Live?'

Grig didn't reply. He was too busy trying to run down the two retreating ships.

'Gee, Grig, I'm not sure I'm ready to ...'

'Within range in five milliparts. Get ready.'

Ahead, the two Xurian ships suddenly disappeared, vanishing from their screens.

'Where'd they go?' Alex wondered.

'Only one place to hide from scanners at this range. Hang on.'

The gunstar dipped as Grig flung it toward a large asteroid drifting nearby. Alex flinched, but there was no rending crash. Grig had plunged them into the centre of a large crater, close on the track of the fleeing Xurians. He slowed immediately, knowing their quarry would be forced to do likewise or risk smashing into the walls of the volcanic vent.

The cockpit was full of beeps and clicks as he navigated a course through the asteroid. The tunnel down which the Xurians were fleeing was curved and smooth-sided.

'Three milliparts to kill zone. Weapons systems armed. Defensive screen armed.'

Alex leaned forward. 'Grig, wait!'

'Fire when ready.'

The images of the two Zurian ships were sharp on the screen floating in front of Alex's face, both of them pinned against the firing grid like tired butterflies. Alex stared blankly, suddenly conscious of what the pair of points represented. This was no two-dimensional microchip-generated picture. Both of those ships were filled with intelligent beings not unlike themselves.

Dimly a voice was shouting at him.

'Fire, Alex, fire!'

'It's no good, Grig! I can't do it. Turn back, get us out of here, I can't!'

'You can and you must.' Grig blinked as the gunstar scraped a barely sensed projection sticking out into the tunnel. 'Steady now, steady. We're still on them, still in range. Use your sensors.'

'It's no good, Grig.'

The tunnel ahead ballooned into a vast open airless cavern. The Xurians whirled and sped back straight toward their pursuer. The cavern was a dead end and further retreat was blocked.

It took only a second or so. 'Shoot, Alex!'

'Grig, I can't!'

If the pilots of the Xurian ships had ignored the gunstar they might both have escaped, shooting past their pursuer on either flank. Instead, they panicked and fired their own weapons. It was just enough to galvanize Alex into action. His fingers danced on the fire controls. Energy shot from the gunstar and the ship rocked as it passed between two expanding spheres of hot gas and vaporized metal.

Grig slowed and turned easily in the cavern. 'You did it! I never doubted for a moment, Alex.' He dropped their speed to a crawl, letting the gunstar coast on manoeuvring thrusters.

Alex sat stunned in the gunnery seat. 'I did it? *You* did it. You almost got me killed. I said I was willing to help fight, but not a suicidal battle against impossible odds. If this is how it's going to be, I withdraw the offer. I volunteered to contribute to a defensive effort, not *be* the defence. I'm not cut out to be a martyr, Grig. I'd rather face Xur's assassins one at a time. The odds are a damnsight better. Take me home!'

Grig was silent a long time before asking quietly, 'Are those your final words on the matter, Alex?'

'I hope so!'

Grig made a gesture of acknowledgement and spoke quietly as they cruised the tunnel. 'My humblest apologies, then. I had hoped that by putting you in the thick of battle, a great Starfighter might emerge, a polished gem from the rough diamond Centauri was so certain he'd found.

'Alas, perhaps there was never one within you to begin with. So it would seem. I cannot make a Starfighter of you against your will, Alex. I will take you back, as you request. You may still be able to live out a long and comfortable life on Earth before the Ko-Dan reach it. Then again, you may not.

'You may relax now. Keep your fingers clear of the fire controls until I can deactivate our weapons systems. There's no need to alert any other Xurian or Ko-Dan vessels to our presence through a burst of unintentional fire.' A sensor beeped, nudging the ship around a large floating chunk of torn ceramic plating.

'Also, I am not trying to make you feel guilty. That would be impolite.'

'I don't feel guilty,' Alex insisted guiltily, thus committing two sins in the space of four words.

'That is good. I do not have the right to manipulate your emotions, no matter how worthy the cause. Let us talk about something else.' He let his gaze take in the smooth ceiling of the tunnel.

'Cheerful, roomy place. With air and gravity and heat it could be made almost homey. Rather reminds me of the town I was raised in.'

Alex frowned as he studied the stone tube. '*This* reminds you of home?'

'Oh yes.' Grig made an effort to appear cheerful. 'My mate and I live below ground with our sixty little Griglings. We're very comfortable. Living below the surface of a world has many advantages, Alex. Stable climate, unvarying scenery, the feeling of your friends constantly around you.'

'Sixty, huh? That's quite a family. I guess you didn't spend all your time preparing to be a Navigator/Monitor.'

'We tend to have large families. The fertile period among us is brief, but most births that occur are multiple. Would you like to see?'

Alex wasn't sure how he was supposed to respond. 'I'm not sure I follow you.'

'My family.'

Alex relaxed. 'Yeh, sure.'

Grig fumbled with his flight suit and harness, extracted a strip of dark plastic. He ran a finger along the right-hand edge. An image appeared on the smooth, thin surface, lit from within. As Alex watched the picture changed automatically, each of Grig's numerous offspring appearing in predetermined sequence. The images changed quickly and it didn't take too long to run through the entire oversized family.

When the last one had faded, Grig slipped the plastic back inside his suit.

'Very nice,' Alex admitted.

'They are a joy to me,' the Navigator confessed. 'I have high hopes for them. That is, until Xur makes them slaves.' This was said in a flat, unemotional tone, which did nothing to lessen its impact on Alex.

'Now tell me, where do your kind live, if not beneath the undisturbed and insulating surface of your world?'

'In houses, mostly. Caves above ground.' Suddenly he shoved a hand into his rightside pocket and removed the contents. He'd switched them from his jeans to the uniform when he'd changed clothes back on Rylos.

Sitting in the fire control seat of a gunstar they looked very out of place. There was his wallet, with its limp, useless currency; a few keys, some coins, a paperclip, a couple of stamps (how much was postage from Rylos to Earth, he wondered?), and a few bits of gravel. Of all of it, he most prized the few fragments of decomposed granite. They were a piece of home.

He returned everything to the pocket but the wallet, unsnapped the catch on the vinyl and flipped through the pictures as he showed them to Grig.

'See, here's where I live. And that's my family. It's a lot smaller than yours.' The picture showed happy younger children gathered around a barbecue. A smiling older man and woman stood together next to the metal utensil. The man had his arm around the woman's shoulder while hers was around his waist. Distant, half remembered images of an ancient time. Even there, in that alien planetoid, they conjured up rarely felt emotions.

'See, that's my mom and my dad before he died. The one with the wrinkled face and the dumb expression is my little brother Louis. The girl, that's Maggie.'

'Your wife?' Grig's interest was genuine as he glanced up and back towards the picture.

'Uh, no, just a friend. A very close friend.' Alex swallowed hard. 'My family lives above ground in a mobile home cave

169

that goes anyplace you want it to. Only we never went anyplace.'

Grig nodded politely. Alex wondered if the gesture stood for the same thing among his people or if, having seen Alex utilize the gesture, the navigator was simply displaying his courtesy through the use of it.

'A mobile cave that never went anywhere. Fascinating, if something of a contradiction in terms. Why call it mobile if it never goes anywhere.'

'That's our fault, not the trailer's,' Alex explained. Aware he'd been staring at Maggie's face for a long time, he removed the picture from his wallet and placed it on a nearby console, copying a gesture learned from watching old black and white war movies. The familiar snapshot was an island of sanity among all the smooth Rylan technology. He put the wallet back in his pocket.

'We do have caves, though. Some of them are pretty big. People used to live in them a lot. A few still do.'

'Ah, then we are not so very different.'

'No, I guess not. We have a lot of below-surface caves near our trailer park. Me and Louis used to play hide and seek in them.'

'Hide and seek?'

'A kids' game. You've probably played it yourself, only you call it something else. Or else it's not translating properly. See, one person or more runs and hides and . . .' He hesitated, thinking.

'Hide and seek,' he mumbled again.

'Alex, what is it?'

'Oh, nothing, Grig. Nothing.'

'Tell me. Anything worth labelling nothing has to be composed of something.'

'Yeah, right. I was just thinking though. We could hide inside this asteroid and let the Ko-Dan armada pass by on its way to Rylos. It would shield us from their detectors just like those Xurians were trying to hide from us. Then after they'd gone by we could come out fast and hit them from behind.'

Grig nodded thoughtfully. 'Yes, it would give us the

170

necessary element of surprise. It might actually have worked. I do not think the Ko-Dan would run an extensive survey of all the asteroids. Any such survey would surely exclude time-consuming internal examinations. The rock here is more than thick enough to block out their sensors. Yes, it might well have worked. What a pity there are no Starfighters left to carry it out.'

'Yeah, but we...'

'Please. It is a waste of time to discuss plans one has no intention of putting to use, and I am not in the mood to discuss tactical theory when reality is at stake. I will take you home now, Alex.'

The gunstar accelerated very slightly. Grig was turning towards another exit. The instant they reached the broken upper lip of the crater the cockpit came alive with half a hundred warning lights.

Neither of them had to resort to instruments to see the Xurian ships resting on the surface of the planetoid. At the same time their presence was detected by the five vessels they had surprised.

'A Xurian base!' Grig exclaimed. 'This must be one of their rendezvous points with the Ko-Dan, or else I was wrong and they're checking out the asteroids after all.' The gunstar rocked as the first wave of fire from the ships below passed close by. The Xurians were too startled by the unscheduled appearance of a stranger in their midst to take accurate aim.

Alex's fingers flew over the fire controls. Grig had not yet deactivated the ship's weaponry and the Xurian vessels exploded silently in sequence. Two of them rose just far enough from the surface for their debris to be scattered out into emptiness.

It was all over so quickly, the fire control computer responding flawlessly to Alex's directions. Now he sat back in his seat as Grig moved them away from the asteroid. Expanding gases burned themselves out. Once again the only external light came from the stars and Rylos's sun.

'That was superbly done, Alex.' Grig was as unperturbed as ever. 'Even taking into account the fact that we caught

171

them unawares and resting on a solid surface, your reaction to their fire was all that could have been expected. Please accept my compliments.'

'I didn't mean . . .'

'Of course you did,' Grig said, correcting him before he had a chance to finish. 'They were shooting at us. They would have destroyed us without a second thought, so you did not permit them second thoughts. Or yourself, either.

'Now that we are safely away, I will program a course for Earth. We will make the jump before any other Xurian or Ko-Dan craft can detect our presence.'

Alex had gone quiet. He was remembering. Remembering the Rylans he'd talked to; the room full of Starfighters who'd never had the chance to fight. Remembering the faces of Grig's offspring, small alien images that came and went in joyful, rapid succession on a strip of plastic. What would their lives be like under Ko-Dan rule?

'Say, Grig?'

'What is it, Alex?'

He was wonderfully calm now that he'd made the decision. He knew he was going to die. Of that he was confident. The knowledge gave him an inner peace he'd never felt before. He was going to shake hands with death. Knowing that the meeting was inevitable, it no longer concerned him. It wasn't important. Grig had told him that. It was only a question of time.

Still, he'd do his damndest to put off the meeting as long as possible. He would . . . and he had to smile to himself . . . he would make a game of it.

'Maybe,' he finished, 'there *is* a Starfighter left.'

Grig did not turn to look at him, did not smile. Not outwardly, anyway.

'Am I to understand that you are changing your mind again? You do not wish to return home at this time?'

'No, not just yet. You know, it's strange. All of you have such confidence in me: Starfighter command, Centauri, yourself. I figure it'd be a real waste if I never found out if that confidence was justified or not.'

'A terrible waste,' Grig agreed, nodding.

Alex looked past him, staring out past the fire control screen at the strange constellations. So far from home. He was so far from home.

'Let's find out if Centauri was right or wrong.'

'As you wish, Alex.' Centauri jubilantly reprogrammed the ship's course.

XIII

The moon was close and full as it sat on the mirror of the lake's surface. It wasn't much of a desert lake compared to such giants as Powell or Mead, but it was big enough to fish in, to ski on, and most importantly to the clustered teenagers laying on its best-beach, to romance on.

The cars remained parked well back from the wooden sign that said Silver Lake. Nevertheless, it was an accepted axiom that before the night was through, some idiot would end up sticking his vehicle in the sand and would have to endure the ignominy of being towed out.

Jack Blake's fancy pickup was one of the assembled cars. It stuck out from the battered chevys and mini-pickups like a cabbage among brussels sprouts. From below the parking area whispers and giggles were interspersed with the sound of the lake lapping against the yellow sand.

The police cruiser that pulled into the lot moved slowly, running on parking lights only. They were extinguished as soon as the driver located a parking place. The engine died as the single trooper inside surveyed the silent ranks of vehicles.

Then he checked to make certain his radio was off and his gun was secure in its holster. He opened the door and stepped out. When he closed the door he held down the lock button on the handle to make sure there wouldn't be any noise.

Eyeing pickup beds as well as interiors, he commenced a careful check of each vehicle. A couple of the cars were locked and he had to fiddle with the doors before they would open.

174

In one car the two occupants were wrapped up in each other on the back seat. They didn't notice the trooper's approach, and didn't look up when he peered in on them. They noticed only each other.

The trooper concluded his inspection and turned his attention towards the beach.

Jack Blake let his fingers do the walking as the cheer-leader moaned softly next to him. The sleeping bag that enveloped them was without its removable goosedown lining and the thin nylon threatened to rip on the gravelly sand. Blake didn't care. If it tore he'd just buy a new one.

His hands functioned independent of his thoughts. They were on another shape enclosed by another sleeping bag. He kept trying to pick out the shape and the other bag in the dim light, but it was difficult to see much of anything in his present position and the confining bag he was in wouldn't let him raise his head very high. Neither would his companion.

Maggie and Alex had settled in further up the beach, away from everyone else. Had he been able to see better, Blake would have been grinding his teeth at the sight of Maggie lying on top of Alex, working her tongue in his ear.

Except that it wasn't Alex underneath her. It was an anxious, quietly desperate simulacrum whose earlier confidence was ebbing rapidly. Its hasty programming included nothing about how to deal with its present situation. The Beta knew Maggie's actions were designed to stimulate pleasure, but how much pleasure it wasn't certain. Furthermore, the entire ongoing procedure appeared to involve a good deal of on-the-spot improvisation. Though versatile, the Beta still relied heavily on preprogrammed information.

Obviously a ticklish confrontation. One wrong move could wipe out his original's relationship with this forceful female. As a professional, the Beta wanted desperately to do the right thing by Alex.

But what was the right thing? He didn't know, and rather than make a wrong move he lay quiet and allowed the female to do as she pleased. Evidently this wasn't the correct reaction, however, since after several minutes of this Maggie rolled off him and straightened her clothing. The Beta had grown sufficiently sensitive to the nuances of human behaviour to sense that she was not pleased. Had he reacted incorrectly by not reacting at all?

It was terribly confusing.

'What's wrong?' he asked innocently. 'Should I put my tongue in your ear?'

She shook her head sadly, staring down at him. 'Don't bother. It's like you're a million miles away, Alex.'

He started, then realized she was speaking metaphorically. Besides, she was more than a few miles off with her guess.

'It's just that I'm kinda new to these gland games.'

'*What?*' (Uh-oh ... wrong thing to say. He was making it worse every time he opened his insufficiently programmed mouth). 'Hey, Earth to Alex. You're not even paying attention to me.'

'I'm sorry, Maggie. It's just that I'm a little preoccupied tonight.'

'A *little*? Alex, you're as cold as a machine.'

'I am not!' he protested, aware that she had to be ignorant of that casual slur.

There had to be a way out of the quandary in which he found himself. He glanced to his right. That big young male down there, he didn't seem to be having any trouble making the proper social connections. He and his partner were whispering without pause, communicating fluidly. Beta listened to their conversation carefully.

'Darling, forgive me,' said the larger human. His name was Blake, Beta remembered. He thought the apology reeked of insincerity.

Not that it appeared to make any difference to the female writhing beneath him. From the information his sensors conveyed, the Beta determined that her thought processes at the moment not only were indifferent to the man's tone, they verged on the unfocused.

Nothing ventured, nothing retained, Beta decided as he turned back to Maggie. 'Darling, forgive me.'

To his considerable surprise, she smiled warmly down at

176

him. Surely she could see through his words the feeble attempt at manipulation? Surely the female of this species was more perceptive?

Apparently not. She moved suggestively against him. The Beta Unit filed this new information emotionlessly. It was not his function to judge the social reactions of other species. Besides, he didn't have the time to render opinions. He was too busy doing his job. He concentrated on the words and accompanying movement of the couple nearby.

Just now they were rolling about on the sand. He promptly began rolling with Maggie. She giggled, which if not the same reaction as the other young female below, at least was not hostile.

'You're my Juliet, my Venus,' Blake murmured to his cheer-leader.

Higher on the sand the Beta whispered throatily, 'You're my Juliet, my Venus.'

Maggie sighed beneath him, her eyes closed tight. This struck Beta as most peculiar, since it seemed logical that now would be just when these creatures would want to see each other. He held off asking Maggie about it, deciding rightly that it would be imprudent.

This was easy, he decided. All he had to do was keep mimicking the words and actions of young Blake, who just then was biting his lady's ear.

This further confirmation of the primitive nature of the human species did not surprise the Beta. He was careful to note the intensity of the bite before duplicating it, reasoning correctly that it would not be appreciated if he drew blood.

He imitated the bite precisely, resigned to carrying on the charade to its eventual conclusion. Again the female beneath him giggled.

'Oh, Alex.'

She kissed him passionately before zipping up the sleeping bag the rest of the way. This occasioned a moment of panic on the Beta's part since it temporarily obscured his vision. He twisted around inside the bag. To his relief his new position did not displease Maggie, and he was once more able to study

177

the activity below.

There wasn't much to see now. Both young humans had all but disappeared inside their own sleeping bag. He could still hear them quite clearly, though, thanks to his advanced audio sensing equipment.

'The other girls,' Blake whispered, 'meant nothing to me. It was you I always wanted with me. You. *You*!' More kissing sounds, followed by the girl's voice.

'Oh Jack, talk dirty to me!'

The Beta tried to interpret this dialogue and organize it as Maggie pulled him deeper into the confines of the sleeping bag, shutting off his view a second time. Her hands were very active. The Beta allowed his human form to respond appropriately (*that* much programming was provided for, at least) while he made mental notes and recorded the information for future use.

'The other girls meant nothing to me,' he whispered. 'It was you I always wanted with me. You. *You*!'

He then kissed Maggie and waited for the next reaction.

There was a reaction, all right, but not quite the one he'd anticipated.

The sleeping bag stopped moving as Maggie suddenly froze beneath him. He could feel the sudden tenseness in her and wondered frantically what he'd done wrong.

What now? He considered repeating the short speech, decided not to since the effect it had produced was not the one expected.

'What... other... girls...?' Maggie inquired through clenched teeth.

Definitely the wrong speech, the Beta decided. It was obvious some sort of reply was expected, but he was at a loss what to say. All he could think of to do was to plunge ahead and hope for the best.

So he said, 'Should I talk dirty to you now?'

Evidently it was not an inspired choice, because a furious Maggie suddenly began fighting her way clear of the sleeping bag's confines while trying to refasten her clothing at the same time. She was still working on the latter by the time she'd escaped the bag. She stood glaring down at him as she worked with buttons and straps, her feet sinking into the soft sand.

'What's wrong?' the Beta inquired weakly. 'What did I do, what did I *say*?'

Her fingers worked on her pants. 'Well if you don't know, I'm certainly not going to tell you!'

Human, he thought. How typically human. How was he expected to cope with such an absurd social fabric? How was anyone expected to handle a race that came forth with statements like that?

As far as the Beta was concerned, Maggie's words closed the last circuit. He was out of patience, out of confidence, and out of control. He climbed out of the sleeping bag and confronted her, and he was at least as mad as she was and twice as frustrated.

'That's it, that's all I can stand! I give up! Let them requisition me for spare parts, let 'em recommission my logic function, let them assign me to quality management... I can't take it anymore, I've had it!' Maggie stared back at him in astonishment.

He finished it. 'I'm not Alex Rogan!'

From his position in the bushes overlooking the beach, the state trooper monitored this exchange with interest. As he listened he quietly removed the pistol from the holster at his hip. It was not a standard-issue .38. In fact, it had no calibre at all, relying for its effectiveness on a silent pulse of contorted electrons.

That was appropriate, though, because nothing about the trooper was standard-issue. Not even his face, which was a latex-like material stretched over false muscles connected to his own. No electronic illusion this time, but a true mask.

Keeping his eyes on the target he raised the peculiar pistol and aimed carefully. It was still unaware of his presence and he waited for it to stop moving. The cluster of adolescent humans did not notice him either, engaged as they were in the performance of their primitive rituals further down the beach.

179

Maggie finally found her voice and with it, the only explanation she could come up with to explain Alex's bizarre behaviour.

'Alex, I thought we'd talked about this before. I thought we'd agreed between us that no matter what any of the other kids tried, *no drugs*.'

'I'm not functioning under the influence of hallucinogens, Maggie, or anything else. They'd have no effect on my system in any case. Nothing would, unless you spiked my receptors somehow.' A sound made him pause, followed by the sight of a half-glimpsed shape moving in the bushes above them. Its silhouette was human, its infrared image decidedly alien.

'Maggie, get down!'

He lunged at her as the assassin fired, catching a single burst in his side just beneath the left arm. Cloth and imitation skin disintegrated. The shot would have killed Alex Rogan or any other organic instantly. It only scorched the Beta's lining.

He tried to turn to get a better view of the assailant while shielding Maggie at the same time. Any other night Maggie would have enjoyed the tussle and would gladly have let Alex come out on top, but just then she was more than a little confused and unwilling to continue without a much better explanation of his behaviour.

One thing she noticed immediately, however. It struck her even more forcibly than his inexplicable actions.

'Alex, have you been working out?'

'Have I what?' Electronic eyes searched the vegetation surrounding the parking lot.

She pushed against him, trying to get up. He didn't budge. Strong as she was, she couldn't move him an inch. It was like pushing against iron.

'When did you get so strong? Damn it, Alex, let me up!'

'I can't, and stop squirming. They're shooting at us.'

Either it didn't register or else she didn't believe him. When they seized on a thought and made it their own, the Beta had learned, humans were impossible to persuade. It was part of the same biological equation that made Alex Rogan a potentially great Starfighter but kept Earth classified among the immature worlds.

'What are you talking about, Alex? I swear, I don't understand you anymore.'

'I told you,' the Beta snapped as he tried to get a fix on the assassin's position. It had to be moving now, wondering why its first shot hadn't turned its target into a motionless mass of smouldering flesh. Confusion would buy the Beta some time. 'I'm not Alex. I'm a duplicate of him, a simulacrum, a Beta unit.'

'Your elevator's not going all the way to the top, is what,' she mumbled, gaping at him.

'I'm an exact duplicate of Alex. I'm covering for him here while he tries to help the League against the Ko-Dan armada and Xur's renegades. It's my job, and it's required by regulations. You can't just yank some primitive off his world without replacing the resultant hole in the social fabric. It could be damaging to local development, especially when it involves someone who shows unusual promise of influencing his society, like Alex.'

Maggie listened to all this quietly, saying by way of reply, 'Huh?'

Exasperated beyond words, the Beta pulled open his shirt. Maggie watched uneasily, wondering what his intentions were, wondering how to cope if she had to with a drug-crazed boyfriend who might say or do anything.

However, those thoughts vanished when that same boyfriend followed the opening of his shirt with the opening of his chest. There was no blood, and after flinching in horror for a split-second she found herself staring at a metal surface spotted with small ports and windows. Behind the transparencies, lights glowed steadily or winked on and off according to some alien pattern.

'Look, I'm a robot. Get it? How detailed a picture do I have to draw for you, you dumb human adolescent?'

'Ggggg-gggg!'

The Beta spoke calmly as he refastened his artificial skin and clothing. 'That is not in my vocabulary, but somehow I get the feeling it means I'm not making much progress. It

181

doesn't matter. Just keep down. I don't want you killed by a shot meant for me.'

There would be no second shot, however. The ZZ-Designate had seen and heard enough. It rose and bolted for the stolen police car. The Beta detected the retreat. The assassin's gait was quite human, but just stiff enough to confirm what was already suspected.

'There it goes!'

He took off in pursuit, cursing the slippery sand that slowed him while wishing Centauri hadn't been too damn cheap to install the optional levitation unit. No point in bewailing that omission now.

'Alex!' Maggie was struggling to follow. After-images of the Beta's internal lights lingered like ghostly fireflies on her retinas. She stumbled up the slope towards the half-buried steps made out of old railroad ties. 'Alex, or whatever you are... wait for me!'

The assassin was having his own problems. Not only had he been sent on a futile hunt, with great difficulty and expense, but his quarry had turned out to be a modern Beta unit. It was quite capable of killing him, the alien knew. What mattered now was reporting back to command and informing them that the switch had been made. As to the location of the real target, that wasn't the assassin's problem any longer.

But he had to make that report.

Back inside the stolen land vehicle, he fumbled with the primitive controls, finally succeeding in activating the smelly internal combustion engine. The police cruiser screeched backward, stopped, then roared out of the parking lot.

Without hesitating, the Beta jumped into the nearest available vehicle. This happened to be Jack Blake's precious pickup. Information raced through storage chips located in the Beta's torso.

Truck, land vehicle, activation of: turn this bit of metal, engine function on, push this lever, push down on this pedal.

The pickup burned rubber as it swung around in a curve that left it facing the exit. As the Beta prepared to shift into drive, the door on the passenger side opened.

'Wait!' Maggie yelled as the truck started forward.

'Let me go! If that assassin reports in to Xur and the Ko-Dan that I'm not Alex and that he isn't here, then Alex is in big trouble. Stay here!'

'I'm not staying anywhere until I find out what's going on!' She pulled herself up into the cab and dared the machine in the driver's seat to throw her out. 'And I am *not* a dumb human adolescent, tinman!'

'Stubborn, then,' said the Beta. There was no time for arguing. No time for anything except running down the assassin before it could file its report. 'You may not like what you find out.'

'I don't like it already.'

He nodded and sent the big pickup thundering towards the access road leading to the highway.

The sound of the pickup pulling out of the lot galvanized Jack Blake into action. The assassin's pistol had done its work silently, and even the Beta's shouts and Maggie's replies hadn't been loud or violent enough to draw his attention away from the heated activity of the moment. But the sound of that particular engine was as near and dear to him as his own heartbeat.

He tried to throw himself clear of the sleeping bag, only to find himself held in check by a pair of clutching hands.

'Jack,' the sultry voice beneath him moaned, 'Jack, for God's sake, not *now!*'

'Damnit, Cindy, let go of me!'

'That's not what you were saying a minute ago.'

'Let me go, Cindy!' It was amazing how strong those perfectly manicured fingers had suddenly become. He tried to stand. The bag rolled. Cindy started laughing as they headed for the lake, Jack Blake's piteous cries fading as his mouth filled with sand.

'Hey! Come back! Scratch that paint and you're dead, Rogan! You hear me, you're dead... Cindy, let *go* of me!'

Activity of a different kind reigned aboard the ships of the Ko-Dan armada. Final preparations were underway. The crews worked in silence, speaking only to give or acknowledge commands. This was to be a landmark day in the history of the Empire, and they were privileged to be a part of it. Their names would be writ large in the history of Ko-Dan expansion and conquest. No soldier could wish for more.

In the command room a suboffider turned from his console. 'All ships are at battle ready, Commander. Probes indicate there has been no re-establishment of the energy shield around Rylos. We are ready to break through.'

Xur smiled and spoke the single word uppermost in his mind for many years. 'Invade.'

Next to him one of the senior Ko-Dan aides spoke to Kril. 'Commander, the Xurian ships have not yet answered the invasion code.'

Kril considered. 'That's odd. They were supposed to wait for our call while concealed on one of the large asteroids in this area. They are to precede the armada in the hope that they can convince the government to surrender peacefully and accept Xur as regent.'

'That is how I understand it to be also, Commander. The lack of a reply suggests some difficulty.'

'What difficulty?' Xur's interruption was an unpardonable discourtesy which the weary Kril accepted silently. 'The Frontier is nothing but an empty phrase now that the shield has been destroyed. As I said, the moon of Galan is eclipsed. The Starfighters are dead. Invade!'

Kril thought further. If anything went wrong, he was the one who would have to answer with his eyes to the Imperial War Staff, not this Rylan harlequin.

'We should wait for word from your people, Xur. It would be best if Rylos could be taken without fighting. It would make the other members of the League see the hopelessness of resistance.'

'Where is your love of battle?'

'My love is for my Emperor, for my family, and for those who serve under me, Xur. And for conquest, yes, but at the cheapest price obtainable. As for attacking at the moment of the Galan eclipse, surely you can forgo that juvenile dramatic

184

gesture?'

'I will forgo nothing! This was planned and timed to the minute. I will tolerate no delay.'

'Where are your ships?'

'I don't know. What does it matter? Delayed, perhaps, or made suddenly afraid by your fleet's demonstration of power. They may be unsure of you even if they remain sure of me, and are simply waiting for your armada to approach within attack range of Rylos.'

'How brave they are,' Kril observed sardonically. 'Nevertheless, what you say makes some sense, and I am directed to obey your orders.'

'Then invade. Now.'

Kril executed a reluctant gesture and addressed his chief communications officer. 'All ships forward at half sublight cruising speed, with all energy probes and detectors on. If there's anything larger than an egg out there travelling in anything other than a standard orbit, I want to know about it immediately! Is that clear?'

'Yes, Commander,' communications replied instantly.

'The same thing goes for any object stable in relation to planets or other bodies that is generating more than a minimal amount of radiation.'

'There may be cargo vessels or transports in the area on their way in-system,' the communications officer suggested.

'If they're heading outsystem we don't need them to give reports of what's happening here, and if they're going towards Rylos it's their misfortune to be in the wrong place at the wrong time.'

'You wish any such vessels detected to be taken in tow, Commander?'

Kril gestured negatively. 'I don't wish to waste the time. If they do not reply to any of the Xurian codes, they are to be destroyed.'

'As you command.'

Xur stood nodding nearby. He was watching the main viewscreen. It showed the starfield forward. In the centre was the slowly enlarging sphere of Rylos.

185

'That is more what I expected from the Ko-Dan.'

'I am glad you are pleased with my tactical decisions.' Kril was careful to keep his tone neutral.

Grig fretted over the gunstar's instrumentation, checking and rechecking every function. Alex could only wait, excited, nervous, but secure in the knowledge that he'd made the decision to fight. He let his fingers flutter over the fire controls, coming so close he could almost feel the smooth surfaces without actually touching them. His seat responded to the slightest movement of his body, always keeping him comfortable and in position.

They waited motionless within the throat of the old volcano, all power off except for sensors and life support.

'Here they come,' Grig finally announced.

'How many?' Alex's fingertips tingled as if they were asleep.

'Twenty to thirty. Small fighters. Indications of more following. Many more.'

'You're not doing a lot for my confidence.'

'Sorry. Should I lie to you, Alex? I've already told you what we're up against. Remember, surprise will be worth a great deal.'

'If we can pull it off.'

'Yes. If we can pull it off.'

They were on Alex's screen now. He was counting the number of deadly shapes when something buzzed loudly on Grig's console, making both of them start.

'*Snash!*' Grig growled in frustration, banging one hand down on a panel. The buzzing and the flashing light that had accompanied it vanished.

'What was that?'

'Automatic engine check. Sounds periodically when the main drive is off. I forgot to shut it down.' He went quiet, then whispered (even though there was no reason to whisper), 'One of them's breaking off. I think it's coming in for a closer look.'

'Surely they didn't pick up on anything as weak as that

buzzing?' Alex found he was sweating.

'Ko-Dan detectors are extremely sensitive. I'm sure they have orders to investigate the slightest disturbance.'

'Why don't we move back deeper inside?'

Grig made a gesture of negativity and stared at his instruments. 'Can't now. Not without sending up an energy card announcing our presence to the whole armada.' He added hopefully, 'Still, as you say, it lasted but an instant.'

The curious Ko-Dan ship cruised low over the broken surface of the planetoid, the pilot watching his instruments intently. He had detected the barest flicker of energy. It had hardly been sufficient to activate his detectors. Now there was nothing. The little airless world below seemed as dead as the ages.

He still conducted his survey with care, employing visual as well as electronic aids. Then his squadron commander called him, wanting to know what he was wasting his time with and why he was still out of formation. The pilot muttered a curse and accelerated to catch up. It would not do to be caught out of formation during the approach to Rylos. Orders were to put on the most impressive display possible to overwhelm the already half-beaten Rylans.

'He's gone,' Grig said softly. Alex let out a deep breath. 'Good thing there's not much gravity here or he might have spotted the debris from those Xurian ships you blasted. As it is, everything's had time to drift off in a dozen different directions.' He smiled, another human gesture his stiff skin was not quite able to imitate properly.

'There's going to be a lot of debris floating around this sector before too long.'

The police car ripped through brush with wild disregard for the large trees in its path. Finally it encountered one tree that refused to bend. The car banged to a halt in a rising ball of dust and dead leaves and was abandoned by its driver.

The assassin dashed into a small clearing that was shaded above by several much larger trees, running towards another parked vehicle. There were no wheels on this one and its

187

range was considerably greater than the police cruiser. Distorted feet pounded the earth as their owner raced for his ship.

Once safely inside, he let himself relax. The craft was small, but more than capable of resisting the minor projectile weapons utilized by the locals, and he had no intention of waiting around until the local military could be informed of his presence.

Now he had ample time to compose a suitable message for his employers. The signal would be reduced to code and sent off to the nearest Ko-Dan relay. From there it would travel from relay to deep-space relay until it was picked up and decoded by the armada. That would put an end to his work here. He would leave for home, his assignment frustrated but his contract fulfilled by the explanatory message.

Maggie clung to the overhead handle as the driver sent the careening pickup hurtling across the rough desert road with complete disregard for maintaining the integrity of the truck's underbody. Or their own.

'You're a robot?'

'A robot.' He searched Alex's memory for additional references. 'Like in the stories by Asimov. Like in the GM factory in Detroit. Like in the song by Styx. More complicated than any of those.'

'A duplicate of Alex . . . I can see that, of course. Then . . . where's Alex?'

The Beta jerked a thumb upwards. 'Out there.'

Maggie looked ceilingward. 'Out where? Up in a plane somewhere?'

The Beta shook his head. 'Considerably farther than that. Considerably farther than you can imagine.'

'Alex . . . out in space. Is this for real?'

'Yes! I've been trying to tell you, it's all for real. Very real. Lethally real. Lethal to Alex if I can't stop that assassin before he tells his superiors what I've just told you.'

'Why would anyone want to assassinate Alex?'

'Because he may be the key to saving galactic civilization as we know it.'

Maggie thought a long while. 'Alex? *My* Alex? Alex Rogan who has a hard time fixing a broken septic tank valve?'

'The same,' the Beta told her. 'Actually, that's not such a bad analogy for the job he's doing now.'

'Then don't talk, drive!'

The Beta did not reply, though it wanted to. What did the young female think he was doing?

'First attack wave closing on Rylos, Commander,' the communications officer announced.

'Any signs of opposition?'

'Nothing, Commander. Monitoring of surface transmissions indicates that the first wave has been detected by the Rylan authorities.'

'Any reaction as yet?'

The communications officer made some inquiries, waited, then replied with barely concealed delight. 'Indications of general panic among the populace despite government assurances that all is under control. Also ultimatums directing us to turn back or be destroyed.'

'They are down to their final bluff.' Kril permitted himself to relax. It was all but over.

'You see?' Xur said triumphantly from nearby. 'I told you. It's been so long since the League has actually had to fight anyone that they've forgotten how to do it. That hidden base was their only source of resistance. All other weaponry is localized.' He sniffed disdainfully. 'Police functionaries. Government security. Weaklings and cowards.'

'I am pleased nothing has materialized to dispute the correctness of your information,' Kril said smoothly, 'though I would still like to know what happened to your own ships.'

Xur turned to stare hungrily at the screen. 'When the time is right they'll show themselves, you'll see. Haven't I been right about everything else so far? You worry too much, Kril.'

'I am aware of that, Xur,' the Ko-Dan replied. 'That is why I was made a commander.'

Off to one side of the spacious command chamber the officer in charge of monitoring fleet communications was staring in confusion at his instruments. He ran the coded message back through the computer, assured himself of its accuracy, and decided it had to be turned over immediately. His superior accepted the transcription with the equivalent of a frown and reluctantly determined to present it to the Commander.

He skirted the Rylan renegade and made his presence known.

Kril turned to face him. 'Yes, what is it?'

'I would not interrupt your triumph if it were not a matter of some ...'

'Get to the point,' Kril said impatiently.

'Yes, Commander.' The officer studied the message one last time. 'We've picked up a signal on an emergency frequency. It's been relayed quite a distance from a primitive world outside League and Ko-Dan boundaries. It comes from one of our ZZ-Designates.'

They were interrupted. 'I know what it concerns,' said Xur. 'Remember that single small ship that jumped to supralight just before we destroyed the base on Rylos?'

'Of course I remember.' Kril was furious at being treated like some green junior officer. One time this Rylan upstart was going to go too far, Imperial orders or no Imperial orders. 'We put a lock on it and estimated its course, then sent Designates to check for activity indicating the presence of League technology at work on any inhabited worlds in line with that estimated course and the jump capability of a vessel that size. As you wished.' He faced the officer.

'What of the message's contents?'

'Rather confusing, Commander,' the officer replied. 'And brief.'

'All Designates file brief reports,' Kril declared. 'They are not utilized because of their ability to carry on lengthy conversations.'

'No, Commander.' The officer swallowed. 'The message from ZZ-Designate 61 says, "The last Starfighter ..."'

The Beta turned off the dirt road and started climbing a steep slope above the clearing, hoping to take the assassin by surprise. It might not be expecting any pursuit, but the Beta was taking no chances.

As the truck bounced crazily over boulders and rills, the Beta held the wheel firmly in one hand while opening its stomach with the other. Maggie observed this bloodless operation with silent fascination. The Beta removed a small box no larger than a pack of cigarettes, stuck it beneath the pickup's dashboard, and refastened his stomach. The box clung to the metal, a single red light glowing brightly on one side.

'What's that?' she asked, her teeth rattling.

'A surprise for our friend below. Isn't it your custom to give presents during the upcoming time you call Christmas?'

She nodded. Actually she couldn't do anything but nod, rough as the ride was. They had reached the top of the low ridge and were starting down the opposite side.

'This will be an early present for our friend. When I give the word, we jump, okay?'

'Do we have a choice?' The pickup was beginning to gain speed as the Beta sent it rumbling down the rocky slope.

The Beta indicated the metal box attached to the dash. 'Not unless you want to be part of the surprise.'

'I don't think so. If this is going to help Alex ...'

The Beta nodded. Maggie put one hand on the door handle, keeping her other on the overhead grip, and waited anxiously for the robot's command.

At the last instant he shouted, 'JUMP!'. Without thinking, Maggie threw herself out the door, covering her face and rolling over a couple of times until coming to rest against a mercifully soft bush. She sat up fast.

It occurred to her then that she hadn't seen the Beta try to jump clear.

Below, she could see the truck roar towards something shiny and strange in shape. The last seconds seemed to pass in slow motion, like something out of an old movie.

The pickup smashed into the vessel concealed by the brush and exploded. The pickup's twin gas tanks erupted in concert

191

with Beta's mysterious metal box. The alien craft, which would have withstood the gasoline explosion easily, turned into a geyser of metal and metallic glass. The concussion knocked Maggie down. Among the vaporized contents of the spaceship were the remains of one very surprised alien killer.

The gasoline and the surrounding vegetation continued to burn long after the ship had been destroyed. For the second time in as many minutes Maggie slowly picked herself off the ground. She wiped twigs and dirt from her legs. She was sore and bruised, but nothing was broken.

She wished she could say the same for Beta. He was down there, somewhere, in small pieces. He'd sacrificed himself to help Alex. Of course, he was only a machine. It wasn't like he was a real person, was it?

Well, was it?

You can't cry over a machine, she told herself. That would be silly. Beta would've thought it silly. So she didn't, but she had to work hard to keep the tears back.

She still didn't understand what was going on, but she didn't want to have to answer a bunch of awkward questions. The fire would bring out forestry service trucks, and Jack Blake would be coming along sooner or later, hot on the trail of his precious, missing pickup. She didn't want to talk to Jack just now. She didn't want to talk to anyone.

She started back toward the trailer park; sore, confused, and concerned.

Just where *was* Alex?

XIV

'Well,' Kril said into the unexpected silence, 'what's the rest of the message?'

'I'm afraid that's all there is, Commander.' The communications officer was apologetic. 'That much came in and then the transmission ceased.'

'Could there have been a relay failure between here and this primitive system the report was being filed from?'

The communications officer considered. 'I do not think so, Commander. Because of the planned assault on Rylos and the rest of the League, all deep-space relays were performance checked just prior to the fleet's departure. All were certified operational.'

'Doesn't make any sense,' Kril muttered. 'There has to be more to the message.'

'ZZ-Designates often find themselves operating under less than ideal conditions for long-range communication,' another officer suggested thoughtfully. 'Obviously this one did not have time to complete its report and intends to do so at some time in the near future.'

Kril repeated the cryptic line to himself. 'The last Starfighter . . . what could the rest of it be?'

'The last Starfighter . . .' Xur declared portentously into the resulting silence, '. . . is dead! That's the message! There was one on that ship fleeing Rylos. As ordered, the ZZ-Designate took care of it. The last Starfighter is dead! The last suggestion of a threat has been terminated. There is nothing to stop us now.' He turned wild eyes on Kril.

'No longer any reason for this display of excessive caution, Commander. We have wasted too much time already. Full sublight speed. On to Rylos!'

Kril found himself hesitating only momentarily. Xur's interpretation of the message seemed so natural, so correct, that truly there was no reason any longer to hesitate. He gestured to communications and engineering.

One elderly officer spoke from his station. 'Shouldn't we do a follow-up on this message, sir, to seek positive confirmation?'

'By all means,' Kril agreed, 'but the time-delay between here and this backward world where the message originates would keep us waiting unconscionably long. We do not want to give the Rylans any cause for hope, much less time to repair their energy shield. This close, it could destroy our engines if reactivated. For a change, Xur makes good sense. By all means put through a request for clarification of the remainder of the message and report to me when it comes in. But I will not delay longer for a formality.'

'As you wish, Commander.' The elderly officer moved to comply with the directive, disquiet nagging the back of his mind.

Alex shifted impatiently in his seat, itching for the fight to begin while aware that Grig would not take them out until just the right moment. Something massive and dark appeared on his battle screen and he stopped squirming.

'The command ship.'

'Yes, that's it,' Grig said. 'Not as well screened as I expected. Most of their attending fighters are well forward, moving in what amounts to review formation. It's almost as if they're on parade. Any why not? There's nothing left to threaten them, is there?'

Alex smiled as Grig activated the gunstar's oversized engines. Slowly they drifted out of the crater under minimum power as the command ship lumbered majestically past.

A large opaque blister was clearly visible against the smooth metal surface of the massive vessel.

Grig pointed it out immediately. 'There, Alex. At the far end. The fighter command centre.'

'I see it.' Alex tried to push himself back into the yielding cushion of the gunnery chair. He strove to blank his mind of everything but the target on the screen, just as he did when he was playing the game back home.

Grig glanced back and up. 'Good luck, Starfighter. The League expects every being to do his or her or its best today.'

It made Alex smile, exactly as Grig had intended. 'Thanks, Grig. For everything.'

'For what? I haven't given you a thing, Alex.'

'You've given me confidence, insight, and a feeling that maybe I've grown up a little out here. For starters.'

The Navigator/Monitor looked away, embarrassed. 'Those qualities were in you all the time, Alex. I merely helped them rise to the surface, just as you have risen to the occasion.'

'You're a good man, Grig, even if you aren't a man.'

'The term is relative, Alex. It translates well. As does your friendship.'

Alex let that warm thought flow over him as Grig turned his attention to the ship's systems. The Starfighter's gaze settled on Maggie's picture, resting nearby. So far away. She was so impossibly far away.

And what was he doing here, a kid with SAT scores barely above average and grades pulled down by lack of sleep and study time? How the hell had he ended up in this position, with so much riding on an ability he'd perfected while playing at it in his spare time?

Something Mr Solomon, his history teacher, had told him in class came back to him now. 'It's always been a matter of debate as to whether great men make history or the sweep of historical events makes great men.'

'Life support, check,' Grig was murmuring.

'Fire control guidance, check,' Alex declared.

'Emergency backup systems, check.'

'Weaponry activated, check.'

'Propulsion, check,' said Grig as the gunstar suddenly erupted from the surface of the asteroid.

'Let's *go*!' Alex shouted, unable to contain the excitement he'd kept bottled up inside him ever since they'd left Rylos. It was for real now. For real and forever.

Long time, forever. He tried not to think about it, tried not to think about dying. If you got philosophical during the game, it would eat your quarter. More than his quarter at stake now. Metaphysics versus reality.

He concentrated instead on the shape looming steadily larger on his battle screen. One chance. Their surprise would probably give him one chance to take out the fighter command centre before the Ko-Dan recovered. The game only gave you one chance.

The universe no longer existed. There was only the image on the screen. He blotted out everything else.

Alarms sprang to life within the command chamber of the flagship as a detection officer announced, 'Unaccounted for craft in central formation.'

'What is it?' Kril turned instantly towards the detection station, trying to divide his attention between it and the main screen. 'Adjust sensors to track.' The view forward blurred momentarily as input was shifted.

'Tracking,' announced an officer.

'Identification.'

'Not possible yet, Commander. It's moving too fast for an accurate reading ... wait; first generation computer image is going up.' A faint outline appeared on the screen.

Xur recognized it immediately. 'A gunstar ... that's impossible!'

Kril turned angrily. 'So: the last Starfighter is dead. I suppose cargo pilots are flying that?'

'It's conceivable,' Xur snapped back at him. 'If one ship remained operational but all the pilots had been killed in our attack ...'

'Whoever's on board that ship knows how to handle it,' said Kril. 'Those aren't amateurs coming at us. Amateurs would have been detected long before this. How they slipped past our fighters I can't imagine, but it wasn't by luck and it wasn't by accident. As for myself,' he glanced towards the head of bridge security, 'I'm sick of dealing with amateurs. This farce has gone on long enough. Seize him!'

A towering Ko-Dan officer advanced eagerly towards Xur, who activated his sceptre and aimed it at the alien. The Ko-Dan halted. Xur backed towards the doorway.

'How dare you? I'm the Emperor of Rylos, by decree from your own Emperor! I command you to . . .'

'You command nothing. This fleet is now on battle standby. I take no orders from this point on from anyone except the Imperial War Staff. It is my opinion that you constitute a danger to the stability and effectiveness of my crew, Xur. Your demented ranting is detrimental to their temperament. I won't have that during a combat situation.'

As Xur reached the heavy doors leading to the first corridor beyond, they parted to reveal not a path of retreat but additional security personnel. They promptly grabbed him from behind and removed the deadly sceptre from his grasp.

'You'll pay for this,' Xur sputtered. 'You'll pay with your lives! All of you!'

Kril turned away in disgust. 'Get the "Emperor" out of my sight. Lock him up until I have time to decide what to do with him.' He dismissed Xur completely from his thoughts as he turned back to face the main screen. It clearly showed the gunstar approaching at incredible speed. 'All defensive systems lock on and destroy the intruder!'

Lights brighter than the distant stars suddenly filled the void around the charging vessel. Alex thought the display was beautiful, like a laser show at a rock concert. All he needed to make the dizzying attack Grig was conducting complete was a good tape of AC/DC or Styx or Def Leppard. Although even if he happened to have one along, he couldn't have done much more than stare at it. He didn't think gunstars were provided with cassette decks.

The eruption of defensive fire from the command ship was so lovely he forgot to be afraid.

'Three milliparts to strike zone, Alex. Don't miss. We won't get another unopposed pass.'

Alex noted the explosions and beams of deadly energy

lighting space all around them and occasionally rocking the ship as the gunstar's defensive screens took the brunt of the fire.

'This is unopposed?'

'Remember what I said; everything is relative.'

'Don't worry. I'm ready.'

'Two milliparts. Wait until you're sure,' Grig warned him.

Then the command blister was in the centre of Alex's floating battle screen and it was so much like the game back home that he almost, but not quite, relaxed. His fingers moved quickly, instinctively over the fire controls. He was no longer concerned. He'd had plenty of practice.

'Now, Alex!' Grig shouted, afraid the moment would pass. Even as he spoke the gunstar's weapons systems fired simultaneously at the command ship as Alex threw everything the powerful little vessel possessed at the target. Flaming gas burst from the surface of the blister, enveloping it completely.

'Got it!' Alex yelled as he continued to pour fire into the flagship.

'No time to finish it off now, Alex. The rest of the armada's nearly to Rylos.' But Alex continued to attack until Grig wrenched them out of range.

The crew of the command ship fought to brace themselves as the big flagship shook from the after-explosions triggered by the devastating attack. The subofficer standing behind Xur was thrown to the deck. Xur kept his balance, threw himself on the unsteady guard in front of him and regained control of his sceptre. As both guards tried to recover they lost their heads to the deadly beam of energy generated by the staff.

Xur vanished into a nearby tunnel, but his destination was revealed by a light that began flashing on a nearby wall panel. The third guard, who'd been temporarily dazed after being knocked against a wall, noted the flashing telltale and staggered to a communications module to report.

'Xur has taken an escape pod and has fled the ship. Repeat, the prisoner Xur has taken an escape pod and has fled the ship!'

The information was relayed to the bridge and was subsumed in the flood of damage reports. Xur's escape troubled Kril, but he had little time to deal with the flight of a single obstreperous Rylan.

He still found enough time to issue a long overdue order. 'Tell the proper agencies to seek and destroy Xur.'

The officer recording the directive looked thoughtful. 'I could order a ship or two out of the middle squadron. They would locate and finish off the escape pod in a few moments.'

'No!' Kril steadied himself as still another explosion rocked the great ship. 'There's a gunstar loose out there with a Starfighter behind its firepower, or haven't you noted that as yet? That is an unpredictable element. There is no room in our plan of assault for unpredictable elements. It must be dealt with to the exclusion of everything else, and instantly.'

'Yes, Commander,' said the apologetic officer.

Kril whirled to face communications. 'Alert all squadron commanders. Tell them what has happened here. All units to function to . . .'

The communications officer replied sorrowfully. 'The fighter command blister is gone, Commander. Completely gone. We have no way to direct our fighters.'

Kril growled something so vile that even under the present desperate circumstances his subordinates were shocked.

'Look at them,' Alex said excitedly as they came within visual pickup range of the rearmost squadron of Ko-Dan fighters. 'They don't know we're here. They don't know they've been attacked yet!'

'They will know soon enough,' Grig said sombrely. 'We have only moments before the Ko-Dan patch through from the flagship on secondary communications equipment. We must make the most of them.'

'Don't worry.' Alex readied himself. 'I know what to do. After all, I've been recruited by the League to . . .'

'Life support intact, weapons systems still functioning at maximum, propulsion at full strength . . .' Grig was mumbling to himself.

'. . . defend the Frontier . . . and this is it . . .'

Grig sent the gunstar swooping down on four squadrons of Ko-Dan ships. Suicidal it might have seemed, but the Ko-Dan expected no trouble as they moved towards Rylos's orbit, and they were used to doing battle under unified control. That control had been taken out by the single surprise pass at the command ship. It should take the Ko-Dan a while to adapt to operating without central tactical direction. Hopefully too much time.

Alex's fingers played over the fire controls. Taken completely by surprise, the Ko-Dan ships were destroyed before they could react. And when they attempted to contact their fighter command centre on the flagship and failed to get so much as a courteous reply, they began to panic. It must have seemed that they were under attack from a hundred gunstars. In every instance their delay in responding was fatal, as Grig wove neatly through the shattered formations and Alex obliterated potential opposition one ship after the other.

One squadron commander finally analyzed the chaotic situation in time to issue new orders just before his own ship vanished in a ball of expanding superhot metal and ceramic fragments. Grig turned the gunstar as two trios of fighters attempted to converge on the interloper from opposing directions, firing blindly at the target with all their weaponry.

The gunstar shuddered briefly under the combined attack but hull integrity was not compromised.

'We're hit!' Grig announced a moment later. 'Engine temperature is climbing, Alex. Drive's overheating.'

'Evade!' Alex shouted, much as he would have hit the evade button back home.

Grig didn't need the advice, sent the gunstar looping radically away from both sets of attackers. The blind charge ended in multiple destruction as the wildly aimed weapons of the opposing fighters blasted their opposite numbers.

Three more ships broke away from the milling, confused armada and dove toward the atmosphere below.

'Sector six,' he warned Alex. 'Three ships making a surface attack. They're going after a civilian target.'

'I see them,' Alex said grimly. The gunstar overtook the three fighters and Alex took them out with a single concentrated burst, using the minimum amount of firepower necessary to accomplish the job.

But now a whole series of warning lights glowed brightly on Grig's console. 'Damned engine temperature won't come down. We need a minute or two so I can cruise powered-down and take the demand off.'

'Take us once around Rylos,' Alex suggested, a conclusion Grig reached independently. The gunstar stayed just above the ionosphere, skimming the outer edge of the Rylan atmosphere as it vanished from the screens of those few Ko-Dan ships alert enough to begin tracking it.

Grig ran the necessary commands through the ship's system and was rewarded when the warning lights began to wink out, one after the other. With the demand down he was able to rechannel the drive and the affected area returned to normal. More important, it stayed there.

'Engine temperature steady, life support unchanged, weapons systems still operating at full efficiency... watch yourself, Alex. We'll be back in attack range again in a minute or two.'

They raced across the terminator... only to have their screens stay blank.

Alex hunted for telltale images, found nothing. 'Hey, where's the armada? They must have run for it.'

'That would not be like the Ko-Dan.' Grig adjusted a control. Immediately both screens filled with ships... at the outer limits of detection.

'Uh-oh. They did retreat, but only to re-establish communication with each other and with the flagship.' He paused as several lights winked on. The multiple targets did not attack, but began to encroach slowly on the gunstar's position. 'Englobement,' Grig murmured worriedly.

Alex switched to a sternward view and saw the Ko-Dan in matching formation moving toward them at the same controlled, steady rate.

'What is it? What are they doing?'

'Spherical attack. Englobement. All ships abandon previous formations and assume positions equidistant from one another at a predetermined distance from the target, then reverse course and move in for the kill while the distance between them remains constant and shrinks. It means there's no way out.'

'Can't we just shoot our way out of the sphere?'

'It's a three level manoeuvre. One sphere inside a second inside a third. Wherever we'd try to break through we'd run into a second and third line of fighters. They would hold us long enough for the others to collapse around us. We can't do battle in every direction at once.'

'This wasn't in the game, Grig!' Alex stammered.

His friend didn't reply immediately, took a moment to adjust their heading. 'The moon of Galan is still within the englobement. If we position ourselves near its surface at least one sector will be protected.'

'Look for another tunnel to hide in!'

'A useless move, Alex. They'd search us out anyway. Besides, Galan's craters are meteoric in origin, not volcanic like the ones on that asteroid we used for cover. There aren't likely to be any tunnels.'

'It was just an idea,' Alex mumbled. 'I'm a Starfighter, not a geologist.'

'Then get ready, Starfighter,' said Grig grimly, 'because we're going to have to use the blossom.'

'That's the experimental, untested weapons system you mentioned? You think it'll work?'

'You have another suggestion?'

'Uh, not at the moment,' Alex confessed as he stared at the slowly shrinking sphere of Ko-Dan ships all around them. 'What do I do?'

'You use your same fire controls, only use them *fast*. Don't even stop to think. At kill range you'll have sixty seconds of overfire . . . theoretically. The blossom has never been battle tested, only demonstrated in simulations. Use of it could overload the ship's drive, and . . .' he hesitated.

'And what?' Alex prompted him. 'What are you worrying

about now?' Alex was amazed at how matter-of-fact he sounded. 'Theoretically we should already be dead.'

'I cannot argue with your logic, but your attitude has turned flippant.'

'Has it?' Alex was feeling euphoric, blindly indifferent to whatever fate the universe had cooked up for him. 'The hell with it.'

He flipped open the protective plate that arched over the red button controlling the blossom. Not that he felt half as confident as he sounded. A gentle shudder passed through the ship. Opening the plate had activated *something*, but from his position in the gunnery chair he couldn't see what. He had the feeling that the contours of the gunstar had been altered somehow.

He wiped his palms against plastic, wishing he could free his arms from the control sleeves but not daring to waste any time.

The images forming the deadly spheres on his screen began to close towards one another. The englobement was tightening. A somnolent green dot lay trapped in the centre of the screen: their own ship.

The first fighters came within range and Alex began firing selectively with standard defensive weaponry. He was selective in his choice of targets, trying to take out ships coming from every direction instead of concentrating on one sector. That would be what they'd be expecting him to do. His football coach had always told him to run the unexpected play, and the same strategy seemed to apply now.

Ko-Dan ships vanished from the screen, obliterated by the gunstar's superior weaponry and Alex's methodical aim. The survivors ignored the losses in their midst and closed up in preparation for the final, overwhelming attack.

'Hold them off a little longer.' Grig was fastened to his instrumentation.

Alex continued to fire, speaking without turning from the display screen. 'How much longer?'

'Wait till they're well within the blossom's kill zone. We have to wait, or else we may as well give up now.' An explosion rocked the dancing gunstar as Grig fought to confuse the incoming attacks while his area of manoeuvrability continued to shrink. Soon part of their defensive screen would fail and one shot would get through. That would be enough to destroy them.

'Grig...?'

'Easy, easy.'

'Now?'

'Steady... hold on, Alex.'

On the display screens the green dot appeared about to be swallowed by a swarm of red gnats. 'Now Grig?' Alex asked anxiously. *'Now?'*

'Now! Fire!'

Alex's thumb hit the forbidden button while his other fingers became a blur on the rest of the fire control panel.

The gunstar became a dervish of destructive energy, throwing off energy bolts and heavy particles in all directions. It was as if a small sun had suddenly gone nova in the midst of the incoming Ko-Dan ships. That wash of unbelievable destruction swept them away as though they'd never been, vaporizing them before they had a chance to escape.

Alex kept firing even though his screen was rendered useless by the quantity of energy being dispersed around the gunstar and kept firing until the brief period of usefulness ended. A warning buzzer sounded loud in the cockpit. Lights dimmed, the ship resumed its standard fighting configuration, and space was once again visible outside and on the screens.

The latter were blank save for a single steady green dot hanging lazily in the centres.

'Engines down, power down,' Grig announced, studying his readouts. 'Except for life support and communications, we're dead.'

Exhausted, Alex pulled his arms out of the control sleeves and indulged in the ultimate luxury of wiping his face and rubbing his eyes. He was utterly drained, physically as well as emotionally.

'It doesn't matter, Grig. We did it. It's over, and we did it.'

'Yes, we actually did, didn't we?' He continued to take readings of ship functions. 'I'll attempt to contact Rylos control. They'll send something to pick us up and recover the gunstar.' He started to spin his chair.

Near explosions suddenly rocked the ship, stopping as abruptly. Grig hastily swerved back to battle position while Alex thrust his arms back into the fire control sleeves.

'Now what?'

'I don't know. Did we miss any? I thought we got them all.' He studied his console.

The oversized image appeared simultaneously on both screens.

'The command ship!' Alex yelled. 'But they've stopped firing at us. Why?'

'Maybe they can sense that our drive is dysfunctional. Maybe they're going to put a tow beam on us and pull us in.' He worked frantically at his instruments. 'Plenty of evidence of damage to their exterior. We hurt them bad in our initial attack.'

Indeed they had. Kril raged at his fire control officer. 'Why have you stopped firing? They are not even trying to evade. They must have engine damage. Fire!'

The officer in charge turned to face Kril. 'Commander, all our weapons systems are down now. It will take time for damage control to repair even the least damaged of them.'

Kril whirled back to face the main screen. It clearly showed the gunstar drifting aimlessly above Galan.

'Sensors?'

'They have minimal power remaining, Commander,' came the reply. 'I would imagine they retain life support since there is no visible sign of hull damage. But all other energy readings are minimal at best.'

'Could it be a deception?' wondered another officer. He was patched from where he'd struck the deck hard during an earlier explosion.

'Why bother?' Kril exclaimed. 'They must know how badly we are hurt. If they could mount the most minimal attack they would be coming straight for us. We must therefore assume they are incapable of attack and cannot even manage their own escape. Could we put a tow beam on them?'

Again the disheartening reply. 'That system is also down, Commander.'

Kril fumed silently. The opportunity was present to snatch victory from defeat, and he was helpless!

Or was he?

He turned to navigation. 'Plot an intercept course. Even at our mutually reduced speeds the impact should be sufficient to reduce them to scrap. Clear all forward compartments of crew and seal off the forward section of the ship.'

'Yes, Commander,' came the replies from the appropriate stations.

Kril was able to regard the screen with satisfaction. This would be like the ancient battles, when Ko-Dan warred against Ko-Dan on the surface of the mother world for control of tribal territories. With the advanced weaponry of both vessels crippled, he had the advantage. He had no intention of waiting until his own weapons were fixed. The gunstar might regain the use of her drive and escape, or worse, mount its own attack.

No, the final outcome of the battle for Rylos would be determined by raw basics: mass against mass. In that primitive equation, the Ko-Dan led.

Alex stared at his screen. 'Grig, they're moving toward us.'

'I know, Alex.'

'What are they doing?'

'I think they are actually going to try and hit us with their own vessel. What a remarkable notion.'

'Remarkable, hell! *Do* something!'

'I am trying, Alex.'

Hesitantly, Alex touched one of the fire controls. All his effort produced was a red warning light on the readout and monitoring system. He tried another. Two red lights glared angrily at him, fiery hostile eyes in the dim light of the cabin.

'Grig we need power. I've got nothing back here.'

'All systems were drained by the use of the blossom, but I'm trying to override the emergency safety system. It's not designed to be overriden, Alex.'

'Well do something. Another minute and *we'll* be overridden!' The Ko-Dan command ship was clearly visible on the screen, leaking glowing gases from the gaping wounds inflicted earlier by the gunstar. It was moving at an infinitesimal speed straight towards the gunstar.

Grig worked with quiet determination. Something behind Alex's seat vibrated awkwardly, stopped.

'All we have left is a little stored power for communications and life support maintenance.'

'Switch it through to the drive and hold your breath!'

Grig tried to do so. The temperature in the cabin began to fall rapidly. No longer continuously recycled and freshened, the air started to foul.

'Hurry, hurry!' Alex yelled, though he knew he shouldn't have wasted the oxygen.

'Power . . . on!' Grig gasped as a battery of lights sprang to weak life on his console. He immediately switched it to the gunstar's manoeuvring thrusters, not daring to try activating the main drive.

The little ship moved. Very slightly and very slowly. It did just dip below the immense ship bearing down on it. There was actual contact between the hulls, a rarity in space, unheard of in combat. The screeching sound produced by the scrape of metal against metal was deafening in the cockpit of the gunstar.

Then they were clear and moving steadily away. The red warning lights above fire control fluttered, went out. Alex pounced on the possibility, hit everything at once hoping *something* might work.

Something did. The gunstar's weaponry raked the underside of the command ship one final time before burning out. Explosions, vast and silent, erupted from the target.

Grig cut the power to the thrusters and rechannelled back into life support and communications. The air began to clear immediately. Feeling like a scuba diver who'd stayed down too long, Alex inhaled deep gulps of the refreshened air. The cabin temperature, which had fallen below a hundred, climbed steadily back towards the comfort range. Only Alex's flight suit had kept him from freezing solid, but he was still shivering even after the temperature had returned to normal. His body remembered.

'What was that?' Kril demanded to know as a violent trembling ran through the deck under his feet. He gazed up at the screen. 'Did we hit them?'

Panic built at the consoles. One officer turned a frightened face towards his Commander.

'I don't know, sir, but our guidance system is gone! We're locked on course.'

'Notify the nearest Imperial ship of our situation and give them our speed and heading. They will rendezvous and help us initiate repairs.'

'You don't understand, sir,' said the officer, all pretence at courtesy swamped by his fear. 'Our present course is not directed outsystem. It's . . .'

He didn't have to finish. The main screen still functioned and Kril could see as clearly as anyone else where the great flagship was heading when drive control had been lost.

All the odds had favoured them from the beginning, he mused while the panic spread around him. He ignored it. Xur and his traitors with their precious secrets to sell, the easy destruction of the Starfighter base, everything had been too simple, too easy.

And now this. To perish because the cosmos had finally determined to even out those odds. With all of immensity open to them, all space to escape into until repairs could be made to the guidance system, they had inadvertantly chosen the one wrong heading to take. Had they retained control of the ship it wouldn't have meant a thing, of course. But they had not.

Through the shouting on the bridge another voice reached him faintly. 'Commander, the Rylan gunstar is now astern of us, still drifting. She must have regained power temporarily and fired on us in passing.'

Kril had already reached that conclusion. He just nodded, smiling to himself. Truly the odds had evened out. The cosmos does not back favourites.

He was still laughing at the irony of it when the command ship plunged into the surface of the moon called Galan, briefly but spectacularly changing a section of the desolate surface from coppery green to a bright, intense hot yellow.

XV

The ceremony was more than a little overwhelming. Previously, all Alex had seen of Rylos had been clouds and forest, distant oceans and extensive mountain ranges.

Now, with the gunstar resting in the central square of the capital city, he had the chance to see what really had been at stake. It was much more than the idea of a Frontier, of a League of united worlds and races. People had been at stake, their lives and futures. Even if most of them did look a little funny.

There were representatives of many peoples standing with him inside the building. Grig stood nearby as the ceremony concluded. Alex blushed at the effusiveness of the translation, until one Rylan official was compelled to wonder aloud if the change in skin colour wasn't due to some allergic reaction to something in their atmosphere. Blushing even redder, Alex assured him that it wasn't.

'Thank you, Ambassador Enduran,' he was finally able to mutter, making the Rylan complimentary sign with his hands as Grig had taught him. The gesture must have gone over well with the onlookers, because there was an alien murmur of approval.

'Thank you, Starfighter,' Enduran replied. He turned and gestured, whereupon the assembled officials, administrators and directors of the government of Rylos, in concert with the visiting representatives of the League, performed a half-bow towards Alex that left him feeling very strange indeed.

To escape the attention he paid a little homage of his own, turning to Grig and saluting. Grig didn't respond in kind. Instead he chose to make a small modification in the carefully rehearsed ceremony, and stuck out his hand. Alex took it and they shook warmly, sharing the private joke.

'Well Alex, you mustn't keep the rest of the crowd waiting. People have come from great distances to honour you. It's the sort of thing heroes have to tolerate,' Enduran told him.

'I'm no hero,' he said softly.

'Whether you are or not doesn't matter.' He nodded towards the doorway. '*They* think you are. As such, you have certain responsibilities. You will stay, won't you?' Alex hesitated, looking over at Grig, who nodded.

He paused long enough to hug the tough-skinned alien, not giving a damn what any of the exalted spectators might make of this peculiar human gesture. Grig understood its meaning readily enough, though, and so did Enduran.

Then the two of them started out of the doorway. The crowd of representatives and officials made way for them. As the door opened an alien fanfare greeted their appearance. They found themselves on a balcony, looking out across a sea of enthusiastic alien faces.

He'd been ready for this. Enduran and the others had told him what to expect. What he was not prepared for was the sight of the elderly figure seated on a nearby mobile platform. Two uniformed Rylan medics stood at attention on either side of the tiny vehicle. Ignoring the crowd, Alex ran towards the newcomer.

'Centauri! You're supposed to be dead!'

The old man grinned. 'I'm supposed to be a lot o' things, my boy, but deceased ain't one of 'em. My people are a tough bunch, and I'm the toughest of the lot, even if I am what your kind would call a cantankerous old coot.'

'What means "coot"?' Grig asked.

'It's a bird that can make a living just about anywhere,' Alex explained.

Grig nodded knowingly. 'How appropriate.'

'But I saw you die . . . after you brought me back to the

base,' Alex insisted. 'The medic working on you...'

Centauri shook his head. 'Oh, I was good and dead, all right. Let me tell you, being dead's no picnic, boy. But my people are tough. The body can expire, but it takes the brain a long time to die. They were able to bring the rest of me back. The important thing was that the memory patterns stayed intact. Just like puttin' a puzzle back together, except the medics had to build me a few new pieces.' He looked Alex over thoughtfully, taking in the new uniform, the new attitude, the recently bestowed decorations. 'What about you? What are you going to do now, Starfighter?'

Alex turned to gaze out across the cheering sea of alien faces, at the impossible skyline of the capital city of Rylos beyond. Everything had happened so quickly. Events had swept him up in their grasp and left him with little time for thinking about such things as 'after'.

'I don't know,' he whispered.

It was cold out. Or maybe it wasn't, but it felt chilly to Maggie. She sat on the edge of the porch that ran across the front of the general store.

Where are you, Alex? Too far away for me to imagine? That's what the machine that looked like you said. Where is that? I don't even know what part of the sky to look at.

'Alex?' another voice called out.

A light breeze stirred the dust in front of the store. A hunting spider scrambled across the open space, searching for some unfortunate arthropod smaller than itself.

'Alex?' the voice called again, a note of concern attached to it now. That was Mrs Rogan. How much should she be told? The machine, the Beta Unit, hadn't forced any guidelines on Maggie, telling her to use her own judgement. It was her world, her people. Her life.

She rose. It was time for Alex's mother, at least, to learn the truth. Mrs Rogan might throw her and her incredible story out of the trailer, but she felt bound to try. She patted Mr President and left.

Behind her: lights, sounds, movement familiar and yet

different. The videogame on the porch was going gently berserk, humming and flashing, vibrating on its levellers. Maggie didn't see, concentrating on how she'd tell Mrs Rogan.

Just as she didn't see the old weathervane atop the store begin to spin wildly, even though there was hardly any wind. It picked up speed and was soon rotating fast enough to be little more than a blur in the night.

Between the trailers Maggie paused, thoughtful. Granny was leaning out of a window nearby, a thick cigar smoking between her fingers.

'Granny, have you seen Alex?'

'Can't say as I have. That boy's been kind of scarce here lately.' She gestured with the cigar. 'You're not the only one lookin' for him, neither.'

'How do you mean? I heard Mrs Rogan.'

'She ain't the only one.'

Figures appeared, exiting from the Rogan trailer and walking towards Maggie. She recognized several of her friends along with Mrs Rogan, and one non-friend: Jack Blake. She stood and waited for them.

'You want to know where Alex is?' Blake was saying as soon as he spotted her. 'Ask Maggie. She knows. She was with him when he stole my pickup.'

'He did *not* steal it,' Maggie shot back angrily. 'He borrowed it.'

'Yeah?' Blake was snarling at her, not the least bit affectionate now. More important things were at stake. 'Then where is it?'

Maggie thought back to the wild chase in the truck and the Beta's little surprise box under the dash and the incinerating heat when the pickup had smashed into the alien assassin's ship, and said nothing.

'Maggie,' Mrs Rogan asked in a gentle but no-nonsense voice, 'where's Alex?'

'Where's my truck?' Blake yelled, without giving her a chance to reply. 'Where's your boyfriend?'

Maggie ignored him, wondering that she could ever have

213

found him even slightly attractive, and kept a lid on her temper as she spoke to Mrs Rogan. It was apparent no one was going to leave until they got some answers. She'd just have to try and explain as best she could.

'Mrs Rogan, it's like this, about Alex. He isn't...'

The dogs began to howl. All the dogs, not just Mr President. They were joined by the cats. If Mrs Edward's goldfish could've howled they would have joined the chorus as well. Suddenly no one was listening to Maggie.

Outside Otis's trailer, Mr President was yowling with puppy-like enthusiasm. His master came stumbling out and was about to berate his fool dog when something on the porch caught his eye.

Oblivious to the fact that he wasn't wearing anything over his pyjamas Otis started for the porch, transfixed by the sight of the rocking, squealing, strobing videogame. Above him, unseen, the weathervane stopped spinning as if shot and all four compass point indicators suddenly bent sharply towards the night sky.

Something blew Otis's sleeping cap off. A descending bright light made him step backward, shielding his eyes. The Starlight, Starbright sign on the front of the store was glowing powerfully, bright enough to be read a hundred miles away.

The falling light came from the underside of something that was lowering itself towards the parking lot. Leaving Mrs Rogan and her friends from school behind, Maggie started walking rapidly towards the light.

Other faces appeared at windows and doors as the residents of the trailer park left bed or TV or bathroom to have a look. The commotion was sufficient to penetrate the brightly painted teepee set up in the Rogan yard. Two small occupants emerged to see what was happening.

'Far out!' said Louis's friend David. 'We been invaded!'

'Klingons!' shouted Louis gleefully as he started towards the descending shape.

The spaceship touched ground, silent except for a deep internal humming. Maggie recalled the Beta's warning words. This might be another assassin, bolder than his predecessors. But she couldn't keep herself from moving slowly towards the faintly glowing ship.

The logo emblazoned on its side looked like the one the Beta had described to her, but she couldn't be sure. She was cautious, but hopeful. Coming down in the midst of a hundred witnesses, primitive or not, didn't seem like the ZZ-Designate's style.

A voice called to her. 'Maggie?' It was Otis, standing in front of the store. She ignored him.

Something was descending from the belly of the spacecraft, a lift of some kind. Mutters rose from the growing crowd of curious onlookers. They stood there by the store in their underwear and bathrobes and watched as a creature stepped off the lift and walked towards them. It wore a peculiar suit and helmet. Its outline *looked* human enough.

Then it stopped in front of Maggie and removed its helmet.

'Alex!' Her face lit up as brightly as the ship's landing lights. 'Alex, is it you? Is it really you?' She took a step towards him, hesitated. 'Or should I open you up to check?'

He grinned down at her, a familiar, warm, guileless grin. 'Nothing in here but us organics, Maggie.'

She jumped into his arms, making him stagger. 'It *is* you! Alex, Alex, Alex...'

'Maggie.'

They kissed, and that was enough to bring the crowd of gaping onlookers shuffling close; Mrs Rogan, Granny, Elvira, Clara... all of them, all talking at once.

'Alex, is that a real spaceship? ... Did'ja meet aliens? ... Where'd you get it, Alex? ... Now what's goin' on 'round here? ... What's this all about? ...'

And lastly, pushing through the others, 'Where have you been, Alex Rogan?' his mother demanded to know.

'Out,' he said automatically. Standing with his arm around Maggie he tried to explain the impossible.

'Take it easy, everybody.' They settled down to listen. He took a deep breath and spoke to his mother. 'I've been on another planet, mom. Helping the Rylans and the other good aliens, protecting the civilized galaxy from the bad aliens.' He gestured over his shoulder. 'That's my gunstar...'

'Like from the Starfighter game?' Louis wanted to know.

'That's right, little brother. See, aliens put the game here on Earth and on other worlds to find people who qualified as Starfighters, to help defend the Frontier against Xur and the Ko-Dan armada. Just like the game always said.'

'Wow!' Louis said expressively.

Otis pushed forward, Jack Blake close on his heels.

'Well then, if you were somewhere out there, who was it broke my antenna trying to put it up?'

'Yeah, and stole my truck!' Blake said accusingly, though much subdued.

'... And ruined my stove... And wrecked my plumbing... Cut my 'lectric...!' other voices inquired.

Alex made shushing motions with his hands. 'That was a Beta Unit, a duplicate of me. A robot.'

'Aw, I knew it all along,' Louis insisted. He looked past his brother, suddenly pointing. 'Hey, what's that?'

The lift was descending again. On it stood a tall, alien shape. The adults in the crowd drew back fearfully, but they had to pull their children along.

'A monster!' one of the women shouted.

'Monster?' murmured Grig as he stepped off the lift and started towards Alex. 'Indeed!'

'Go easy on 'em, Grig,' Alex asked him. 'Remember, they're just immature primitives. Like me.'

Grig nodded, stopping short of the crowd.

Granny was trying to push her way forward, clutching her old shotgun. Alex hastened to cut her off.

'Wait! Put down the shotgun, Granny. Everybody, come back. I want you all to meet Grig. My best friend.'

The children were first, breaking away from their parents' paranoid grasp to crowd unhesitatingly around the alien's long legs. Urged on by shame and curiosity, their elders timidly joined them.

'Grig,' said Alex brightly, 'I'd like you to meet Mr and Mrs Boone... that means they're mated... Elvira, Otis...'

He led Grig down the impromptu reception line. 'And this is Granny, and Maggie, of course.' Grig nodded, shook hands with each in turn before they stopped in front of the young female. She regarded him with a lopsided smile.

'Er, hi...'

'Remember the English I taught you,' Alex murmured to him. 'There are no translator buttons here.'

Grig nodded and took Maggie's hand. The crowd murmured. Grig made an effort to smile in the human manner and said with perfect diction, 'Charmed.'

Louis once more pushed his way to the fore and began doing strange things with his fingers. Grig found this puzzling, which was not surprising since he hadn't seen the movie Close Encounters of the Third Kind.

But he recognized the resemblance immediately. 'And you must be Louis. I've heard good things about you.' He bent to shake the small hand, marvelling at the softness of the flesh, so different from his own.

Louis stepped back, eyeing his hand as though it had just magically materialized on the end of his wrist, and turned to his friends.

'Hear that, you slimes? I'm famous!'

Mrs Rogan was next. She eyed Grig warily.

'And this is my mom,' Alex said.

As Alex had instructed him, Grig took Mrs Rogan's hand. But instead of shaking it, he bent and put his lips to the dorsal side. A peculiar custom, though no more so than half a hundred he'd acquired in his travels.

It certainly had the intended affect. Mrs Rogan was rendered speechless. Alex had warned Grig this might be the result, so he resumed the conversation himself.

'You should be proud of your son, Mrs Rogan.' He looked past her at the assembled crowd. 'You should all be proud of him. He saved the League and hundreds of worlds, including Earth. He is the greatest Starfighter ever. He will teach other potential Starfighters and help us to build a permanent core of citizens ready to insure that such attacks as we have just suffered will not occur again. Their very existence will be a deterrent to future war.' He glanced solemnly at Alex.

'Which reminds me. We are expected back to begin work. It is time to leave.'

Maggie frowned. 'Leave?'

'Alex?' said Mrs Rogan.

He kissed her gently on one cheek and nodded.

'I have to, mom. I promised. You heard Grig. I have a job to do. An important job. And I'm the only one who can do it.'

She sighed. 'I always knew you'd leave here, Alex. I just never wanted to face that moment. I don't imagine any mother does. Still, I guess it's not so very different from going off to the University. What are you going to do about your studies?'

He grinned, waving towards the starfilled sky. Just like his mom, trying to couch the impossible in everyday terms.

'Somehow spending four years preparing to be a computer technician doesn't seem quite as important as it once did, mom. Don't worry. I've got plenty to learn, out there.'

'Yes, I suppose that you would.' She looked meaningfully towards Grig. 'You'll watch after him, won't you?'

He nodded. 'It will be a pleasure. I hope only to do one-tenth as good a job as you have done.'

For the second time that night Jane Rogan found herself speechless.

'Gee, can I come too, Alex?' Louis wondered, staring worshipfully up at his brother.

Alex knelt until they were eye to eye. 'Sorry, squirt. But I'll be back to visit, lots of times. You didn't think I was going away forever, did you? But you can't come.' He gestured back at the gunstar. 'There's only room for me, Grig, and Maggie.'

She swallowed. 'Me?'

'Of course.' He took a step towards the gunstar, but she held back, uncertain, and he turned to her again. 'Why else do you think I came back? I told you that we'd always be together.'

'Yeah. Together here, or at school, or in the city. Not... out there, Alex.'

'You always told me you wanted to travel and see faraway

places.'

She didn't met his eyes for a moment. 'I meant San Diego, or maybe someday New York. This Rylos of yours... you can't even see it from here.'

'You can't see New York, but you *can* see Rylos, Maggie.' He put his arm around her and turned her so they both faced the sky, and he pointed. 'There it is... right there.'

'Oh. It's bright.'

'You gotta come with me, Maggie. I'll be back, but I don't know when. Setting up this training programme's going to be a lot of work, and I promised. Don't you see? This is our big chance. It's like Otis said. When it comes, you gotta grab it with both hands and hold tight. I can learn a lot and help a lot of good people at the same time. It's something I have to do.'

'What about Granny?'

Alex gave her a look easily interpreted to mean, 'Not that old excuse again', and she knew that he knew what she really meant. So why continue hiding it?

'You're right, Alex. I'm scared of leaving here. I'm scared of leaving this trailer park, for all my big talk about travelling and seeing the world, never mind other worlds. Why can't you stay? Someone else could start that school.'

'It's not just that, Maggie. Don't you see? I'm not just a kid from a trailer park up there. I'm a Starfighter. I'm *the* Starfighter, and I've got new friends who are counting on me. I can't let them down. This is... Maggie, this is a lot bigger than me, or even you and me. It's bigger than anything.'

From inside the ship a voice sounded over a speaker, gentle but insistent. 'Alex.'

He whirled and replied almost angrily, though Grig would know it was only Alex's frustration speaking. 'Just a minute!' A low whine rose as the drive was activated.

'I can't talk anymore,' he told Maggie. 'Anyway, I've said everything. I gotta go.'

He hugged her hard, forcing himself to move on to his mother, to Louis. The he waved goodbye to the others, the assembled faces he'd known since childhood. They stared back at him reassuringly, solid as the desert, alive with the light from the gunstar.

He turned and headed for the waiting lift.

Haze filled the air as the ship's drive disturbed the atmosphere and irritated dust particles swirled above the parking lot. Granny held Maggie tight, saying nothing. It wasn't her place to. Not this time.

Finally Maggie looked anxiously into that weathered face. 'Granny?'

The old woman smiled knowingly, running her fingers through her granddaughter's hair. Once for luck, and a second time to remember. No reason to cry. Hadn't Alex said he'd be back to visit? And Alex was a good boy . . . no, not a boy anymore. Alex was a man of his word.

'Be sure to write, darlin'. Or whatever it is that they do out there.'

Maggie broke out in a wide smile, fighting back her own tears. Then she turned and ran for the ship, shouting and waving frantically.

'Alex, wait! Alex!'

The lift was nearly into the belly of the gunstar, but nearly isn't all the way. It stopped and lowered to the ground a third time. Alex helped her onto the platform and she knew it was all right as he kissed her tenderly, knew that everything was going to be all right from now on. Because they were together.

The residents of the Starlight, Starbright trailer park knew it was going to be all right too. They watched and sighed, and Mr Boone surprised Mrs Boone with a long kiss. A warm feeling spread over them all as they watched the youngsters. Louis expressed the feelings of the prepubescent contingent by making a face and grumbling under his breath.

The whine from the ship intensified. Otis started shooing the crowd away.

'Everybody back! Keep your distance. These babies really pack a punch.' *I think*, he added silently to himself.

'Must be an optical illustration,' insisted one still-disbelieving resident.

'Nope,' argued Mrs Donovan. 'It's a one o' them UFOs. I saw one of 'em back in '58.'

'Ha!' snapped Elvira. 'You been seein' 'em all your life, Bessie.'

'Lord,' mumbled elderly Mr Franklin, 'I swear I'll never touch another drop as long as I live.' Then he remembered the half-full bottle of Jim Beam back in his trailer and added hastily, 'After tonight, that is.'

'I figure we're a cinch to make the Carson show,' Mrs. Donovan added confidently.

'I can see the headlines,' murmured Elvira. '"Martians Land at Trailer Park". We're famous now, eh, Otis?'

'Yessir,' he said proudly, watching the ship. 'The whole world's gonna know about it. Starlight, Starbright Trailer Park. The place where Alex and Maggie left for the stars.'

Everyone was staring at the transparent canopy at the forward end of the ship. Alex and Maggie stood there, close against each other, waving and smiling back at them.

'Spaceships... spacepeople... oh, I'm so confused!' Elvira murmured.

Granny came over and put a comforting arm around her neighbour. 'Trouble with you, Elvira, is that you're laggin' behind the times. You got to look to the future and quit living in the past.'

'You mean...?' Elvira asked worriedly.

'Yep. No more *I Love Lucy* reruns.'

'Oh, Granny!'

The gunstar rose skyward more quietly than any of them expected, the humming of its drive a muted thrum instead of the fiery thunder of the rockets they'd seen on television. A small figure pushed its way through the rest of the crowd, heading for the mob of kids clustered around the Starfighter video game sitting silently on the general store porch.

'Hey, lemme in, you guys!' Louis demanded, shoving between the small bodies. 'He's *my* big brother.'

'But it's my quarter,' David protested.

'I'll pay you back, Davey.' Louis thumbed the 'play' button. A familiar synthesized voice responded immediately.

'GREETINGS, STARFIGHTER. YOU HAVE BEEN RECRUITED BY THE LEAGUE TO PROTECT THE

FRONTIER AGAINST XUR AND THE KO-DAN ARMADA.'

'Go get 'em, Louis,' yelled David. Around them the rest of the kids pushed for a better view and cheered Louis Rogan on.

Otis had moved to stand close to Jane Rogan, who was staring silently at the sky while her excited neighbours jabbered behind her.

'Otis, did I do the right thing? Letting him go back out there?'

'Course you did, Jane. Course you did. Time for the young 'uns to flee the coop. When it's that time there's no way you can hold 'em to the hearth.' He grinned softly and put a reassuring arm around her waist. 'No way on Earth.'